MAKE ME

Yours

USA TODAY BESTSELLING AUTHOR

TIA LOUISE

Anita~
Dreams do
come true!
Tia xoxo

This book is a work of fiction. Names, characters, places, and incidents are products of the author's imagination or are used fictitiously. Any resemblance to actual events or locales or persons, living or dead, is entirely coincidental.

"You aren't wealthy until you have something money can't buy."
–Garth Brooks

For Becca, Sarah, and all lovers of fairytale princes.

Contents

Prologue

Ruby

Fifth grade

It's a truth universally acknowledged that little girls know by fifth grade whether they're bitches or not.

Okay, I just made that up based on the intro to Jane Austen's *Pride & Prejudice*. I don't really know if it's a universal truth or not, but in Oakville, our tiny bedroom community of Charleston, it was real clear the day Serena Whitehead emerged as queen bitch of our fifth-grade class.

A lot of families had migrated to Oakville from Charleston for the small-town schools and the perception of safety, so we were meeting a lot of new girls. Still, we'd known Serena since Kindergarten...

"My mother says your dad was voted Most Handsome in high school." Her voice comes from behind my left shoulder. "Too bad you look nothing like him."

She's right.

My father, prominent Charleston neurosurgeon Kenneth Banks, is tall, with light brown hair and flinty blue eyes.

Stepping back, I smooth my finger along the fair brow framing his round eyes, thinking how they look disappointed even in charcoal. "My mom was voted most beautiful in her graduating class."

"Where was that? Suzy Wong Manicurist Academy?" Serena laughs, and I turn to face her.

Bitches don't scare me.

"Clemson Magnet. Her degree was in accounting."

I leave out how she then met my dad and gave it all up to stay home and raise her family, also known as me.

"You are so good at portraits." My best friend Drew's voice is a sweet interruption, and the fist in my chest relaxes.

"I'm too literal." Leaning my shoulder against hers, I speak quietly. "Your technique is good—"

"They just never look like the person I'm drawing."

Serena isn't done. "What a pair," she quips. "The fallen princess and the daughter of a geisha."

My jaw tightens, and I turn quickly, stepping right into her face. "You'd better watch your mouth, Serena Whitehead."

"Why, banana brains?" Her eyes flash, but I don't flinch.

"My family are Bak Mei kung fu masters. Since the age of seven, I've perfected the Five Finger Heart Exploding technique."

Serena's green eyes narrow slightly. "What the hell is that?"

"Piss me off, and I'll show you."

"I'm telling Ms. Hughes you threatened me."

"I'm telling Ms. Hughes you're a foul-mouthed bully."

We glare at each other as the second-hand ticks, *one... two... three...*

Until our teacher's voice breaks the stand-off.

"Girls, what's going on here?" Ms. Hughes puts her hand on my shoulder, and Serena skanks off to her side of the classroom.

Drew pipes in. "Just packing up, Ms. Hughes."

Our teacher gasps, clutching her chest. "Why, Ruby Banks, this portrait of your father is outstanding. It's an amazing likeness. You have to take it home and show him tonight."

"Oh, no..." The confidence in my chest deflates. "My dad's not really into art."

Or anything I do...

"Nonsense!" She spins off toward her desk. "I'll send them a note. I'm recommending you for the artistically talented program at Oakville High. You have real potential!"

It's no use arguing. I've tried explaining to teachers before, and they never believe me. Everyone thinks my dad is some cultured philanthropist because he grew up in the city and Charleston General named the children's surgery wing after him... Maybe even because he married my mom.

The truth is, he's kind of just an absentee jerk.

"Sure." I smile and nod.

When I meet Drew's eyes, her smile is sad. "You should go to the artistically talented program. You really deserve it."

"We both know it's not going to happen."

The bell rings as we finish collecting our books. Serena glares at me from across the room, but I have more important things to worry about.

"Bak Mei kung fu masters? The Five Finger Heart Exploding technique?" Drew whispers, and we both start to laugh.

"I guess somebody never watched *Kill Bill*."

"Or *The Amazing World of Gumball*."

We do a low five, and I follow her to the door.

"Ruby, wait!" Ms. Hughes hurries to give me a business-sized envelope. "I want you to give this to your parents tonight. Have them sign it."

"Yes, ma'am." A knot tightens in my throat.

I wish people wouldn't jump to conclusions.

Unless they need the exercise.

Drew and I walk our regular route home from school. We live in the same neighborhood, but developers have been adding to it so long, it's more like three neighborhoods connected by long, winding streets.

Her family's historic mansion is in the oldest part of Oakville Estates. It was one of the first homes built here. My family's house is on the other, newer end. It's not a mansion, but it's still pretty big.

We reach the fork in the sidewalk, and she hesitates, looking in the direction of her house. Since her mom died, all her daddy does is drink, and her brother Danny gets in trouble all the time.

"If your dad hates art so much, why'd you pick him for your portrait?"

"Daddy issues." I joke, kicking the grass with the toe of my shoe. Neither one of us really wants to go home.

"Seriously?"

"I don't know. His face was in my head." I squint up at her. "Why'd you pick Danny?"

She shrugs. "Same reason."

She opens her large portfolio, and we both study her portrait. It doesn't look like Danny at all. It looks more like his best friend Gray. Our eyes meet, and I laugh again.

"That's the face in your head?" Her cheeks flush, and she doesn't have to answer me. Drew and I know each other better than anybody in this town. "See you tomorrow, Drew-poo."

"Don't call me that, banana brains."

I give her a push, and she pokes me in the ribs. Our pretend-wrestle turns into a brief hug. "Good luck."

"You, too." She waves and marches slowly toward her house.

I wonder if a drunk dad is better or worse than an absentee jerk. Either way, I can't put off the inevitable any longer.

Dad's stuck at the hospital and won't make it in time for dinner again. Ma and I sit together eating kimchee and spicy dumplings with chopsticks as she recites the events of her day.

Her neat beige dress stops at her knees, and a thin black belt is around her waist. Her dark hair is smoothed back into a low bun at the nape of her neck, and her shoes are sensible black pumps. A neat strand of pearls is at her neck, and her lips are a pale shade of pink. My mother's skin is flawless.

She is the very model of a small-town church secretary.

I'm dressed in ripped jeans and a graphic tee, and my hair is styled in a fluffy bob that ends right at my ears. While I do look more like her, thanks to my Anglo dad, my hair has a little wave in it, and my dark eyes are slightly rounder. It's clear I'm half-Korean, but I appreciate these little perks from the man with whom I otherwise have nothing in common.

We finish eating, and Ma goes to the bar separating the kitchen from the dining area. "What is this?" She picks up the envelope I left behind.

"Ms. Hughes wants you to sign and return it."

Ma opens the letter and her dark eyes quickly scan

the page. "It says you'd leave school early? To draw pictures?" Her brow furrows. "What about your science class? Your math? You should leave school early to take accounting."

"It's just a recommendation, Ma. I don't have to do it."

"Your father will not like this."

No shit. I don't say that part out loud. I don't want her putting soap on my tongue again.

"What won't I like?" Dad's stern voice makes my insides jump.

Ma jumps as well. "Kenneth! Welcome home." She steps over to peck his cheek. "I saved you a plate. Sit."

He goes to the wet bar at the window, and ice clinks in a crystal tumbler as he pours his daily scotch. "Ruby?"

My stomach clenches. "Yes, sir?"

"What is your mother saying I won't like?"

Blue eyes fix on me, and I wonder how he can make me feel so cold with just a look.

"We had an art assignment at school. My teacher sent home a note."

His brow lowers, and my frozen insides splinter in painful shards. "A reprimand?"

"A recommendation." I speak fast. "She wants me to take this art program. I told her I wasn't interested."

He goes to the letter my mother left on the table and scans it even faster than she did. "Art." His perfectly straight nose curls. "What gets into these teachers? What kind of job would you get with a degree in art?"

Swallowing the pain in my throat, I nod. "I know, right?" My voice sounds too small.

"What's this?" He reads out loud. "See portrait. What portrait?"

"It's nothing." I stand, collecting my plate. The last thing I want is to continue this conversation.

"Ruby Banks, what portrait?"

Depositing my plate in the kitchen, I go to where I left my school things in the mud room. My art folder is in the back of the long cubby behind my raincoat. I take it out and carry it slowly to the dining room where he now sits at the head of the table, holding his scotch.

My mother stands behind his right shoulder, and a steaming fresh plate is in front of him.

"It's nothing, really." I hold out the brown folder.

He takes it, and my breath stills.

My stomach is sick.

What will my father see when he looks at my representation of his face? Will he see the anger and disapproval always looking back at me? Or will it do something to his heart, break the stone wall around it? Or will he only see what he sees every day in the mirror? Are disappointment and frustration how he views the world?

The heavy brown cover opens, and his expression doesn't change as he studies the lines and shading, the positive and negative space.

My clasped hands squeeze tighter. I don't want him digging deeper, turning the page and seeing my attempts at copying Klimt or Degas.

The truth is, I agree with Ms. Hughes. I'm so proud of my art. The portrait of my father is an amazing likeness, even if it is distant and cold. When I'm drawing, I feel like I'm alive, and the harder I work, the more it turns out exactly as I'd hoped.

It's exciting and fulfilling…

I don't want him to take what I love and kill it.

He closes the cover and tosses it aside. "A useless

degree."

"I told her I wasn't interested." I speak quietly, submissively.

He hates that.

His eyes don't leave his plate. I watch as he slices a sticky dumpling with a knife and fork and puts the piece in his mouth. My father refuses to use chopsticks.

"That is all."

I'm dismissed, and my artistic dreams fall away, like the portrait inside that folder.

Like the letter, which is never returned.

Chapter 1

Ruby

Twelve Years Later

"I've hit rock bottom." I flop on the couch in Drew's office at the Friends Care clinic where we both work.

Yep, I'm a licensed therapist... with two clients, both shared with Drew, who has like twenty.

So I'm not the resounding success I'd expected, but Drew keeps telling me it takes time to build my practice, especially in a town the size of Oakville...

Trust me, based on the dating scene alone, I get it.

"What's wrong now?" She stands and walks to the closet at the back of the room.

"HookUp4Luv matched me with Ralph Stern."

"The Almond King!" My best friend laughs for the first time in a week. "Did you know he has a plan for revolutionizing Oakville's economy?"

Clutching my forehead, I groan. "Gah—yes! He's told me his plan five hundred times."

"Almonds are the fruit of the future." She pauses. "Are they fruits or nuts?"

"Who knows? They grow on trees..."

"I'll tell you who knows."

"Don't say his name."

"The future king of your little almond patch."

"If you're referring to my vagina, that's just gross." She laughs more, and I feel a twinge of guilt. "Am I being a bitch?"

"Umm… No."

"Good. Because Ralph is a hard no."

It's not that he's a bad guy. He's just so… so… Sheldon Cooper. Still, my mom is in my head giving me a disapproving look. *Be kind to everyone, Ruby Banks.*

"I've dated every match in the tri-county area, and this is it. Ralph Stern is the last man on Earth."

Drew laughs even more, and I have an inspiration. "Screw the dating apps. We're going out tonight—just you and me."

Her laugh disappears, and she's shaking her head before the words even start. "Nope. Not interested. No."

"Yes." I'm off the couch and catching her by the arms. "You've been cooped up alone in that big old house since your dad went in the nursing home. You're going out with me." I pull her trench coat on her shoulders. "Anyway, I'm your ride, so you can't argue."

"You're kidnapping me?"

"If that's what it takes." I lead her out the glass entrance, waiting as she locks the doors, then she follows me to my lime-green Subaru.

"Do you think it's responsible to blow your paycheck on a night out?"

"Yes, my sad little paycheck only covers one night out. Thanks for reminding me." We're in the car, and I drive us to my mom's house. "Kenneth Banks was so adamant about a useful degree. I'm a licensed therapist, and I can't pay my bills."

"Stop it. You're building your practice." Drew looks out the window, adding under her breath.

16

"Kenneth Banks was a royal ass."

"It's okay. You can say it out loud." Five turns, and we're at Ma's. "I'm confronting my daddy issues." Her eyebrows shoot up, but I hold up a hand. "The first step is admitting you have a problem."

"Drew!" Mom meets us inside the door, giving my friend a long hug. She pretty much adopted Drew after her mother died when we were eight. "We prayed for your father this morning at church, and I burned incense to the Buddha when I got home."

"All the bases covered!" I lean to let Ma kiss my cheek, before swinging through the kitchen for a plate of dumplings.

"Eat in the kitchen, Ruby Banks!" Mom yells, but I keep going to my bedroom.

"We're going out for a little while, Ma. We have to get ready."

"Church tomorrow!"

"That woman, I swear…" Rolling my eyes, I close my bedroom door. Drew flops on my single bed with the plate, and I take a dumpling while inspecting my wardrobe.

"Here, you can wear this." I pull out a super-short, high-waisted mini with a cute long-sleeved crop top. "You'll look hot and totally on point."

She takes it and frowns. "I don't know why I'm dressing up. I'm not looking for a date."

"You're dressing up because it's Saturday night, you just got paid, and you're going out with your best friend!"

"You're feeling good tonight. What are you not telling me? Did you get into your mom's herbs?"

"Ha ha, very funny." I laugh, but her question makes me pause. "You're right, though, I do feel good… like something's coming. Maybe the planets

17

shifted."

"I'll take that forecast." She goes into the bathroom to change. "Lord knows I could use a shift."

Nibbling on the dumpling, I study my wardrobe, finally settling on a velvet sheath with a sheer black top and built-in bustier. "Velvet is supposedly out… now it's lamé. And track suits."

"I am not wearing a track suit." Drew's back looking like a hot tamale, and we freshen our makeup, pushing each other side to side with our hips in front of the mirror and laughing.

Next, I sit as she uses the curling iron to touch up the waves to my long, brown hair. "Maybe I should mix it up. Wear a wig?"

"No." Our eyes meet briefly before she returns to checking my head for curl-holes.

With a sigh, I take another dumpling. "I've got to get a better job, D. I can't live in this house anymore. It's embarrassing."

"Be patient. The clients will come." She releases a smooth spiral across my eye, and I push it behind my ear. "Anyway, your mom likes having you here, especially since your dad died."

"I'll be twenty-three next year, and still living with my mother."

"At least you're gorgeous. Let's go!"

She shakes her long, naturally wavy blonde hair — which I do not hate her for having — and we head for the door. "Just don't completely lose it and go out with Ralph Stern."

"If you're truly my best friend, you will never let that happen."

"I am your best friend."

"Thank God."

Patrons spill out the door of The Red Cat as we walk up. It's the only bar in our tiny town-square, and the interior hasn't been updated since Frank Sinatra was alive. Lava lamps dot around the inside, and blood-red shag carpet covers the floors, running all the way up the bar. The scent of cigarettes permeates the room, even though smoking in bars has been banned for years, and an ancient jukebox playing real records is blasting "That's Amoré."

"Are you kidding me?" Drew recoils. "The Red Cat is where old men hide out when they don't want to go home."

"It's the hot new place!" I grab her hand and drag her through the door. "Strong drinks served cheap."

We make our way slowly through the crowd when a loud male voice makes me cringe. "Ruby Roo!"

I spin around fast, pissed as hell at Dagwood Magee. He's been calling me that Scooby Doo nickname since we were in high school.

"Stop yelling that! You're messing with my hustle." He only laughs and gives me a hug, leaving sweat on my face. I growl, wiping it off. "Gross."

Drew is weirdly pleased to see him. "At least we know a big guy here... just in case."

I order us two tequila sunrises while we wait at the bar, and even though it's pretty packed, I'm not seeing anyone I know besides Dag. "How is it possible I don't know anybody here?"

"That's a good thing, right?"

Our drinks are in front of us, and I lift mine, taking a long sip. "So you're not even looking for a man now?"

"You know how I feel."

Drew has been pining after Grayson Cole since we were in high school. She waited for him all through

19

college while he was overseas with the military, and then when he came back, he didn't stay.

I can't help being protective of my bestie. "He ghosted you, Drew."

"He didn't." Her eyes are fixed on the drink she's not drinking. "He's doing what he has to do. Getting help."

"You know I love you, and I think you're a great therapist." She nods, stabbing her drink with the skinny straw. "I just worry sometimes all your understanding and empathy ends up making you a doormat."

"I'm not a doormat. I love Gray. I'll love him forever."

We're quiet a few minutes. My chest hurts at her confession, and I wrap an arm around her shoulders, giving her a squeeze. "He's a lucky guy. I wish I felt that way about someone."

As I say it, I realize it's true.

She puts her head on my shoulder. "What will you do if you're not a therapist?"

"No idea." I shake off the sudden melancholy mood and take another, longer sip of my sweet drink. "Search for my insanely rich Asian husband?"

"Not in Oakville," she straightens, looking around the room.

She can say that again. It's a fantasy football sausage fest in here. The guys are all big and boisterous, and when the juke box starts blasting "Fly Me to the Moon," they all start singing loudly.

"You've got to be kidding," I mutter, when my eyes land on a guy sitting alone at the other end of the bar.

Lava lamps don't provide much light, but I can see he's wearing a tailored gray blazer over a white shirt, and he's nursing what looks like a scotch. His brown hair is just long enough to be messy, and it has a sexy little wave across his forehead, which he pushes aside with an elegant hand.

He glances up, and when our eyes meet, he gives me a brief smile. Heat shoots all the way to my core. *Holy shit,* he has a dimple in his left cheek!

I give him a shy smile and turn slowly to face my friend. "Holy shit, I'm in lust." I hiss, grabbing her arm fast. "Who is that?"

"Who?" Drew is talking way too loud, and now she's looking all around the bar dramatically.

My jaw clenches. "Stop it. He'll know we're talking about him."

"How am I supposed to know who you mean if you won't let me look?"

"The Jamie Dornan clone in the corner." The music is blasting, and we have to shout.

"You think every hot guy looks like Jamie Dornan."

"I do not." Her eyes slant, and I defend my position. "Jamie Dornan has a very standard, hot-Anglo guy look."

"Are you saying all hot white guys look alike?"

"I am not saying that. It's racist. You're saying that."

"Good thing I'm white."

Rolling my eyes, I shake her arm. "Whatever. He's hot as fuck. Who is he?"

She finally looks, then she starts bouncing up and down. "Oh! That's Remington Key! I tried to introduce you to him at church, and you couldn't be bothered."

My fingers clutch her arm tighter, and I pull her to me. "Please stop jumping and screaming his name. He's not in BTS."

"You with the K-pop." Her expression turns excited. "Just think, Mr. Right was waiting for you in a bar all along. It's like the olden days!"

"Ma says Mr. Right is waiting in church." *I'm still not sure if she meant Jesus...*

Drew's eyes go even rounder if that's possible. "You met Remi in church *and* now at a bar—that's got to be a sign!"

I steal a glance over my shoulder again, and he's reaching into his back pocket for his wallet, giving me a glimpse of his cute butt.

"I'll tell you what's a sign—that ass. You did not introduce me to him. I'd remember it." Drew starts to argue, but I cut her off. "I'm going to investigate. Stay out of trouble."

She yells after me. "Don't do anything I wouldn't do."

"I never follow that rule."

She laughs, and I shake my head.

Come to mamma, cute butt...

Chapter 2

Remington

I'm alone in a bar on a Friday night.

Okay, technically, I was invited here by Dagwood Magee to join his fantasy football league. The only problem is I've been so buried in getting my investment business off the ground, researching new applications, studying industry trends, the market, rising stars, I can't remember the last time I even saw a football game.

I don't have a team, I only know one person here, and I'm in an ancient, smoke-scented, crowded bar with a bunch of sweaty jocks. No joke—it's a fucking sausage fest.

At the same time, I'd rather be here than home right now.

After another ridiculous fight with Eleanor, my increasingly overbearing mother-in-law, about spending time with my daughter Lillie, I've decided something has to give.

Hell, all I'd wanted to do was watch *Guardians of the Galaxy* with Lillie, but no, Eleanor insisted it was too violent for a four-year-old.

Lillie ended up crying, and I ended up furious.

Sitting here now, I concede Eleanor was probably right.

Still, I just wanted a fun daddy-daughter date,

something we could both enjoy. Now I feel like a heel, and I'm alone in a bar. *Dammit.*

Four years ago, after Sandy died, I didn't mind if her mother moved in and took over the childcare. Lillie was her granddaughter, and I had no idea how to be a single dad to a newborn baby. I didn't even know if I was going to survive losing my wife…

I'd left the Navy, invented a series of apps to organize intelligence data then locate enemy combatants based on that data, sold it, made a billion, married Sandy, we got pregnant, and when the pregnancy turned high-risk, she wanted to move here to be closer to her mother.

I thought my life was so perfect, so planned out… then it all fell apart. I was alone, and I didn't know how to keep moving forward. I didn't want to keep moving forward.

I pulled away from everybody, burying myself in work, until a year ago. My daughter was walking, talking, needing a father, and I realized I had to make a change.

Polishing off my whiskey, I think about the past year. The haze of grief had slowly lifted, and I saw my home life was a mess.

My mother-in-law drives me crazy, and I need to regain control of the situation.

I've considered returning to Seattle, but as much as I want to strangle her sometimes, I know being that far from Lillie would kill Eleanor.

The old jukebox starts playing "Fly Me to the Moon," and the bar erupts into drunk males singing loudly. I signal to the bartender to bring me another drink.

Getting drunk is not a responsible solution to any problem.

Which is why I'll worry about this one tomorrow.

I push my hair off my forehead and look around the room. If I'd known it was going to be all guys...

My throat goes dry when I see her.

She's standing at the bar looking at me, and it's like everything stops.

Dark hair flows around her shoulders in silky waves, her eyes flash, and her body... *Jesus*. Soft shoulders, perfect tits, narrow waist, shapely legs... Our eyes meet again, and heat filters through my pelvis.

I smile. She blinks and gives me a shy smile in return. When she turns away, I fish out my wallet to settle my tab. I want to go over and say hi. Maybe offer to buy her a drink.

I'm just putting my wallet in my pocket when a sassy voice catches my attention. "Hey, sailor, new in town?"

She's standing right in front of me, and I lower slowly to sit on the barstool. She's even prettier up close. Her eyes are so deep, and when she smiles, she has a little dimple right below the corner of her mouth. I want to kiss it. Then I want to make my way lower, biting her chin, tracing my tongue down her neck to those perfect little tits.

Jesus. I don't know if it's the whiskey or the testosterone in the air, but I'm feeling thirsty for the first time in years.

A year ago, when my therapist released me from grief counseling, she said I should try dating again. She said I should be open to moving forward with my life. She said I was ready. I disagreed with her... I didn't think I could feel this way about another person ever again. Now, all I feel is *it's been so long*.

Clearing my throat, I grab the reins. "Sorry. I've

25

lived here about four years."

Her slim brow furrows, and her voice changes. "Four years? You're kidding me. What's your name?"

"Remi... Remington Key. I live in Eagleside Manor." As the words come out, I wince a little. I don't want her to think I'm bragging about living in Oakville's only gated community.

"Oh, really?" her eyebrows rise, and she turns as if to leave.

I can't help a laugh. "What is this? Reverse discrimination?" Carefully, I reach out to touch her arm. Despite my internal conflict, I don't want her to go.

She stops and faces me again, narrowing her eyes. "What are you doing in the Red Cat, Remington Key? Slumming?"

"What are you doing in the Red Cat... I don't know your name." Although, I swear she looks familiar.

"Ruby Banks." She holds out a slim, ivory hand with perfectly manicured nails.

Gently, I take it in mine, covering it with both of mine. She studies our connection, and her cheeks turn a pretty shade of pink.

How can I not know everyone living in Oakville? It's a testament to how little I get out these days, I guess. If it weren't for Eleanor's nagging, I wouldn't even bother with church.

"Nice to meet you, Ruby Banks." Right as I say the words, it clicks. "We *have* met before."

Her shoulder rises, and she slips her hand out of mine. "I don't think so."

"We did. I remember it now. It was after church one morning." I look toward the bar, and I recognize her blonde friend, a.k.a., my former therapist. "You were with Drew... Isn't that Andrea Harris?"

She does a funny little fast-laugh. "That wasn't me."

"But... it was." I study her face. She won't meet my eyes, so I try to lighten my tone. Maybe I'm being too forceful? "I was the guy with the squirmy four-year-old."

Another wince. I know admitting I'm a single dad probably kills any chance of getting a date with her.

Wait... Is that what I want?

It doesn't matter.

Loud commotion breaks out on the other side of the bar, interrupting our conversation.

It's hard to see what's happening as the bodies crush together. The guys form a tight circle, and voices are raised. It sounds like a fight is breaking out. I hear the crash of what sounds like a body being shoved against the opposite wall.

An unexpected surge of protectiveness grips me. Standing, I put my arm between Ruby and the chaos. "We should leave before it gets dangerous in here. Do you need a ride?"

Her head whips back and forth. "No, I have my car... I've got to find Drew." She pushes past my arm.

"Wait... Ruby!" I do my best not to panic as I watch her disappear in a mass of oversized guys shoving back and forth.

I try to follow her without starting a fight of my own. Interesting how guys are so quick to let girls pass in a crowd. Not so much for other guys.

When I finally make it to her, she's hugging Drew, who's holding hands with another guy I know. Grayson Cole owns the garage in town. I thought he'd left.

I can't tell what's happening, but it all seems to be

resolved. Gray puts his arm around Drew, and they head for the door. Ruby watches them go with her hands clasped at her chest, and I recognize something in her face.

It's a feeling… A longing so familiar, an emotion I remember once having. One I want again. Could Drew be right? Am I ready?

Once again our eyes meet, and again, it's electric, She walks straight to me, a small act, but it feels significant.

"What happened?"

The crowd slowly disperses while Mose the bartender holds what looks like a Louisville slugger.

Her hand slips into the crook of my arm, and she exhales a little sigh. "Do you believe in true love, Remington?"

"You can call me Remi. And I think so…"

I don't say I've stopped believing in *one* true love. At least, I hope we're allowed more than one. Otherwise, I'm fucked.

We go to my old spot at the bar, and she releases me, taking the stool beside mine. Blinking away the dreamy expression, she tilts her head to the side. "What do you do for a living to afford a McMansion in Eagleton Manor?"

I signal for drinks. "It's not a McMansion, and I've done a lot of things. What's your poison?"

"Tequila Sunrise, and don't dodge the question."

I grin and place our order. "I wasn't dodging. I left the Navy and started working in tech."

"Ahh…" She nods. "Military guy. We get a lot of those around here."

"Right, because of Charleston."

"What did you do in tech?"

"I sold a program to a group of investors, who in

turn sold it to the government. It made a lot of money, and now I'm an investor looking for guys like me with great ideas."

I think about how hard I worked in those early days, how hard I work now. I should be more involved with Lillie. I've acted just like my dad. Shit, these past four years, I practically turned into a clone of the man.

The bartender puts a whiskey in front of me and a salmon-colored mixed drink in front of Ruby. She takes a long sip, and I do the same.

"So you're like a philanthropist?"

"I'm an investor. I give developers money to finish their work, and when it becomes successful—if it becomes successful—I get a nice payday. Whatever money I put up, plus profit."

"That is some serious first-world shit right there. Some serious illuminati shit. Are you trying to control the world, Remington?"

I laugh, shaking my head. "I wish. I feel like I can't even control my house."

She nods, taking a long sip of her drink. "I hear that."

"And what do you do, Ruby Banks, who doesn't remember me from church?"

Her small nose wrinkles, and she shakes her head. "That wasn't me. It was some other, irresponsible person. I'm a very responsible, licensed therapist. Or at least I was."

That explains how she knows Drew. Leaning my elbow on the bar, I'm intrigued. "What do you mean you were?"

"I can't afford my client list." She copies my move, putting her elbow on the bar. "Or my lack of one. Too bad I'm not in tech or you could throw some money my way."

"Call me as soon as you develop an app."

"I'll do it." She grins, and I notice her studying my left hand. "You're not married, but you have a wiggly four-year-old. How's that?"

"My wife died."

"Oh!" She pulls back quickly. "I'm so sorry. I had no idea."

"It's okay. It was a long time ago." My hands go to my lap.

"Do you still miss her?" Her brows are pulled together, and when I look up, I see genuine concern in her eyes.

"Yes." Then I scratch my head. "I'll always miss her…" But maybe it's time to stop being alone? I don't know. "I'm starting to think I need help."

She leans forward. "It just so happens I have a lot of openings in my schedule. And I mean *a lot*."

"I think my most urgent concern is my daughter, Lillie."

"Does she have special needs?"

My bright-eyed little sunbeam flickers through my mind. "No, she's just four. She goes to preschool half days and then she's home while I'm working. She's active and playful, and my mother-in-law doesn't believe in listening to me—"

"Because she's the grandmother." Ruby nods as if she understands completely. "Grandparents are supposed to spoil them, feed them cake for breakfast. Not make them mind."

"Eleanor doesn't feed her cake, but Lillie's schedule is erratic. She never naps, so she's cranky in the evenings. And the Barney videos—"

"Oh, stop! Barney is the worst." She holds up her hand, making a horrified face.

"Tell me about it."

30

"He's a big purple freak with weird eyes and a creepy voice."

I snort in my glass. "You clearly have strong feelings about him."

"Why does he move his arms like that? Goody goody!" She pins her elbows at her waist and does a hilarious T. Rex flap. "If I were a kid, I'd pee my pants crying."

It's all too perfect. I know in that moment, this must happen.

"Come work for me." The words are out so fast, I can't stop them. I don't want to stop them.

Ruby freezes mid-T. Rex flap. "You're drunk."

"I'm serious." Sitting straighter, I snap into boss mode. "You're a licensed therapist. You're clearly qualified, and I need help."

"Do you know what therapists do?"

"I know what I do. I'm a problem solver, and we have parallel problems."

Her arms lower slowly, and I can tell she's curious. "What would I do for you?"

"Be Lillie's nanny." Her full lips quirk down, and I keep going. "You would live at my house, drive Lillie to and from school, do educational things with her in the afternoons... help with her meals and light housekeeping, bathe her, put her to bed..."

"You want me to be a live-in nanny?" She's not convinced, but I'm liking this idea more by the minute.

"I've got plenty of room. You'll share the whole top floor with Lillie, and that way if she needs anything during the night, you'll be there to help her."

"Why can't you help her?"

"I have to work."

Concern lines her pretty face, and I decide to sweeten the deal. "I'll pay you five hundred dollars a day."

She straightens so fast, she almost falls off her stool. I swallow a laugh and jump forward to catch her. The move puts us shoulder to shoulder, chest to chest, and heat surges through my waist. She smells good, like flowers in the spring... she feels even better in my arms.

In that moment, I'm vividly aware of how long it's been since I've had sex.

Her hands grip my biceps, moving higher as she regains her balance. She blinks up, and our noses almost touch. It's amazing... until she steps back, out of my embrace.

"You said five hundred dollars a day."

"That's right."

"And you're serious?"

"I am."

"I don't care if you're drunk." She sticks out her hand. "When do I start?"

I catch it in a nice, firm handshake. "How about Monday? You could move your things tomorrow evening, meet Lillie, get a feel for the place... Is that too soon?"

"We should have a contract or something... lay some ground rules. I've never been a nanny before."

I study this beautiful girl with bright, intelligent eyes. Her lips are red and full, and she smells like new roses. Not old lady roses, nice clean and crisp ones. I want to hold her in my arms again. I want to bury my face in her hair and slide my hands from her narrow waist, over her slim hips, cupping her ass and lifting her against the wall...

In my current state, I see no conflict in having these feelings and offering her a job. In hindsight, I probably am drunk. Still, I know my instincts are always good.

"I'll put a contract together, and you can look over it tomorrow. If you're at church, you can meet Lillie and let me know."

"One month." She holds up a finger, and I tilt my head to the side.

"What about it?"

"We'll have a one-month trial period." Then she nods, standing in front of the bar and picking up her small bag. "We'll meet tomorrow, and if the contract looks good, I'll do a one-month trial period. After that, we can decide if I stay."

"You sure you've never done this before?"

"I'm a professional. I cover all my bases." Her phone is out, and she taps the pink Lyft app.

"Give me your number."

She starts to object, then she backs down. "I was going to make a joke, but you're right. You'll need to be able to reach me."

Even if she decides not to work for me, I want to be able to reach her. Everything about this night is different, special. I'm sure it won't happen again... like it's the second chance I can't let slip away.

Her digits are in my phone, and I send her a quick text. "Now you have mine."

"My ride's here. See you tomorrow."

I follow her to the door, holding it as she steps out into the night. "Text me when you get there."

She pauses at the door and squints up at me. "Oakville's pretty small. I'm sure I'll get home just fine."

"Still, I'd like to know you made it."

"You know I've been taking care of myself for a while."

"Please?"

She does a little eye roll before hopping into the waiting car. I get one last look at her pretty legs before the door closes, and she's gone.

Inside the bar, five minutes later, I've just settled up my tab when my phone buzzes in my pocket. Sliding it out, the text shining on the screen tightens my stomach.

Made it home, boss. Happy?

I quickly tap out a reply. *So far, you're an exemplary employee. Looking forward to tomorrow.*

A few seconds pass, and I'm walking to the door as the gray bubble floats, indicating she's typing a reply. For as long as it takes, I'm a little surprised it's only two words.

Me too.

Chapter 3

Ruby

"Wake up! Wake up! Church time!" My ears flash with pain as my mother stomps around my room, opening the blinds and talking way too loud. "You want to hoot with the owls all night, you have to fly with the eagles all morning."

"That's not how that saying goes." I growl, pulling a pillow over my head. "Stop being so loud. And turn off the sun!"

I can't wait to get my own place.

"Get up, Ruby Banks!" She takes the pillow off my head and tosses it aside. "You live in my house, you go to church. Now go and take a shower. We leave in fifteen minutes."

Rolling onto my side, I look at the clock. It's not even eight yet. "Church doesn't start until ten!"

"We signed up to help with the senior breakfast this morning. It starts before Sunday school. Eight thirty."

"We signed up to help? *We?*" *I like that…* I grumble as I stomp to the shower. "I didn't sign up for anything."

Warm water rouses me, and the first thing I remember is Remington Key. Hell, what did I agree to do last night? I've lost my mind. Or have I?

Remington Key has a straight, white smile and an

adorable dimple in his left cheek. He has warm hazel eyes and wavy, caramel brown hair. His hands are long and elegant, and when I slipped off my stool last night, he caught me in the strongest embrace.

His muscles were hard and lined through his shirt, and I didn't want to let him go. I slid my hands slowly up the hard ridges, imagining what might be under that soft fabric. Water runs down my face, and I tilt my chin up, picturing his sexy lips touching mine, threading my fingers in those soft waves, wrapping my legs around his narrow waist... *Damn, that's hot...*

My hand slips between my thighs, and I finger the little bud hidden there. I move my hand back and forth, circling, massaging, rising onto my toes as I imagine his hard dick teasing my entrance, nudging, pushing, pillaging my insides, sliding in and out, all the way to the hilt, pushing me higher, higher...

My jaw drops, my eyes squeeze shut... Oh, god, I'm coming...

"Ten-minute warning!" My mother's loud voice jumps me out of my orgasm.

"Jesus!" I shout, my heart flying, and my entire body on edge.

"Do not take the lord's name in vain!"

"Or what?" I shout back, shutting off the tap and feeling *very* frustrated.

Drying off quickly, I think about what I've done. Have I lost my freakin' mind? I just spent the last several minutes rubbing one out while I dreamed of screwing my new boss...

That does it. I can't work for Remington Key. He's too hot.

Then I remember the carrot: Five hundred dollars a day.

Holy shit, that's fifteen thousand dollars a month!

How loaded is this guy? And why the fuck didn't I remember meeting him at church?

Shaking my head, I apply light makeup — powder on the nose, cat eyes, pale pink lip. He was drunk. He's going to call me today and apologize, and I'll be back on the job market.

Still... He seemed pretty serious. What if he doesn't back out?

My stomach squeezes, and I swallow a squeal. I could do a lot with fifteen thousand dollars a month. Standing in front of the mirror, I take a few deep breaths and evaluate my appearance. I look responsible, competent, professional. I would trust me with my kid.

If this is for real, and ridiculously hot Remington Key really wants to pay me an insane amount of money to be his nanny, I will do it.

He said he needs help, and it's the right and Christian thing to do.

I can do this.

Leaning forward, I softly order, "Don't fuck it up."

By the time we finish cleaning up after those messy old people, service has already begun. I don't mind being late, because Pastor Hibbert's sermons always put me to sleep. Also because it means Ma and I get to sit in one of the open pews near the back, rather than her favorite spot right up front.

The congregation is singing "Turn Your Eyes Upon Jesus," and I take this opportunity to turn my eyes upon Remington Key sitting beside a silver-haired woman who I assume is Eleanor, his mother-in-law. She's dressed in a pale blue suit, and she looks very formal and strict. She's vaguely familiar. I'm sure I've seen her at one of Ma's many Bible studies.

Remi's wearing a tailored brown suit, and now that he's standing, not sitting on a barstool, I realize he's tall. He's also slim, but not skinny. I bet he's hiding a hot, athletic bod under all that expensive-looking material. A Jamie Dornan in *Fifty Shades Freed* kind of bod.

I do a quick scan of the backs of heads. Dagwood is here, sitting with his wife Dotty. Mrs. Stern and her son Ralph are behind them. I do a shiver and continue looking, but I don't see Drew anywhere. Not that I'm surprised.

We're instructed to sit, and I watch as Remi makes sure Eleanor has everything she needs. *What a gentleman.* Just before he takes a seat, those hazel eyes sweep the room, and when they meet mine, a shot of adrenaline sizzles in my lower stomach.

A tiny smile curls my lips, and the side of his mouth moves upward. That dimple appears briefly, and I have to shift in my seat. *Damn*, he is so effing good-looking.

No, I don't think the F-bomb in church.

Yes, my mom is in my head.

Back to my hot boss... I can't believe he's lived here four years. Granted, I don't make it to church every single Sunday, but hell, I must be sleeping through a lot of sermons. Maybe he misses the Sundays I'm here and vice versa. Yes, that has to be what happens.

His head is turned to the side, and I admire his square jaw as he listens politely to Pastor Hibbert talking about helping others. A few natural highlights are right at the tips of his brown hair. I didn't notice it in the bar last night, and I bet as soon as he gets a haircut, they'll be gone. The thought makes me sad.

I tune in for a second, and the verse is about some

deaconess who helped the apostles. Finally, the pastor tells us to close our eyes and ask God to help us see people in the community who need a little time, a little friendship, a little faith.

Clearly, this is a direct sign God wants me to accept the job working with Remi. I was meant to see he needs help and offer to give it to him. *Mission accepted, God.*

The *Amens* ring out, and we're on our feet, headed to the door as the organ plays the Doxology. Once we're outside, I linger on the front lawn, wondering if Remi might want to chat while we're all here together.

"What are you waiting for?" Ma stops her progress toward the parking lot and walks back to where I stand.

"I'm meeting someone... Do you know Remington Key?"

"Remington?" Her head cocks to the side like a bird.

"Um.. yeah. I'll explain later." I don't really want to go into the details with her. No telling what she'll say when she hears I'm moving into his house and how much he's paying me.

Anyway, here he comes, and my heart beats faster. *Why the hell am I nervous?* I don't know.

"Thanks for waiting." He walks quickly to where I'm standing, and thankfully Ma falls silent.

"Hi." I feel like I'm smiling too big, so I clear my throat and glance down at my black platform shoes. I'm so glad I wore them, since he's tall. "I thought I might hang around and meet Lillie."

"Eleanor went to get her from Sunday school." He reaches up to rub the back of his neck while he looks toward the building running parallel to the sanctuary, and I can almost see that bicep flexing in his arm. "I guess that's something you could do. If you still want the job, I mean."

I glance across the lawn at the dozens of children, from toddlers to elementary school-age kids, running out the doors of the other building to meet their parents.

More nerves flutter in my insides. *Am I really doing this?*

Fifteen thousand dollars, Ruby.

Yes, I am.

"I can do that." I don't want to make it seem like I'm not worth it. "It'll be one of my many tasks."

Those golden-hazel eyes meet mine, and the flutters turn to butterflies. His eyes graze over my white lace blouse, and I swear I can feel them touching my skin. It's like he's undressing me, but carefully, delicately…

It's fucking hot.

What? We're on the church lawn.

Blinking away, he pulls a long, white envelope from his breast pocket. "I took some time this morning to write up the contract. You can look over it and bring it back this evening. Once you've decided."

"Sure." I take it from him and slip it into my bag. "I'm about a hundred percent decided."

Or fifteen thousand percent.

At last Eleanor emerges holding a little girl's hand. As soon as she sees us, she tosses her grandmother's hand aside and takes off running toward her dad.

Light brown pigtails bounce around her shoulders, and she's wearing a cute green dress with a navy bow and a white collar. She has a little white cardigan on top, and when she reaches Remi, she jumps.

He lifts her to his chest almost as if it were choreographed, and she throws her arms around his neck. "I made you a picture, Daddy, but Gigi said she has to hold it because it's all wet."

"I can't wait to see it." He kisses her cheek, and I swear to God, my insides are just all mush at the cuteness overload... and possibly a teensy bit envious.

I can't imagine doing what she just did with my dad.

Not that I care anymore, of course.

"I want you to meet someone." Remi turns to me, and I see how much they look alike. Her hair is lighter than his, but they have the same eyes, the same cute dimple in their cheeks. "Lillie, I'd like you to meet Miss Ruby Banks."

She squirms forward, and I totally remember meeting them six months ago. *Holy shit.* She was squirming all over him, and I took one look and looked the other way. I could kick myself in the pants. Whatever. We're here now.

"How do you do, Miss Ruby Banks?" Lillie holds out her little hand, and I squat down to her level to take it.

"Very well, thank you." I shake her hand, and we both smile. "You're very polite."

"My Gigi said good manners show people you care."

My eyebrows rise, and I glance up at her father. Remi shrugs.

"You're very smart, too. I bet you make good grades in school."

The little girl nods. "I do. You're pretty." Lillie looks up at her dad. "Is Ruby coming over for a playdate?"

"Ruby might be coming over to stay with us. If that's okay with you." He lifts the little girl to his hip again just as Eleanor reaches us.

"Like for a sleepover?" Lillie's voice is loud, and Eleanor's face is pure shock.

"I'm sorry. What did I miss?" A fake smile stretches her cheeks, and Eleanor's voice sounds exactly as I expected it would—old, refined, and a touch bitchy.

She places an elegant hand on the top of her chest as Ma finds her voice as well.

"Ruby?" Her tone makes me wince. "What is he saying?"

"Sorry." Remi steps forward. "I'm Remington Key."

Ma takes his hand briefly. "June Banks, Ruby's mother." She looks at Eleanor. "We met at the ladies' auxiliary brunch."

"Yes," Eleanor nods. "You're the church secretary."

Ma hated that brunch. She talked about it for two days, how the ladies there were not very Christlike. I never knew exactly what she meant, but now I think I have an idea with the way Eleanor says *secretary*. Like it's a dirty word.

What she doesn't know is just because my mom is tight-fisted and works as the church secretary, she has a shit-ton of money socked away. Still, even though my dad made us wealthy, Ma never allowed us to act materialistic or better than anyone. To her, valuing people simply because of how much money is in their bank account is as bad as lying.

"Remington." Eleanor touches her son-in-law's arm. "What is going on here?"

Remi's eyes meet mine, and I swear in that moment, the decision is made. "Why don't we discuss it over lunch."

I follow his lead, taking my mom by the arm.

"Come on, Ma. I'll tell you everything over dumplings."

"I made Sundubu-jjigae," She is not amused, and I know she didn't miss a thing.

"Sounds great." I love her spicy tofu soup. "I'll fill you in at home."

Elegant bowls of steaming brown soup sit in front of us, and the Asian Inquisition continues. "A babysitting job?" Disgust permeates her tone.

"A full-time nanny position." I have the contract out on the table beside my bowl, and I'm quickly scanning the list of duties. It's exactly what he said they would be. "I'll take care of his daughter, basically like her mother would."

"You are not her mother." She spoons the soup, keeping her eyes on mine. "What about your work at the clinic?"

"I've been there almost a year." My lips tighten, and I say what I haven't even told Drew yet. "I'm not sure I like the work."

She accepts this, lifting her chin after she takes another bite. "Still, childcare is a step down."

Nodding, I eat some of my own lunch. "Normally, I'd agree with you, but this is different, bigger than just babysitting, and he's paying me a lot of money." That yearning is in my chest again. It makes me feel like I can't breathe. "I'll actually be able to pay my own bills. I can get my own place. After all, I can't live with you forever."

I add the last bit with a laugh, but Ma emphatically objects. "Nonsense! I lived with my parents until I married your father."

"You were twenty-three when you married Dad."

"And we had a long and happy life together."

"Did you?" I can't keep the skepticism out of my

voice. It's hard to believe Dad was nice to anybody.

"Ruby Banks. Your father was a good man. He had very high standards."

That's one way of putting it. "Well, I'm taking this job."

She shakes her head. "Remington Key is a good-looking man. You cannot work for him."

I snort a laugh. "That's just... Looksism!"

"You made up that word." Her voice is stern as she sips another spoonful of soup. "You don't know how to cook."

"I'll learn." *How hard can it be? I also don't know anything about kids, but Lillie's not a baby.*

"You will be living in sin with him."

"I will be living in the lap of luxury, getting paid a lot of money I will then use to figure out what I want to do with my career."

She sits back in her chair and crosses her arms, still not smiling. "What you will do is get in trouble."

My stomach squirms, but I won't give in to this feeling. I will not let her be right. Emotions come and go, and I will not blow a great opportunity just because the guy holding it out to me happens to be obscenely handsome.

I've dated more guys than I can count, and I've always been in control of the situation. There is no reason this time should be any different.

Even if it is, I will not let my hormones or Ma's negative attitude screw it up. Steeling my resolve, I focus on my vow to myself in the bathroom mirror.

"Will you have a little faith? Please?" I can't believe how calm my voice is. "I will not get in trouble. I'll get what I want."

"Only if you know what you want."

That's the problem—I think I do.

Chapter 4

Remi

Lillie chases a macaroni noodle around her bowl with her fingers, and Eleanor grabs her wrist, wiping her small hand with a cloth. It's the only thing that breaks her lecture.

"Use your fork, Lillian." Just as fast, she's back on me. "You cannot hire that girl to live in this house."

"I can do whatever I want." My voice is level. "It's my house."

Eleanor's voice goes low. "I saw the way you spoke to her at church. You have chemistry with that girl. It's a bad idea."

"If I thought it was a bad idea, I wouldn't have given her a contract and asked her to start this evening."

Lillie looks up from her plate, where she's putting mac and cheese on her fork with her fingers. "What's chemistry, Daddy?"

Her question makes me grin. "Remember Bill Nye the science guy?"

She nods quickly, that cute little dimple appearing in her cheek when she smiles. I wasn't sure I could love someone this much until she was born. Now I can't imagine my life without her.

"Well," I continue. "He does chemistry."

Her little eyes widen. "He makes things go boom!

Will you make Ruby go boom?"

I cough a laugh, shifting in my seat and imagining how that might go... and how it might sound. "It's different with people, honey."

Of course, Eleanor's face is a disapproving, *I told you so*. "Lillian, take your hands out of your food." She wipes my daughter's hand again. "What are her qualifications?"

Sitting back, I cross my arms over my chest. "She has a master's degree, and she's a licensed therapist."

"Therapists are all crazy. It's why they do what they do."

"She is not crazy." *A little nutty, maybe, but not crazy.*

"We don't need her."

"We do." I fight to keep the edge out of my tone. "Friday night was the perfect example."

"I was right Friday night."

Anger rises in my stomach, but I fight it down. I won't let her bait me.

Instead, I take a different approach. "You're her grandmother, Eleanor. You should be spoiling her, not worrying about following my rules."

She sits back, daring to act offended. "I guess you think I was a horrible mother."

"I do not think you were a horrible mother. I think we need boundaries, and you need a break. You've been taking care of Lillie for four years now."

"So it's not about me?" Eleanor huffs, straightening her blouse.

I don't respond to the snark in her tone. I don't say it's very much about her, and that I wouldn't have been in that bar last night if it wasn't for her.

"It's about making things easier for all of us."

"I just hope you remember those boundaries when

that girl is in this house."

"I'd rather not discuss that here." I tilt my head toward Lillie, who's studying her plate, but who I know is not deaf. "My goal is to have more time to focus on my work. I need to get more accomplished if I'm going to grow the business. It's what I hope Ruby allows me to do."

Lillie's head snaps up. "I like Ruby. She talks to me. She shook my hand and said I was polite."

My smile to Eleanor is conclusive. "*That* is what matters most to me."

I pace the large foyer of my house as I wait for Ruby to arrive.

She texted me earlier saying the contract was agreeable, she would sign it, and arrive here with her things at seven. It's seven, and I can't sit down. I have to move.

I've prepared the room down the hall from Lillie. They're on the third floor of the house. My suite and offices are spread out on the second. Eleanor's master suite is on the first.

As I walk back and forth in the large entrance, I realize this house probably is considered a McMansion. The grand staircase curves up to the second-floor landing, which has a balcony overlooking the downstairs.

Doors close it off from my quarters, and the stairs continue up to the third floor. When she was a baby, we had Lillie's bedroom and playroom on the first floor near Eleanor's. As she got older, she wanted to move to the top floor. She went through a *Tangled* phase, and I guess it made her feel like a princess in a tower. Naturally, we have monitors in her rooms.

Her playroom is still on the first floor, however,

and I hear her little voice talking to her dolls. She won't be awake much longer. My hands are shoved in the pockets of my jeans, and the tail of my button-up shirt is untucked.

I didn't want to appear too formal when she arrived or make her feel uncomfortable. Honestly, the only thing I know about nannies is from what I saw as a kid in *The Sound of Music*, which my mother made me watch one day when I was sick, and which I mostly slept through.

Still, I remember whistles blowing, kids marching like soldiers, and running from the Nazis.

I'm pretty confident none of that will happen in my house, so I have no basis for what to expect.

A knock sounds at the door, and my boat shoes squeak on the marble as I rush to open it. Ruby's hair swirls around her shoulders when I do. Her brown eyes widen, moving up and down my body quickly. *God, she's so gorgeous.*

"Hi." I manage to say.

The air hums and crackles between us. I wonder if she feels it, too. Then her cheeks flush that pretty shade of pink, and I know she does.

Jesus. I want to fuck the nanny. Don't get a boner. I cannot adjust my fly right now.

"Hi!" She smiles nervously. "I… um… wasn't sure where to park. My car is down there."

She points to the right, along the circle drive, and I step out on the flagstone landing to see a lime green Subaru almost at the street behind Eleanor's Crown Victoria.

"That's fine." I nod, stepping back and holding the door for her to enter. "You can park in the garage next time. I'll make sure we have a remote for you."

"It's the little things." As she passes me, I catch the

faint scent of roses again. I wonder if it's her hair or her perfume.

A navy backpack is on her shoulder, and she's rolling a white suitcase with a pink kitten outline on it. Everything she does turns me on.

"Can I help you with your bags?"

"It's okay, I've got them." She looks up, all around the entrance. "Your home is beautiful."

I close the door, leaning my back against it as I study her. She's dressed in black leggings and a white tank top with a long-sleeved chambray shirt unbuttoned over it, and she looks perfect. Her hair is up in a high ponytail, and the ends fall just past her shoulder. She turns in the entrance to face me, and for a moment I don't know what to say.

The long, white envelope is in her hand. "I guess you'll be wanting this." She holds it out to me, and I step forward to take it. "I signed everything."

"I added the bit about the one-month trial period. To be sure you're happy here."

"Right." She nods slowly, her eyes staying on mine. "It looked like you covered everything we discussed."

"I tried to be thorough."

It's like a low current hums between us, silent but powerful. As much as I try to dismiss Eleanor's lecture, keeping my hands off this girl might not be as easy as I anticipated. I feel like I'm waking up from a long sleep...

What? No. Of course, I'll keep my hands off Ruby. I'm not some creepy 1950s-era sexually harassing male employer. This is a business arrangement. A mutually beneficial business arrangement. She is here to help care for my daughter. That is all.

"Is something wrong?" Her soft voice is higher,

and I realize I'm frowning.

"Oh, sorry, No. I was just thinking about…" *I can't tell her what I was just thinking about. What's wrong with me?* "Have you had dinner?" Her expression is slightly startled, and I hasten to add. "We've all eaten, but you're welcome to help yourself if you're hungry."

"Oh," she exhales and smiles, seeming relieved. "I already had something. Thanks."

It feels so stiff and formal. I'm not sure what to do to ease the tension. "Eleanor has gone to bed." *After sulking around the house all evening*, I don't add. "Lillie is still awake. She wanted to show you her room… And yours."

"Okay!" Ruby seems as eager as me to do something, anything to get out of this foyer, where we're awkwardly trying to pretend like we're not checking each other out.

I lead the way through the open living room, with the large kitchen and dining area to the right and Lillie's playroom on the opposite end to the left. My daughter is still happily chattering away with her dolls.

"Travis," Lillie speaks with an exaggerated southern accent, shaking a doll in a pink dress at a sitting Ken. "When a woman says lay-tah, what she really means is not EVAH!"

What is she saying? I start to make some sort of apology, when Ruby laughs. *"The Princess and the Frog!"*

She drops her backpack at my feet and leaves her suitcase, going to where Lillie sits on the floor and kneeling beside her.

"Ruby!" My daughter jumps up and hugs her, holding out a doll in a green dress. "You want to be Tiana?"

"Sure!" Ruby takes the green doll and shakes her at the pink one Lillie's holding. "Lottie, don't eat all the beignets."

"Give me napkins!" My daughter grabs five tissues out of the box on the floor and shoves them under her doll's arms. "I'm sweatin' like a sinner in church!" I cough a laugh, and she keeps going. "My prince is never going to come!"

"Lottie, wait!" Ruby calls after my daughter, who runs to the small daybed. "Calm down and take a deep breath."

"I just have to wish harder!" Lillie looks up at the ceiling. "Please please please please…"

Ruby goes to where my daughter is chanting, and they continue this scene. I'm stuck at the door, watching as they bond over some crazy movie scene I don't know.

Satisfaction filters warm through my stomach. This is good… better than good.

I watch as she smooths a silky, sand-colored curl off Lillie's shoulder. "Wishing is fun, but you have to work hard to get what you want."

Lillie puts the doll down and turns to her, and I don't think they're playing anymore. "Did you have to work hard to get what you wanted?"

Ruby smiles. "I've worked hard, but I'm not finished yet. I still have things I want."

Interesting.

"I like your hair." Lillie crawls around the bed to thread her fingers in Ruby's long ponytail. "You're like Mulan."

"Mulan is Chinese. I'm half Korean."

Lillie's eyes widen. "What's that?"

"It's a whole different country. We can talk about it later." Ruby looks back at me, where I'm silently watching, wondering where she's been all my daughter's life. "I didn't know if it might be bedtime?"

"Yes," I snap out of it, straightening. "I'll show you your room."

Reaching down, I slide out the handle on her rolling suitcase and lift her backpack from where she left it at my feet.

Ruby hurries to stop me. "I can carry my bags."

"You'd better let me. Your room's on the third floor."

"We're at the very top!" Lillie grabs her hand, practically skipping. "All the princesses live in the top of the castle."

"Is that so?" Ruby smiles down at her, and the two take off ahead of me.

Lillie chatters all the way up the stairs, and I follow, feeling better about this situation by the minute. Lillie acts like Ruby belongs to her, leading her up the stairs and down the hall to her room.

Ruby gasps as she steps inside, looking all around the same way she did in the foyer. "It's beautiful." She looks back at me. "And so big!"

I can't resist. "That's what she said."

Ruby snorts a laugh, but my daughter frowns. "That is what Ruby said?"

"It's a joke." Ruby smooths her hand down Lillie's hair, and I place her backpack on the queen-sized bed against the wall.

The room has been furnished and empty since we bought the house. I look around at the white walls and sand-colored comforter on the bed with tan pillows. White cordless shades cover the windows, and the French doors facing the front drive are covered with long, white sheers. Even the bathroom suite is all white.

"You can change the décor if you'd like."

She goes to the beige-wood corner desk. "It is a bit monochromatic. Maybe after my first month?"

Lillie takes her hand. "Come see my room!"

I stop them before they leave. "I'm heading downstairs." Turning my attention to Lillie, my voice gets serious. "No more playing. Brush your teeth and get ready for bed. Lights out in ten minutes."

"Okay." Her bottom lip pokes out, and I scoop her up in a hug.

"Goodnight, princess."

She melts and gives me a hug then starts wiggling to get down. I release her and straighten to catch Ruby's eyes on me.

Her expression is a mixture of curiosity and something more... desire? I don't know. Hell, maybe it's just what I want to see there. I can't stop these feelings of desire from flaring up.

I will stop them.

"I'll be awake a bit longer if you need anything." I leave them, stopping by my bedroom to kick off my shoes before continuing down to the kitchen for a drink.

Chapter 5

Ruby

Remington Key has perfect feet.

After watching Lillie brush her teeth, reading her a princess picture book, singing as much as we could remember of "Almost There" from *The Princess and The Frog*, and saying the "Now I lay me down to sleep" prayer, I left my new little charge snuggled soundly in her bed.

Then I returned to my giant room and unpacked my folded clothes into drawers and hung my few blouses and skirts in the large closet. My toiletries are arranged in the large bathroom, and all I need is a glass of water for bed.

Lillie's right. Descending the enormous staircase, past the second-floor landing, to the first, I can't help feeling like I've been whisked away to some castle like one of those princesses.

I'm in the kitchen searching for a glass, when I notice my boss standing in the lamp-lit living room, looking out the French doors toward the man-made lake in the center of this posh gated community.

He's still wearing those sexy, loose jeans and that pale blue button-down, untucked. A crystal tumbler is in his hand, and his feet are bare on the hardwoods. *It's on, Jamie Dornan.*

Nope. I put the brakes on that and tell my

hormones to take a rest. As Tiana says, *I'm almost there*. No distractions. But when he turns and sees me watching him, I swear, my entire body flushes as hot as his hazel eyes.

Blinking fast, I force a smile. "She's adorable."

A smile ghosts across his lips. "She's always had a lot of personality." His brow quirks. "You're no slouch in that department. How did you know all of that stuff she was saying?"

"What can I say?" I do a shrug. "I'm a sucker for Disney princesses."

"You'll be her favorite person in the house."

My stomach is tight and tingly. "It'll come in handy when I have to make her eat broccoli."

"She actually loves broccoli. Dipped in ranch dressing."

"Little weirdo." I'm thinking how much I like this kid already until he laughs, and my jaw drops. My face flushes. "I mean... I didn't mean it like that. Your daughter is not a weirdo. I actually love broccoli myself—"

"It's okay." He holds out a hand. "It *is* weird for a kid to like broccoli." He takes a step away from the window, toward me. "So? What do you think? Got any questions?"

"Um..." I look around the large living room, the soft white sofa and huge flat screen television over the wide, dark fireplace. "You have such a beautiful home."

"Think of it as yours while you're here."

"Right..." I wonder how long that will take. "I guess... do you need me to make breakfast in the morning?"

"Just for Lillie... and you, if you eat breakfast. Eleanor does her own thing, and I usually grab a yogurt or a power bar."

"Should I make coffee?"

"We have a Keurig."

"Right." *Easy enough...* "I saw preschool is at eight to noon. Do I make lunch?"

"Again, just for the two of you." He smiles. "Dinner's really the only meal we eat together. Eleanor has a private chef who comes three times a week. She's very particular about her diet... Our diet."

"Ah." I nod. "Explains why she's so thin."

We've been moving closer as we speak, and now we're in front of each other. I can feel the heat radiating off his skin. I can smell the earthy fragrance of his cologne—sandalwood, leather, and soap. I remember it from the bar when he caught me.

"She's very particular about a lot of things, but I'm hoping to ease her into her own place."

I think about my own mother. "Let me know how that goes."

"I guess you'll be here to witness it." The dimple in his cheek causes the space between my legs to heat. Our breath is warm, and we're so close. My lips are full and heavy, and if I lift my chin, I'm certain his would dip, and our mouths would caress...

Or maybe I'm daydreaming.

Stepping back, I do my best to break the spell. "I'd better go on up. Morning comes early."

His eyes hold mine, warm and inviting. "Let me know if you need anything."

Jesus take the wheel, if I told him what I need right now...

"Thanks." I'm retreating fast, while I still can. "And thanks for the job."

"You're helping me, remember?" He smiles, and that dimple almost scrambles my brain.

"Right. Although, it looks like you've got everything pretty much under control."

"Things aren't always how they appear."

He can say that again. I turn, leaving as fast as possible without running. If I stay here, so close to him one more minute, I'm not sure what might happen.

In my room, I strip off my leggings and toss the chambray shirt on the back of a chair. I grab a notebook from my backpack and crawl into the super silky sheets, beneath the thick duvet, and bend my knees.

At the top of the page, in all capital letters, I write GOALS. Under it, I make a numbered list.

1. Get my own place.
2. Pay off my credit card.
3. Save for new career options.

Yes. This is what I need to do. Focus on my goals. This is how I'll resist the temptation sleeping one floor below me and *not fuck this up.*

"Penny cakes!" Lillie sits on the stool across from me with a plastic cup of orange juice in one hand and a fork in the other.

I frown, studying the box of pancake mix. *Mix with water, drop onto hot griddle, flip when bubbles appear.*

I take a sip of coffee. I'll have to get up earlier for this. It sounds so easy, but I'm not convinced. "Let's just have go-gurt and toast today."

Her little lip pokes out, and even pouting, I swear, she's the cutest thing. Leaning forward, I speak softly, our faces close. "Remember how Tiana can cook anything in New Orleans?"

Her pout turns to a big smile, and she nods excitedly.

"I am not Tiana. I'm more like… Lottie."

Her shoulders drop, and I nod, pressing my lips into a frown. "But I'll learn. Maybe we can learn together?"

Her excitement returns. "Yes!"

"In the meantime..." I pass her a plastic pouch of yogurt and pull a loaf of bread out of the small box on the counter. "Go-gurt and toast. I'll put some peanut butter on it."

That satisfies her, and Eleanor breezes into the room wearing beige pants and a navy sweater with a neat Chanel scarf tied at her neck.

"Good morning, Lillie, Ruby. I trust you slept well?" She places a mug in the Keurig, pops in a pod, and hits the brew button. "Sorry I had to turn in early. I was very tired. Guess I'm getting older."

I don't believe that for a second. She's studying me like one of those predator birds, searching for signs of weakness. Too bad she's not going to find any.

"No worries." I smile as I spread peanut butter on Lillie's toast—all-natural, of course. "Lillie showed me my room." I wink at my little charge as I hand her the toast. "Remi filled in the rest."

Her eyes narrow, and I know what she's thinking.

I'm just going to let her think it, too.

"Ready to go to school?" She turns to her granddaughter, who's stuffing toast in her mouth and nodding. "My goodness, Lillian, that's not what you're wearing is it?"

For a moment, I'm confused. Lillie is dressed in a sea green skirt, made of layers of thick, sparkly tulle and a white tee with a glittery *Make Waves* and a blue-green-lavender mermaid. On her feet are iridescent silver Uggs.

"Ruby said I could!" Lillie cries.

"I'm not surprised." Eleanor sneers at my outfit.

"What?" I glance down at the flowing purple skirt I'm wearing with a white tee that says *Stay Gold* on the front and black converse tennis shoes. I put on light makeup, pink lips and mascara with just a touch of blush.

I'm very nanny-chic, if you ask me.

"I'm confused." I look up at Eleanor again. "Is she not supposed to wear those boots to school?"

I imagine she'll be running and jumping and climbing and doing whatever else little kids do all day with their friends. Maybe tennis shoes are more appropriate.

"I placed out a lovely smocked dress for her to wear last night, and her black patent Mary Janes and lace socks."

"Oh…" I did see that. "I thought that was for Sunday."

"Yesterday was Sunday." Blue eyes level on mine. "Lillian has many nice dresses. At the rate she's growing, she'll hardly get to wear any of them before they're too small."

I pinch my lips together, thinking. When she got dressed this morning, Lillie was very excited about putting her outfit together.

I think she's adorable in it.

Still… this is our first crossing of swords and how I handle it is going to set the tone going forward. I choose my words carefully, keeping my voice level, firm, and not aggressive.

"I imagine it's hard to run and play in those dresses and shoes… And I don't think they show off her personality."

Eleanor's gaze narrows. "Lillian is four. Her personality is still ours to mold." That statement makes me bristle. "Besides, Oaklawn is a very prestigious school. She should look the part."

Now I understand what she's worried about, and I remember my mother's complaint. Eleanor wants Lillie to look like a catalog model and not a real, live four-year-old. I also see what Remi vaguely referenced in our earlier conversations.

"I think Lillie's outfit is adorable and perfect for a day at preschool." I'm not backing down.

"She looks like a vagrant." Eleanor's annoyance is barely hidden.

Remi walks in the room at that exact moment, looking fine as always. "Morning, ladies." He goes to the Keurig, oblivious to the tension crackling in the air.

"Daddy!" Lillie rocks on her stool, finishing her toast, and seeming about as oblivious as her dad. "I'm eating toast."

"What's that? Peanut butter?" He tweaks her nose. "You're a little peanut butter."

"I am not!" She cries, giggling.

His smile turns to me, and damn, it's the same as last night—interested, focused, irresistible. "Did you sleep well? Got everything you need?"

Hardly. I feel the heat in my cheeks, and I don't want to respond to him this way in front of Eleanor. Especially not in the middle of a power struggle.

"I'm good." I take a sip of cool coffee. "Everything is perfect."

Eleanor takes advantage of our fizzy moment to reassert her power. "Lillian, go to your room and change. Now. We don't have time to waste."

Lillie whines and looks to me for help. My eyes go to Eleanor's, and I pick up my car keys. "You're right. We don't have time if I'm going to meet her teacher. We need to leave now."

"She will *not* go to school dressed this way. She

61

looks like a... a—"

"Mermaid princess!" Remi scoops his daughter off the stool into the air.

He's wearing a short-sleeved tee, and the muscles in his arms line and flex. As if that wasn't enough, Lillie's tummy peeps out, and he lowers her to his mouth for a loud, sloppy raspberry.

"Dad-day! Dad-day!" Lillie screams, laughing and squealing so shrill, dogs cry.

A smile splits my cheeks, and damn him. I might have just fallen in love in that moment.

He laughs and lowers his daughter in his arms. Her cheeks are pink and her laughter contagious. "You'd better get out of here before you miss the first bell."

"No!" In a flash, her little face goes serious, and she wiggles to get out of his arms. "I'll have to move my monkey!"

I have no idea what that means, but Lillie grabs my hand, pulling me to the door. I snatch my bag off a nearby chair. My keys are in my hand, and I look to see if Eleanor is still planning to ride with us.

"Have a nice day, Lillian, I'll see you this afternoon." She turns on her heel and stalks off in the opposite direction.

A smile teases my lips, and it takes all my willpower not to do a little fist pump. At the same time, I know this isn't over.

Oaklawn Preschool looks more like an expensive boarding school than a school for kids five and under. It's another new addition to accommodate the wealthier families moving into Oakville from Charleston—much like Eagleton Heights.

Parking in the small lot, I notice the Audis,

Mercedes, Acuras, and other fancy cars lined in the circle drive. I'd feel inferior, but I guess I'm the high-priced nanny. That gives me a certain level of clout.

"You'll have to show me your room." I look in the rearview mirror at Lillie sitting in her booster in the backseat.

She's so cute in her mermaid getup. Right before we walked out the door, she grabbed a headband with feathers and a tiara on top.

"Ms. Terry is in the E hall." She takes my hand like a regular little adult and leads me across the lawn and up the stone steps.

Walking past mothers in starched skirts and blouses, scarves, and Prada bags, I get Eleanor's insistence on Lillie's attire. All the little girls are wearing smocked dresses and patent leather shoes. Hell, I'm starting to wonder if they even play at this school.

Lillie's teacher, by contrast, is delightful. A petite young woman with light blonde hair and a bright smile, Ms. Terry is round and huggable and clearly in love with her class.

"Good morning, Lillie! My, you look fancy! Are you a mermaid?" Lillie nods excitedly, and her teacher continues. "Get your things from your cubby. Today we're learning red monster number two or *cinco*."

I'm impressed. Colors, numbers, and Spanish. "Hi, I'm Ruby, Lillie's new nanny."

"Nice to meet you!" She shakes my hand, and we spend a few short minutes getting to know each other. I give her my cell number, and she gives me the syllabus for the semester. A syllabus in preschool? Walking away, I search the sheet for where they get dirty.

"Lillie has a new nanny?" That voice doesn't

sound friendly.

Turning, I can't believe it. "Serena Whitehead? I thought you moved to Charleston."

"Ruby Banks?" She does not smile. "It's Serena North now. My husband Dr. Phillip North and I just moved back to Oakville with our daughter Whitney. I see you're still here. Working as a nanny now? Is that right?"

The way she says it makes me want to crawl under a rock.

Which I will not do.

"Remi needed help, so I agreed to do this for a month."

"Remi?" Another woman, slightly older steps up to join us. She's wearing a starched white shirt, a floral, tea-length skirt right out of the 1950s, and a condescending sneer. "What's this about Remi? Who are you?"

"It appears Remington has hired a new nanny." Serena says. "Ruby Banks, this is Anita Flagstaff."

"Hello." I nod. "Nice to meet you. I have to go."

"Just a minute." Anita is still scowling, looking me up and down. "You're the new nanny? Where's Eleanor?"

"I'm sorry. Why are you asking?"

"I was best friends with Sandra Burnside Key. I want to be sure Lillian and Remi aren't being... taken advantage of."

"Is that so?" One thing's for sure, this woman won't bully me. "Did someone ask you to do that?"

"Of course not. I consider it my duty as Sandy's friend."

"Perhaps this is something you should discuss with Remi. I don't feel comfortable discussing family matters with strangers."

Turning on my heel, I square my shoulders and walk with purpose toward the door.

Anita Flagbitch speaks in a whisper loud enough for me to hear. "Looks like a live-in geisha to me."

"All I know is Phillip better not get any ideas." Serena's voice is rude as it ever was. "Ruby Banks is trouble."

My face tries to get hot, but I fight it. For starters, I'm a nanny, I'm not Japanese, and by definition geishas did not all sell sex. Many of them were artists, musicians, and educated companions…

Whatever. All that explaining would be "casting pearls before swine," as Ma would say.

Instead, I push through the door and through my feelings of embarrassment. I'm not doing anything wrong, and I'm too old for these women to hurt me.

Chapter 6

Remi

Hiring Ruby might be the best decision I've made all year.

When I walked into the kitchen this morning, I could tell something was up by the way Lillie was dressed. Since she started preschool, Eleanor has had her walking around looking like an escapee from *Toddlers and Tiaras*, minus all the makeup. And the tiara.

I think my daughter might have liked that part.

Seeing Lillie laughing, brimming with excitement, and looking like a regular little kid this morning, melted my insides. The stress is off, and she's having fun again.

Don't get me wrong. If Lillie were the type of kid who wanted to wear smocked dresses and patent leather shoes all the time, I could deal with it. I want my daughter to be happy, but this morning I saw her true personality.

I also saw Eleanor's attempts to control it, whether it's because she doesn't know how to let Lillie express herself or because she sees that expression as a threat. I don't know.

Ruby, by contrast, lets my daughter shine. She gets on her level and plays with her. She talks to her, but she doesn't force her to be an adult.

It's incredible how it affects me. She's like a gift.

Walking around my office, I toss the stress ball in the air, giving it a squeeze every time I catch it. I stop at the French doors facing the lake in my office.

All three floors have them. They're lined up parallel to each other, with balconies on the second and third levels.

Ruby's right, it's a beautiful home, and the layout works well with my family situation. Each floor has privacy, like its own quarters... I never noticed it before.

I haven't noticed a lot of things.

Gazing out at the calm waters, the cranes stepping carefully along the banks, I dismiss any second thoughts I might have had about hiring Ruby.

Sure, it was impulsive and seemingly out of the blue, but I'd been researching hiring a nanny for weeks. I had planned to go through a service, but trusting my gut has gotten me this far, and Ruby is clearly the right person for the job.

She's a smart, independent woman who isn't afraid of Eleanor and who also happens to be great with Lillie. It's a stroke of luck I'm not sure a service would have provided.

My mind drifts to the way she took Lillie's invitation to play that Disney princess scene last night. Ruby didn't care who saw her. She didn't care if it was silly. She only cared about getting to know my little girl and making a friend.

Seeing her that way did something more, though. It found a crack in the wall I'd built around my heart. It took all the feelings I'd set aside and stirred them up, twisting them into a new and unexpected emotion.

I realized in that moment... I am different.

Before, I didn't believe I could ever move on

without betraying my wife's memory, no matter how many self-help books I read. It didn't matter if I was thirty, with more than half of my life still ahead of me... I felt guilty if I responded to the sight of a beautiful woman.

Hell, I felt guilty for being attracted to Ruby.

Despite everything Drew said, I couldn't let go and learn to live again. What changed?

I don't have to ask. The answer struts around this house with bouncing curls and sparkly mermaid shirts. Lillie is the key to it all, and now I have to decide how I'm going to handle this new information.

Before, when it was only attraction, I could dismiss it. I'm a mature adult, I'm five years older than Ruby, I can handle myself.

Now that she's become my ally, now that I know she's smart and tough as well as sexy, now that she's stolen Lillie's heart and treats my daughter like I would...

It's a pull I'm finding hard to resist.

I turn from the window and toss the stress ball on my desk. I will resist it. I'll focus on something different, what I hope to accomplish. The reason I hired Ruby in the first place.

Sure, it was so I could move Eleanor into her proper place, but it was also so I could focus on my work and move my investment firm to the next level.

I've been following a few tech startups. One even has a bid from the military that could bring in a huge windfall in the coming months, but I've fallen out of the mix. Now I'm ready to get back in there and start doing more. Having more time means I can keep the investments rolling.

Picking up my phone, I tap out the old, familiar number. It only rings once before my friend and investment scout answers.

"Hastings here." Stephen's voice hasn't changed. It's as impatient and arrogant as always. "What's on your mind, Remington? *Psychology Today?*"

"I want to know the latest on the Stellan project."

I tried to acquire the communications security app a year ago, but I confess, fighting with Eleanor and my own apathy probably lost me the deal.

He exhales as if he's bored. "You haven't asked about Stellan in six months."

"I'm asking about it now."

I hear his fingers tapping on computer keys. "Looks like he took some time off. Probably found a glitch or bumped into a patent issue."

"Let's hope it's the former. Send him a note. Say I'm still interested if he'd like to talk to me and see if there are any rising projects along the same lines out there. I want to be the go-to guy when it comes to military security."

"You always were. Until you dropped out of sight."

"Right. I'll be doing research on my end, and Stephen, get me an invite to the Empire Investments annual gala."

If anyone can get me to the capital investors' Manhattan party of the year, it's my old Navy buddy.

"Are you saying you're back?"

"I'm back."

With Ruby taking care of Lillie, I won't be fighting with anyone. I can work uninterrupted. I'll dig in and make the most of my time, not having to check in and intervene every few hours.

Still, Eleanor's voice is in my head. "Your daughter is only four once. A large inheritance won't make up for spending time with her father."

As much as it grates my nerves, she's right.

I grew up with a dad who chose work over me. He was never around for anything I did. He missed every baseball game, every science fair, and every awards ceremony. Yet, he always showed up to let me know when I was getting off track. He always managed to assert his control without ever showing me his love.

Lillie will not have the same lonely childhood I did.

Pulling out a post-it, I hastily scribble a note across the front: *Time for Lillie.*

I slap it on the bulletin board and stick a pin in it to be sure it doesn't fall off.

Every day, no matter what, I'll make time for her, spend time with her, make sure she knows no matter how important Daddy's job is, it's never more important than her.

A close second: *No sex with Ruby.*

My hand goes to my stomach, and I rub the sting away. Yeah, she's pretty great. Her smile warms my insides and everything she does feels special. The worst thing I could do is have a casual fling with her.

For starters, what happens when it's over? How could she continue working here with us seeing each other every day? How could she continue living in the house? It's too much of a risk to expect things to go back to normal after something like that.

I suppose it could happen, but I can't take the chance. No matter how strong my feelings are for her, I will not act on them.

I don't write it down, obviously, but it's decided.

The rapid thud of footsteps on the stairs draws my attention to my open door just in time to see the woman in question on her way to the third floor.

Her purple skirt swishes around her legs, up to

her narrow waist. Her silky hair falls around her shoulders and her small breasts bounce... *Damn*, I reach down to adjust my fly.

Turning quickly, I swipe the mouse back and forth to bring my oversized Mac to life. A large colorful bar graph is on the screen.

Yes, market analysis is what I need. The perfect boner-killer...

I refocus my thoughts.

I've always been good at tests. No reason to think I'll fail this one.

Chapter 7

Ruby

"Wait. How long have I been gone?" Drew's voice is all the comfort I need after my run-in with the elementary school bitches turned preschool mean moms. "You're a nanny?"

I'm pacing my enormous bedroom on the third floor. "And you're not going to believe how much he's paying me."

I tell her, and she shrieks again. "That's... a hundred eighty *thousand* dollars a year!"

"I know!" I walk to the French doors facing the lake. "I was going to flip out, but then I googled it. Most celebrity nannies make like two hundred a year."

"So you're not the highest paid nanny in America. I guess you'll have to keep looking..." She's playing it off, but I can tell she's impressed. "You know, I had a feeling Remi was well-off, but hell. I didn't know he was that rich. What is he? Bill Gates's kid?"

"I don't think Bill Gates is old enough to have a son Remi's age. He's only thirty."

"Have you slept with him yet?"

I almost choke. "He's my boss, Drew."

"Well, have you?" She's laughing now. "He's hot as fuck."

"You can say that again." Leaning against the window sill, I remember him in those bare feet and faded jeans last night. "But I'm a professional childcare provider."

"Why should that stop you?"

"I couldn't keep working for him if I was sleeping with him." My voice goes soft, and my stomach sinks at the truth. "I'd have to give up this amazing job... give up the chance at finally being financially independent."

We're quiet, and when she speaks again, I'm reminded why Drew and I have always been so close. She just gets me.

"So are you going to sleep with him?

We both start laughing harder. "I'm hanging up now."

"Love you, hooker."

"Love you more."

Only Drew would know exactly the predicament I'm in—brain versus hormones.

Isn't the brain controlled by hormones?

I'm in trouble.

A glance at the clock tells me I have about an hour before I have to pick up Lillie. Walking down the stairs, I stop on the landing at the second floor and see Remi at his impressive workstation, frowning at an enormous computer screen. Those hazel eyes quirk up to meet mine, and the frown is replaced with that smile.

My stomach tightens.

"Hey!" He slides back and stands, walking to where I'm waiting. "Did you meet Lillie's teacher? She seems great, but I don't know. What's your professional opinion?"

That makes me grin. "She's amazing. Lillie's going to learn a lot this year."

He nods, and I notice his bare feet again. He's in

those jeans, but this time he's wearing a maroon tee that shows off his toned arms. Those biceps... I remember him lifting Lillie this morning at breakfast and how they flexed. It takes all my willpower not to exhale a delighted sigh.

"Seemed like something was up with Eleanor this morning." He walks back into his office, and I follow, noting that ass, wondering how much I should share with him about my earlier power struggle.

I guess he did say Eleanor was driving him crazy, too. "I didn't mean to have a run-in with her on my first day here."

"Technically it was your second day." He stops at his desk and looks up at me with that panty-melting smile. "What happened?"

The way he says it, it's almost like a joke, like he knew it was coming all along. I guess that makes me feel less guilty?

"Apparently, she'd put out this fancy dress for Lillie to wear to school. I didn't know, so I let Lillie wear what she wanted."

"I thought Lillie looked great—exactly like herself. Mermaid princess."

"Right." Now I'm confident he'll understand. "I guess I could have made her change. What she wears isn't so important to us... but it's a big deal to her."

"I think it's great how you treat her. It's how I would."

"She's a lot like you. She's adorable." The words are out before I realize what I've just said.

"Is that so?" His smile changes from panty melting to flat out want.

His hand twitches, and I can imagine going to him, putting my hand on his shoulder and pulling our mouths together. I imagine straddling his lap, him lifting my shirt over my head, pulling on my nipple with his lips... Oh, hell, I'm already wet.

I want to bone my boss.

Bone my boss...

Yes, please.

"Don't you think she's like you?" My breath is shallow, and he returns to where I'm standing.

"I hope she's not."

"Why? What's wrong with you?"

His chin drops, and it's like he's baring his soul. "You're a therapist... tell me what you think—unless that's not allowed... Can you treat your boss?"

"Of course, I can." *Can I?* "What's bothering you?"

We're so close, and today his scent is less earthy and more soap and sexy man-scent. It's delicious.

"Is it inevitable... Do we all eventually turn into our parents?" He looks up at me from under his brow, and *Oh, sweet Jesus,* those eyes.

"Lord I hope not." I gently tease. "My mom is a piece of work... and my dad, well..." I don't want to get into that.

"Dads." He exhales deeply. "I can't be that man... Absent, distant, always distracted by my work, missing Lillie's childhood. Showing up only to criticize."

The tone in his voice pulls at my chest, and his eyes are so earnest. They capture my heart.

I swallow the tightness in my throat. "Well, I know a little something about distant fathers. You are *not* like that."

"I try not to be." The muscle in his jaw moves, and he looks over my shoulder. "Eleanor says I work too much. She says I'm missing my daughter's most important years... Sometimes I think she says it to get under my skin. I mean, I have to work, or I'll fall behind. Other investors will get ahead of me."

Reaching out, I touch his arm. It feels so good, warm and strong. "Everyone has to work, Remi. You can't feel guilty for providing for your family."

He puts a hand on top of mine. "I'm too close to judge my own behavior. If I start neglecting her or putting my work first again—"

"Lillie loves you. She's so excited every time she sees you, which means you're doing something right." Our hands lower. He's still holding mine, and instinctively our fingers thread. "I've been here less than a day, but you seem to have a great relationship with her. You seem to be there for her... as much as she needs you to be. I think it would be okay if she turns out like you..."

"Will you let me know if I let her down?" His voice is lower.

"I will." His eyes drop to my mouth, and my tongue slips out to touch my bottom lip.

His gaze stays there, and his lips part. *God, I want to kiss him.* Tightness fills my stomach, and I sway forward, lifting my chin. Warm breath skates over my cheek...

It's happening.

We're going to kiss.

My heart beats so fast. He leans closer. My chest aches from the pressure. Perhaps we'll meet in the middle.

His eyes move across my cheek like a caress, up to my eyes. "I don't mean to offend you. I hope you don't mind me saying this..."

"What?" The word floats out on an exhale.

"You're so beautiful."

"So are you..."

Because, yes. Yes, he is.

He leans a little closer, and the heat between us is

right there. It's fire, a burning ring of fire, like the song. Our hands are still joined, an electric connection, sparks in our fingertips. I exhale a whimper, a plea for more. I'm slippery and wet, vibrating and magnetic.

He inhales again, placing his hand on my shoulder. "You smell like roses."

My shirt is so thin, I'm sure my nipples will rip through the fabric. I want to reach forward and slide my hand along the front of his pants, feel the erection I know he has.

One step forward, my chin lifts. My eyes slide close, and my breath stills...

"Ruby!" Eleanor shouts my name so loud, we both jump apart.

"Oh my god," I whisper.

"If you're late to pick up Lillian, they fine us a dollar a minute."

She's coming up the stairs. She's almost to the landing, and I go to the door. Remi turns his back and steps out the open French doors onto the small balcony.

He didn't even touch me, but I smooth my hair and straighten my blouse. I'm hot and bothered and breathing fast. "What's that?" My voice is wobbly.

"Here you are." Eleanor pauses at the door, and her eyes narrow suspiciously.

I pass her, going out to the landing, without a backwards glance at my boss.

My boss.

Remi is my boss.

"I must've lost track of time." My voice is light, not breathless.

Eleanor pivots and follows me down the stairs. "You might set your watch —"

"That's a good idea." I lift my wrist and tap on my

Apple watch.

"That's nice." She leans forward to look over my shoulder. "I looked at one of those a while back, but it seemed so expensive..." Her tone makes it clear she wants to know how I could afford an Apple watch. Like it's any of her business. "And I'm so old, you know."

"It was a Christmas present from my mom."

"Oh... of course."

Checking my watch also shows I have twenty minutes left to get Lillie. "I guess you drive slower than I do, too."

She grins, and her eyes narrow as if she's sizing me up. "Tell me, Ruby, why does an educated, attractive young woman like you want to be a nanny? I'm sure there's something you'd rather be doing besides babysitting someone else's daughter."

"Being a nanny is not the same as a babysitter." I already had this conversation with my mother; now I'm having it with the Dark Lord. *Lordess*? But while Ma is overly helpful, Eleanor is manipulative, controlling, and pouty. "Anyway, I like Lillie. She's adorable."

"We don't need you."

"Remi seems to have a different opinion on the matter. He said he needed help, and I'm here to help. It's the Christian thing to do."

I couldn't resist tossing in that jab.

Church ladies love being so holier than thou.

"I know you, Ruby Banks. I've seen you at church, and you've never struck me as particularly Christ-like." I'm pretty sure she's trying to insult me, but I've never worried about my reputation in Oakville. "Do you even know CPR?"

"Do you?"

Her eyes flare. "What is it you really want?"

I pause, considering her question, how to answer, and I decide to give her the truth. "I want what I think everyone wants—to be useful, to help others, to be independent."

"To find a husband?"

"When the time is right. Speaking of time... Don't want to get fined!" I pat my watch and give her a perky smile as I walk out the door.

Nice try, Eleanor.

Chapter 8

Remi

I'm deep in a proposal Stephen forwarded me about a new developer in Manhattan when I hear singing downstairs.

At once, I'm on my feet, hustling to the kitchen so I don't miss lunch. Rounding the corner, the sight hits me again, right in the stomach.

Lillie follows Ruby to the microwave while they both sing "Be Our Guest"—another Disney princess song. I happen to know this one.

Watching her, I'm completely mesmerized, and I can't help remembering our near-kiss less than an hour ago. Despite all my logical, reasonable decision-making, the moment I was alone with Ruby, I found myself a breath away from taking her.

We came so close... Seriously, if Eleanor hadn't interrupted us, I can pretty much guarantee, I'd have done more than kiss Ruby.

The heat between us is so strong... It doesn't help I can see she wants me as much as I want her. Now here she is, dancing and singing with my daughter, and I'm completely helpless.

I'm totally at her mercy.

"Don't believe me?" Ruby sings, popping the plate in the appliance and pressing a button.

Lillie's right behind her. "Ask the dishes!"

Ruby holds her hand while Lillie turns, and a smile splits my cheeks. "What's going on in here?"

"Daddy!" Lillie screams and runs to where I'm standing, leaping into my arms. "Ruby's making me pigs in blankets! Only they're not really pigs. They're little bitty hot dogs!"

She's so excited, she's bouncing on my waist, and I look over at Ruby. She blinks down, and her cheeks flush. I'm not sure if it's me or all the dancing.

"It's crescent rolls around cocktail weenies. I hope that's okay." She looks up at me, and her eyes are so bright.

"I think it sounds great. Are there enough for me?"

Her expression melts into a genuine laugh, and I'm a goner. "I think so. I've got baby carrots to go with them."

She holds up a bowl with carrots and another with ranch dressing.

"My favorite."

A minute passes, the microwave beeps, and I'm at the table with my daughter, crunching carrots and hearing all about her day.

"Then Louie said girls couldn't play with toy soldiers. Only boys could, and I said that's stupid. Hasn't he seen *Mulan*?"

Lillie hasn't stopped talking, lifting a small hot dog and pulling the crescent roll off it. "Look, Daddy. My pig lost his blanket." She starts giggling, and I grin, smoothing a hand down her head.

Ruby isn't with us. I noticed when we sat down, she slipped out of the room. I don't know where she went, and it bothers me she's not here.

"Wrap him up again." I kiss her head. "I'll be right back."

The living room is empty as is Lillie's playroom.

I'm about to jog up the stairs when I see her outside the back doors, standing on the patio.

When I step through the open door, she seems startled. "I'm sorry. Is lunch over?"

"Not quite. Don't you want some pigs in blankets? Did I eat your lunch?"

Her cute nose wrinkles. "I had a late breakfast. I'm good. By the way, having lunch with your daughter pretty much confirms you're not a distant or detached father."

"It's something I try to do every day. You're welcome to join us."

"I think it's better if you have that time with her." She tilts her head and gives me a little smile. "She gets you all to herself."

I don't know why that pleases me so much. Still... "What are you doing?"

"Would it be okay if we set up easels out here?" She gestures toward the lake. A bridge arches over one end, and cranes stand beneath it. "That's a really nice scene. I'd like to try painting with Lillie."

"Do you paint?"

"Just for fun." She shrugs, seeming embarrassed.

"I think it's great. I'd love you to give Lillie art lessons."

"Okay." She starts for the door, and I catch her hand. Her eyes fly to mine, startled, and I release her. "Sorry. I just wanted to say I think you're doing a great job with her. I hope you like it here."

Her shoulders relax, and she smiles. "I do. I like it very much. More than I thought I would."

"Daddy?" Lillie's voice is serious. "I finished my lunch. I think you'd better finish yours and get back to work."

She's standing in the French doors with her little

hands on her hips, and I can't resist picking her up again. "Is that so? You think I need to get to work?"

I tickle her, and she laughs. Ruby's hand goes to her mouth, and she's laughing as well. Our eyes meet, and those feelings are so strong. I was going to apologize for almost kissing her. I wanted to make it clear I'm not trying to crowd her or make her uncomfortable.

Her answer to my question gives me some relief, but I'll make a point of clearing the air later, once Lillie's not around to misunderstand.

Giving her a wink, I put my daughter on her feet. "I guess I'm getting back to work now."

Ruby holds out a hand to her. "How do you feel about painting?"

It gets about the exact response I'd expect. Lillie starts jumping up and down, clapping and cheering. Walking to my office, all I can think is this is exactly how I want it to be.

Chapter 9

Ruby

Dinner with Eleanor is an unexpectedly formal event.

I didn't get the memo to wear a ball gown, so I showed up in the same outfit I've worn all day—my purple skirt and "Stay Gold" tee. Eleanor's wearing a fancy beige pantsuit with another one of those little scarves tied at her neck.

Lillie changed out of her sparkly mermaid costume, and now she's wearing a fancy version of Belle's dress from *Beauty and the Beast*. It has sparkly gold tulle and a full skirt and looks nicer than anything I own.

Remi's drop-dead gorgeous as always in his jeans and tee, but he pulled a navy blazer over it. When I enter the room, he gives me that swoony smile, and I swear, I'm never going to get used to it.

Everyone's standing behind their chairs looking at me. "Were you waiting for me?" My face gets hot. "I was…"

The sentence is started, but the way Eleanor glares at me, the words die on my lips.

I was on the toilet.

"You were saying?" She raises her eyebrows, but I only wave my hand.

"It was nothing."

We take our seats, and I nearly jump up again when a woman I don't recognize appears at my elbow. "Roasted beets with organic kale, avocado, and a splash of balsamic vinaigrette."

Wow. She moves down to Remi, and I watch as a male server puts plates in front of Lillie and Eleanor. The woman who served me opens a bottle of white wine and pours Eleanor a glass. She stops by Remi's seat and he holds up a hand.

"I have a little more work to do tonight. Thanks."

"You work too much." Eleanor's voice is condescending, and I see him bristle.

The server is at my side. "None for me, thanks!" I cover the rim of my glass. "I still have work to do, too." Eleanor glares at me, and I smile. "Lillie won't put herself to bed!"

"Honestly," she shakes her head. "One glass of wine won't hurt you. It's actually good for you."

"What's this red thing?" Lillie pokes at the beet on her plate.

"It's called a beet." Eleanor touches her small wrist. "Don't play with your food."

Holding my breath, I watch as Lillie stabs the dark red slice and pops it in her mouth. Her little eyes widen, and I have no idea what's about to happen.

"It tastes like dirt!" She announces, and I bite my lip to keep from laughing.

Eleanor is undeterred, calmly taking a bite of her salad. "And how do you know what dirt tastes like?"

"Louie made us all eat dirt to prove we could be good soldiers." Lillie stabs another beet. "I can eat dirt. I'm going to be a general."

Remi laughs as he shovels another bite of salad into his mouth. "Take it from me, soldiers don't eat dirt, honey."

Eleanor puts down her fork. "While I admire your fortitude, Lillian, you are not to eat dirt at school or anywhere. That's how you get worms."

My smile is tight, and while I hate being on Eleanor's side, I don't want Lillie eating dirt either.

Her little brow furrows, and she stabs the last red beet on her plate. "What kind of worms? Earthworms are friendly worms, but they wiggle so fast when you touch them."

She holds up a little hand and squiggles her fingers wildly.

"I'm going to have a talk with your teacher," Eleanor huffs, leaning back with her wine as the male server reappears to collect our salad plates.

"Miss Terry says dirt has minerals in it."

Eleanor glares at her, but I jump in to redirect. "It's true. *Pica* is a medical condition where patients crave dirt and other non-nutritive substances. Researchers later found many of them were anemic and deficient in other minerals like iron and zinc."

"So you're saying Lillian should be allowed to eat dirt?" It's not really a question. It's a stabby little barb from Eleanor to me.

"Of course not." I force a laugh. "I only mean it shouldn't hurt her."

"Lillian," Eleanor turns to her granddaughter. "I forbid you to eat dirt."

Lillie looks at me, and I nod. "It's not a good idea."

The female server enters the room with two plates of meat and a swirled cloud of deep orange fluff. "Free-range pork chops and mashed, organic sweet potatoes locally grown right here in Pike County."

I'm across the table from Lillie, but the male server stays at her side, slicing her pork into tiny pieces before leaving. *Good to know.*

"This ought to be good for us." Remi cuts a slice of the perfectly cooked pork and pops it in his mouth. "It's delicious."

The female nods and leaves the room.

"Daddy and I had pigs in blankets for lunch!" Lillie announces proudly as she pushes the sweet potato mash around her plate.

Eleanor's eyes go wide. "Who in the world gave you that? Remington?"

He starts to answer, but Lillie cuts him off. "Ruby made them, and I helped! Ruby's not like Tiana. She can't cook everything in New Orleans."

My lips press together, and I'm not sure if I want to laugh or crawl under the table.

Eleanor puts her fork beside her plate and glares at me. "You might just as well have fed her dirt. Do you know how many chemicals… how much sodium is in a hot dog?"

"Ruby said they were cocktail weenies." Lillie starts to giggle, stacking her sweet potatoes higher on her plate. "She said *weenie*."

"Lillian, stop playing with your food. It's bad manners." Eleanor clears her throat and turns to me. "Perhaps we should sit down and create a menu for lunches each week."

Remi puts his fork beside his plate. "It was a delicious lunch, complete with baby carrots —"

"And ranch dressing!" Lillie cries.

Eleanor puts her hand to her chest as if she'll faint.

My lips press into a frown, and I push my own sweet potatoes around. Ma was pretty much Suzy Homemaker when I was growing up, but all I know how to make is spicy dumplings and kimchee. Drew's house was where I got American food, and we ate all the things I know how to prepare… none of which are free-range or organically grown.

"I appreciate your feelings about a healthy diet, Eleanor," Remi continues. "I also appreciate Ruby's effort preparing a fun lunch for Lillie, even if it falls outside your nutritional norms."

He's kind of awesome sticking up for me, and I give him a grateful smile.

"Remington, you can't let her eat that trash. Too much sodium is bad for her heart, juvenile diabetes is at an all-time high, obesity is —"

"We can talk about it later."

Looking down at the fancy meal before us, I guess pop tarts are off the list. I'll have to do some research on healthy eating and step up my game a little bit, maybe pull Ma into the mix. I don't want to make Lillie unhealthy.

Finally we're done, and I lead my little charge up two flights of stairs to her elaborate bedroom. It's like a room in a palace with an ornate headboard and thick, fluffy duvets and loads of pillows.

She's bathed and dressed in her Elsa nightgown, searching for a book to read as I pick up her clothes and put them on hangers.

"You're old enough to hang your own clothes now." My tone is gentle, and I pull the sleeves of her coat out of the body. It's when I notice a crinkly ball in the pocket.

Reaching inside, I pull out three packets of ketchup. The kind that comes from fast-food restaurants. "What's this? Where did you get these?"

The minute she sees me, her face flushes with shame. She runs to where I'm standing and takes them from me. "Don't tell Gigi. She'll never let me get a puppy."

My mouth drops open, and I watch as she reaches

under her bed for a plastic, heart-shaped box. It looks like the one the evil queen gave the huntsman for Snow White's heart, and I pause for a moment to consider just how gruesome that storyline is for children.

She opens it, and it's stuffed with ketchup and mustard packets. I'm completely bewildered by all this new information. *A puppy?* And what the hell is up with all the condiments?

"Where did you get all of these?" I rake my finger through the little foil pouches.

She shrugs, taking one out and squishing it in her hand. "Feel it." We sit together, and I give one a squish. She squishes hers back and forth in her little fingers, whispering, "Gigi says I can't have them."

Pressing my lips together, I think about what a little scientist she is. Or a little weirdo. "You need to mind your Gigi." Her brow falls, and I lean closer. "But I'll let you keep them. Don't get them in your bed. They might pop, and that would make a huge mess. We'd probably have to get a whole new bed."

She jumps forward, throwing her arms around my neck. "I love you, Ruby. You're my best friend."

It pretty much seals the deal. "I love you, too. Now put these up and get in the bed."

"Maybe if I get all stars I can get a puppy for Christmas like Darling in *Lady and the Tramp*."

Chewing my lip, I look around at all the super nice furniture. I think of the polished wood floors. "Have you talked to your dad about getting a puppy?"

"Gigi says puppies are a lot of work. She says they're babies that never grow up, and I'm the baby for now."

I think about this a minute, and as much as I hate to say it… "She kind of has a point. Dogs are a lot of work, and you might be too little to help walk it and teach it to do tricks."

"Would you help me?" Her little hazel eyes go round, and I won't lie, it squeezes my heart. How can I say no to that?

"This isn't like the ketchup packets, Lil. You're going to have to ask your daddy about this one." Her little shoulders drop, and I tuck the blankets tight all down her sides. "Now you're a well-rolled dumpling." She nods slowly, her eyes still downcast.

I exhale a sigh. "Tell you what. If your daddy says you can have a puppy, I'll for sure help you with it."

Her expression flips to excitement so fast, I start to laugh. I'm pretty sure this little con artist knows exactly how powerful her own set of puppy-dog eyes are.

We read a quick story and finish the night singing "Bella Notte" from *Lady and the Tramp* before "Now I lay me" prayers and turning out the light.

I'm standing out on the landing trying to figure out how to handle this situation when I notice Remi on the floor below looking up at me. My heartbeat picks up, and I walk down to where he's standing.

"Don't you have work to do?" I can't resist teasing him.

"I'm at a stopping point." He grins and that dimple makes a special appearance. "I like listening to you sing with her. She never sang so much before you came here."

"The songs are the best part of those movies."

"Want to have that glass of wine now?"

It feels like a risky suggestion, but hell if I'll say no. "I'd love it."

Chapter 10

Remi

The lights of the neighborhood reflect across the lake, and the moon is full.

"You picked a good song for tonight." We walk through the French doors holding glasses of wine, and I stop in front of the two easels.

Lillie's painting is bold black lines and large patches of dark and light blue, but Ruby's looks like something out of a gallery. It's delicate abstract with short brush strokes and subtle gradients of color.

"This is really good. Did you minor in art?"

"Heck no." She laughs and shakes her head as she sips her wine. "My dad would never approve of such a useless degree."

"Art's not useless."

"It's not something Kenneth Banks was willing to fund, and I caved just like the pushover he always said I was. Always second-guessing myself..." She steps up beside me looking at the canvas, her slim brow furrowed. "But never mind all that. Earlier today you said something that confused me."

I'm still trying to get over this little reveal she just gave me about her childhood. I can't help wondering how much we have in common.

"How did I confuse you?"

"You said your dad criticized you. What in the world could he criticize? You've done really well. You served in the military, then you were a huge tech success..." Her dark brow furrows, and she seems almost protective—of me. It's completely out of left field.

My father is not my favorite topic, but I'm intrigued by her interest. "I was successful because I followed the plan he approved."

"You're saying there was an alternate plan?" Her eyes narrow, but a smile hints at her lips, those full, kissable, rosebud lips.

"A plan my father called absolutely ludicrous." Glancing down, I clear my throat. Not many people know this part of my history. "I wanted to be a singer."

Her jaw drops and her pretty, pretty eyes go round. "Shut up."

"It's true." I walk over and sit on the sofa in the center of the patio.

She follows me and sits on the table in front of me, excited. "You can sing?"

"I was in a band in college... for about a minute. Until Howard found out." I take a sip of the dry wine. "Naturally, he was horrified."

"I take it Howard's your dad?" I nod, and her lips press into a knowing smile. "That explains it."

"What?"

"Lillie has a great ear for music. She never gets off key, and she keeps the tempo steady, even a capella. That's really huge for a four-year-old."

Not what I expected, although I like hearing it. "I thought all children could sing those songs. They all seem to."

"Um, no. Most little kids are all over the place. Lillie's special." Her voice turns soft. "Like you."

An unexpected compliment. It sends my mind flying down that old familiar rabbit hole, but she changes direction quickly. "What kind of band were you in? Rock and roll?"

"Classic country."

She almost chokes on her sip, covering her mouth and laughing. "No way!"

"Way."

"You are a very unexpected man, Remington."

"Call me Remi." I give her a wink and polish off my glass. "I'm sure you wouldn't know a song on our set list."

"Ha! That's where you'd be wrong." She points her finger as she polishes off her wine. I reach for the bottle and pour us each another glass. "My mom is a huge classic country fan. It's how I got my name."

Now it's my turn to be surprised. "You're named after the Kenny Rogers song?"

"I am indeed. Ma loves it. She's fascinated by the Asian war angle."

"It's kind of depressing." I sip my wine, thinking about the lyrics. "Ruby leaves her crippled husband at home to cat around in town."

"First, it's not clear he was her husband." She's counting off on one hand, holding her wine in the other. *Absolutely adorable.* "Second, a woman her age has wants and needs."

"Still, she leaves him to... take her love to town." I cock an eyebrow, and she raises hers as she sips her wine. "We should have dinner with your mom. I'd like to discuss our shared love of Kenny."

"Do you love Kenny Rogers?" She gives me a skeptical look, and I take her hand, singing the first line of his song...

"Everyone considered him the coward of the county..."

She laughs, and it's sort of magical. We're out on the flagstone patio under the stars, singing, drinking wine under the moon with the lake gleaming behind us. I want her to sit beside me so I can put my arm around her shoulders and pull her close, kiss her head, her lips...

"My favorite is *The Gambler*."

"He made a life out of reading people's faces." I study hers, wondering if I'm reading it right. *If so...*

"I thought it was weird how they made a whole TV series out of that song. It's really sad. He dies." She whispers that part as if it's a secret.

"He broke even."

A breeze filters through, sweeping a long dark wave over her shoulder. Her chin drops, and I'm fascinated by her. She's so pretty. When she looks up at me again, her eyes are deep, like she's contemplating telling me something.

"What?"

"You said you don't want to be like your father, but when you sing, when you listen to your daughter sing and love it, you're already not like him."

Her words flood my chest with warmth. "You said you'll help me be sure I'm not."

"I will." She smiles and stands. "If I can keep my vision of you clear."

I stand with her, and we're face to face again, close. "What does that mean?"

She puts her hand on my chest. "It means you tend to cloud my vision."

I put my hand over hers, loving the flow of electricity between us. "How do I do that?" My voice is low, confident.

"You're a good man, Remi, and you're so sweet to your daughter." Her chin lifts and the moon bathes her face in silver. "When you look at me, I find it very hard to be objective."

"Objectively, I enjoy looking at you, so good to know."

She exhales a laugh, taking a step back. "Sing me your favorite Kenny Rogers song."

"Wow... okay... I have to think about that one." I set my wine glass on the table, retracing our conversation, the things she said. Then I have it. "She believes in me. I'll never know just what she sees in me..."

I hold the note and her eyes close. "Mm... that's nice. You have an amazing voice."

Her eyes blink open slowly, and when they meet mine, I want to carry her to my bedroom.

I'm caught off guard by what she does next. She steps forward, and the hand on my chest slides higher to my collar. At the same time, she places her other hand on my cheek. Before I'm fully aware of what's happening, she rises on her toes and lightly presses those full, pouty lips to mine.

It's a closed-mouth kiss, but my hands are on her at once, pulling her closer, sliding higher to hold her face, threading my fingers in her silky hair, as I open her mouth with mine.

She makes a little noise when our tongues touch and curl together, and heat floods my torso, centering in my pelvis. I'm instantly hard, and *God, I want her in my bed.* She tastes like expensive dry wine, and she smells like heaven.

Sliding my arms around her, I can't help noting how perfectly she fits against my body, shoulder to chest to stomach. I chase after another, deeper kiss, but she turns her face, pressing her palms against me.

I release her at once, and when she glances up, her eyes are brimming with emotion.

She blinks fast, turning away again. "I'm sorry. I didn't mean to sexually harass you." Her tone changes to shaky humor. "I might be a little drunk."

"I think sexual harassment is premised on who has the most power, and you only had one glass of wine."

"Now you're a lawyer?" She holds the chair and steps around the easels, going quickly toward the house.

I'm not ready to let her leave. "Hang on... where are you going?"

"It's time to walk away. Or maybe run." She lets out a nervous laugh.

"I don't want you to walk away."

"You're right, I'd better run."

"Ruby, wait." I catch her hand, stopping her progress. "Why are you running from me?"

My hand goes to her waist, and I pull her against my chest. Right where she belongs.

She reaches up and touches the center of my top lip with her thumb, slipping it down to the bottom. "I've wanted to kiss you since that first night..." Then she shakes her head. "But you're too tempting, Remington Key. You'll ruin everything."

"What would I ruin?" I catch that hand touching my face, holding it to my mouth and kissing those slim fingers.

She chews her lip as she watches me. "My plans... my goals." She eases her hands out of mine, and my stomach sinks. "Thank you for the wine. Morning comes early."

I watch as she disappears into the house. Her kiss is still warm on my lips, and I can still feel her body next to mine, the scent of her hair all around me.

She says I'm too tempting. She has no idea how tempting she is to me. I'm not sure how we come back from that kiss. I'm not sure I want to...

Chapter 11

Ruby

"It's official. I'm my own worst enemy." I flop on the couch in Drew's office, scrubbing my fingers on my forehead.

"I feel like we've been here before... Just a week ago, actually." Drew is sitting behind her desk, typing her client notes into her computer. I've watched her do it a thousand times.

This morning, I came straight to her office after I dropped Lillie off at preschool.

As soon as Lillie was up, I had her dressed and out the door. We drove to the only McDonald's in Oakville and had Egg McMuffins. *Suck it, Eleanor.* Then on the way out, I picked up two more ketchup packets so Lillie wouldn't tell where we ate.

The last thing I wanted was to bump into Remi after I attacked him last night. *God, that kiss...* My toes still curl at the memory of his mouth, his tongue... not just that, his arms around me, holding me so close, kissing my fingers. His voice when he sings. I had to go straight to the shower and turn the cold water on full force...

"Now I'm bribing small children with ketchup packets."

"I can't even begin to guess what that means." My best friend flips her yellow legal pad closed and turns her attention to me. "Make it fast. Hunter will be here in fifteen minutes."

"Oh, screw Hunter and his Watergate stories!" I'm on my feet, still scrubbing my forehead. "I've got a real problem. One that doesn't involve Richard Nixon or the Cubans."

Hunter is one of our shared clients—or I guess, *was* one of our shared clients. They're all Drew's now. He has a paranoid obsession with government surveillance.

Her lips press into a knowing smirk and she nods. "You slept with Remi."

"Nooo!" I flop onto to my stomach, burying my face in my hands. "But I would have. I sure as hell wanted to. It's only a matter of time before I do it, and then I've blown the whole deal."

Drew tosses her pen on the desk and leans back in her chair. "What happened?"

"I kissed him."

"Oh." I hear the squeak of her chair as she leans forward, and I carefully turn my head to meet her eyes. "That's serious."

"It is, right?" Swinging my legs around, I'm on my feet and pacing. "Kissing is almost worse than sex... It's like in *Pretty Woman*. Never kiss a client."

"It's definitely more intimate. You're all up close and personal, breathing each other's air, noses touching, sliding your tongues together... sliding your bodies together."

"Drew!"

She starts to laugh. "Was it a good kiss?"

"Oh sweet mother..." I drop to sitting on the couch. "It was the greatest kiss of all time. I think I'm in love with him."

"You've known him three days. You are not in

love with him."

"Have you ever seen him with his daughter? It's the most adorable thing." I wrap my arms around my waist and fall to the side. "I think he might be the perfect man."

"No one is perfect." She's using her therapist voice. "You're idealizing him, and you know that means you're setting yourself up for disillusionment."

"He sings."

Therapist-voice gone. "What does that mean?"

"It means he's a singer. He was an actual lead singer in a country band in college. And his voice…" Another shiver. "It's like butter."

"Huh." Drew tilts her head to the side. "I had no idea Remi could sing. That's really neat."

"So now you're thinking it might be an appropriate idealization?" I nod my head being very I told you so.

"I'm thinking we'll have to take him to karaoke next time they do it at the Red Cat."

"They do karaoke at the Red Cat?"

"It's something new they're starting. Now that all the college kids are coming over from Charleston. Gray told me about it—apparently Billy told him."

"Oh shit, I suck." I stand and walk over to her desk again. "I've been so knocked out by this tsunami named Remi, I haven't even asked. How's it going with Gray?"

"You know, I'm going to let that slide." She taps her pen on the notepad. "Because you're right. Remi did sort of come out of nowhere."

"So Gray's back… and things are good?"

A smile curls her lips, and the light in her eyes makes my personal concerns take a momentary backseat. I love seeing my friend so happy—especially after all the shit she's been through, how long she's waited, and all the assholes who tried to destroy her happiness.

"I can tell things are good." I give her a wink. "You're glowing."

Her lips press together, and she makes a sneaky face. "I am glowing, but not just because I'm so happy."

It takes me a second to catch up, but when I do. "Holy shit, you're pregnant?" My voice is a shriek, and I'm on my feet jumping up and down. "You're pregnant!"

She starts to laugh, and she's out of her chair hugging me. "I am."

"We're going to have a shower and we're going to pick out all these cute little baby clothes... What are you having?"

"Don't know yet. It's super early, so don't tell anyone." She leans on her desk and her expression dims slightly. "They say in the first six weeks anything can happen."

I'm not hearing any of that. "The only thing that's going to happen is we're going to have a blast! I can't wait... and let me know if you need help with anything. Lillie's in school every morning, so I can run errands." My lips twist and I nod. "It might actually be helpful not to be lurking around the house most mornings alone."

"Don't you have things to do? He can't be paying you all that money just to drive Lillie around."

"Everything's pretty much Lillie-based. I feed her, change her clothes, help her clean up, do little activities with her, do her laundry..."

"What a sweet gig!"

"Which is why I cannot fuck it up." Walking over

to collect my things, I get an idea. "Maybe if I got my own place. I'll be able to afford it... Hell, by next week."

She rearranges her notebook and pen getting ready for her next client. "Will he go for that plan? I thought he hired you to be there at night in case she needed you."

Chewing my lip, I toss my bag over my shoulder. "I guess I'll have to ask." I hear the noise of people in the lobby and blow her a kiss. "Thanks, bae. Take it easy and let me know everything that happens with the new baby. How far along are you?"

"Five weeks."

"So next week we can tell everybody?" I'm excited.

She waves, shaking her head and laughing.

I say hello to Hunter on the way out, and he studies me with that always-serious expression.

"You look really happy today." His eyes move around my face, and I await some comparison to Martha Mitchell or Dorothy Hunt. "Perhaps you shouldn't be a therapist."

Nodding, I pat his arm. "Or maybe I should be a different kind of therapist."

"There are five broad approaches to psychotherapy—"

Drew steps to the door. "Hunter, your appointment has begun."

He tells me a quick goodbye and starts for her door. Dotty is the clinic receptionist. She shakes her head as Hunter leaves, and I give her a quick wave before heading to the door.

"Let me know if she needs anything or starts looking tired."

"Something wrong?" She's frowning, and I do a

little zipper motion across my lips.

"You'll know soon."

"Miss you around here!"

I don't want to say Hunter's right, and I don't really miss talking to patients. Instead, I give her a squeeze, and I'm on my way to pick up Lillie.

The rest of the week goes pretty much the same. I sneak out with Lillie before everyone's up, we eat Egg McMuffins, and I get her extra ketchup packets.

"Are eggs bad for me?" Lillie picks at the corner of the cheese slice on her perfectly round poached egg.

"It's more about how they treat the chickens." Not that I'm one hundred percent sure the eggs on our breakfast sandwiches are real.

It's better than Taco Bell, I guess.

"How do they treat the chickens?" Her little brow furrows, and I'm not about to get into the ethics of poultry farming with her.

"Some people prefer getting eggs from chickens who run around farms. They're called free-range chickens."

Her little eyebrows go up. "Like in *Chicken Run*? They all made a big airplane out of their cages and flew to a valley."

I'm not super familiar with that movie, but it sounds good to me. "Sure."

"I'd like to have a chicken." She walks her fingers along the ketchup packet, back and forth, squishing the contents as she plays.

First a puppy, now a chicken... It gives me an idea. "Why don't we plant a little garden in the backyard? You could grow beets and Chinese cabbage and broccoli..."

"I love broccoli!" She jumps out of her chair.

"I heard." Taking a napkin, I wipe a spot of grease off her cheek. We can't keep doing this, I know. "When we have a harvest, we could eat our crops at dinner. Or lunch."

Speaking of dinner, even though I've lain pretty low, it hasn't stopped Remi from giving me hot looks across the table. He's given me space since that amazing kiss we shared... or I've been avoiding him like crazy. Every time he smiles, my skin tingles and my brain says, *Oh, shit*.

Still, I can't avoid him forever.

She jumps out of her chair again. "Can we do it today?"

"I don't know if we can start today, but we can scout a good location after lunch. I'll see what I can find at the garden center while you're at school."

We collect our trash, and I walk her to the bin. I'm just buckling her in her booster seat in the back of my car, and she's happily squeezing ketchup when she suddenly brightens.

"I'll tell Daddy I want a puppy!"

That gives me another bright idea.

Chapter 12

Remi

Lillie appears at my door carrying a basket. "Ruby said we're having a picnic!"

She marches in like she's on a mission, and I hop up and run to the door, looking out, all around. "Where is Ruby?"

I swear, she's been dodging me all week, and while I'm getting a lot of work done, it's making me kind of sad.

"She said she's scouting out a good spot for our garden."

Today my daughter is wearing oversized black pants with large white polka dots, and a matching white shirt that has a nose and long whiskers. She's adorable, and her personality shines through. I love it.

"A garden? That sounds fun. What made you think of making a garden?"

"Ruby said we can grow beets and broccoli and Chinese food."

"Is that so?" I start to laugh. "I didn't know Chinese food grew in gardens."

She's struggling with a blanket twice as big as she is, and I walk to where she's setting up shop in the middle of my office. I take the quilt and spread it over the floor.

"I like having a picnic with you. What's in the basket?"

My daughter sits on the quilt and takes out two plastic containers. "I helped make these." She hands me a green tortilla wrap filled with what looks like tuna salad. "I'm supposed to tell you it's organic tuna…" Her little face scrunches as if she's trying to remember her lines. "E-C-A-B and a little salt and pepper."

I touch her nose. "You mean E-V-O-O?"

Her eyes roll around and she drops her head backwards. "I said it was too hard to remember."

"You did a great job." I inspect our very healthy lunch, complete with organic milk in glasses with plastic lids and metal straws. Organic, environmental… Ruby's a fast learner. I don't see anything Eleanor could complain about.

Lillie dives in, taking a big bite of wrap. We also have small containers of cucumber slices, without the ranch dressing. I open the lid on her cup and slide the straw inside before handing it to her.

"Ruby can't drink milk." My daughter takes a long swig. "She's galactically int…" A worried expression crosses her face.

I cover my mouth with a napkin and swallow my laugh. "Lactose intolerant."

She shakes her head. "That's not what she said."

"Oh, it's not?" I grin at how serious and grown up she's acting.

We're sitting cross-legged across from each other, and the warmth in my chest as I watch my little girl happily nibbling a cucumber slice is undeniable. Ruby was right about one thing. My father did not stop what he was doing to have lunch with me ever. Although, seeing this little cherub with her golden curls arranged in two ponytails, maybe he would've stopped. Who could resist Lillie? …or Ruby for that matter.

"How'd it go today at school?" I give her a playful frown. "No more eating dirt, I hope."

Her eyes remain fixed on her food, but she shakes her head. "I don't want to get a worm in my tummy."

"Well, I don't want you to get sick." I'm not sure about the worm part.

Her head cocks to the side, and her brow furrows. "If we plant our garden in the dirt and then we eat the broccoli, how come we don't get worms that way?"

"We wash it first." The mechanics of drainage and modern waste disposal are way too complicated to get into over a picnic lunch with my four-year-old.

She thinks a minute then nods slowly, seeming okay with that answer. We munch a few minutes longer, and I feel her watching me. I look over, and she's giving me a cute little grin.

"What?"

"I have a very serious question to ask you, Daddy." She finishes her last piece of wrap, and I grab a napkin to wipe her hands.

"Okay..." I have no idea what's coming.

"I want to get a puppy." She sits for a second, watching me with that smile firmly in place.

"Is that so?" Looking around, I try to imagine what having a dog in the house would be like. I'm not entirely opposed to the idea. "Have you talked to Ruby about it?" Don't know why that matters...

"Ruby says I have to be very responsible to have a pet. She says I have to ask you." My daughter crawls across the blanket and puts her hand on my leg. "Can I have a puppy, Daddy?"

Round hazel eyes blink up at me, and I have to put down my food. It's like an invisible fist punched me straight in the gut. How could I possibly say no to that face?

"I... well, I don't know, sweetie." *Shit.* I can't get a dog without talking to Ruby. Why am I thinking this way? Why does Ruby's opinion matter so much to me? "We need to do a little research first. Be sure nobody's allergic."

"Like Ruby can't drink milk?"

"Yes—just like that. Are you finished?" She nods, and I quickly pick up the plates, shoving everything into the basket. I'm ready to find her absentee nanny. "Carry your milk."

Lillie takes off ahead of me running as I jog down the stairs. Every day little things have changed around here. I've watched their paintings get more detailed until I assume they're finished. I've searched for Ruby every morning to tell her how much I like them, and I've been beyond frustrated to find her gone without a word each time.

When we find her on the patio, my stomach tightens, and a surge of desire rises in my chest. Maybe she was right to stay away? I wasn't expecting to feel like this when I saw her again. I'm acutely aware of how long it's been since I've touched a woman. *Four years...*

"Ruby! Daddy said we have to talk to you about the puppy!"

When she looks up, I swear, it's almost too much. She's wearing black pants and an oversized white shirt I assume doubles as a smock over her black tank. Her long hair is up in a ponytail, and she looks like fresh air and sunshine and everything good. I want to go to her, pull her into my arms, and devour those pretty pink lips again.

Her cheeks flush when she sees me, but she squats in front of my daughter. "Why did he say that?"

"He said you might be allergic!" Lillie is talking so

loud, and I can tell she's excited. I'm not sure we're ready for a pet, but telling her no is going to be hard.

"I'm not." Ruby looks up at me as I walk to them. She quickly picks up one of my old button-up shirts and starts putting it on my daughter.

"I told her we needed to do some research." I see her fingers tremble slightly. *Is she nervous?* I want to cover those hands with mine and tell her she has no reason to be. I never want to hurt her.

"Your daddy's right, Lil. We need to do some research. Eleanor might be allergic."

"Aww!" Lillie mixes a whine with a little stomp, and I watch as Ruby fishes out a small pair of gardening gloves.

Reaching out, I give my daughter's little ponytail a gentle tug. "I never told you I love your cat suit."

Lillie's smile is only half-hearted and she picks up a small trowel.

Ruby speaks to her softly, giving her a little nudge. "What do you say?"

My daughter's reply is pouty. "Thank you."

"Lillie, don't act like that. You have so many nice things." Ruby starts, but I touch her arm.

Her eyes meet mine, and I shake my head. "Are your paintings finished? I've been looking at them all week. I think you have real talent."

That distracts her, and she proceeds to tell me about brush strokes, showing me how to flick the brush to make it look like a leaf or a cloud. She's clearly a beginner, but I see Ruby watching her and smiling proudly. It's just another reason on my growing list of why I'm falling for this woman.

As much as Eleanor spends her days worrying and fretting over what my daughter eats and wears, I'm trying to remember if I've ever seen her step back and simply observe Lillie doing things with as much pride as Ruby does.

It's Friday before I get my wish to speak to Ruby alone. Dinners have leveled out to mundane chatter — the weather, preschool activities, the prospect of a fall harvest. Eleanor doesn't have as many barbs to throw since Ruby started preparing healthier lunches, although the details of breakfast have been a bit sketchy. If I didn't know any better, I'd say my daughter is trying to be sneaky, which only piques my curiosity even more. Naturally, I run interference when Eleanor gets too pushy.

I floated the idea of my mother-in-law potentially finding her own place, to which she responded as I expected — shock, dismay, concern for Lillie, concern for her finances. I don't really mind paying all of Eleanor's expenses. I do mind her being in my house, hovering over Lillie, and meddling in my affairs.

All of this is on my mind as I stand outside Ruby's bedroom door. *What am I doing here?* After the way she's acted since Monday, I decided she must need space. That kiss was amazing. It's been on my mind all week, distracting me from my work, making me think about all the possible ways we might be able to act on these feelings.

I've also been puzzling nonstop over what she said... *You'll ruin everything.* What plans is she afraid I'll ruin? Is she already thinking of leaving us after a month? It's only been a week, and I can't imagine this house without her in it.

My muscles are tense as I take a deep breath and tap softly. Her room is quiet... no immediate response, so I knock again.

On the other side of the door, I hear her hesitant

voice. "Who is it?"

"It's me... Remi. I'd like to talk to you if that's okay?"

The door opens halfway, and I have to catch my breath. She's wearing a silky green robe, and possibly nothing else. Her hair is down, hanging in long waves around her shoulders, and she's fucking sexy as hell.

My stomach tightens, and all I can think of is touching her, sliding my hands all over her skin, cupping her breasts and rolling her tight nipples between my fingers.

"Is everything okay?" She's speaking just above a whisper, and I'm reminded my daughter is down the hall.

"Yeah, I wanted to... I..." *What do I want?*

I want to pick up where we left off Monday night. I want to kiss her hard and back her into the room, lay her on the bed, and spread her thighs. I want to lose myself in her, tasting her, teasing her, then plunging deep, feeling her break around me as she comes apart, screaming my name.

"Sorry. I've just been thinking." *Obsessing about you all week* is more accurate. I clear my throat, passing a hand over my mouth. "Remember Monday, when we were talking, you said something about your dad—how he made you second-guess yourself?"

"Oh." Her shoulders drop. She seems to relax, taking a step back, into her room. "Yes, my father excelled at that. We have something in common. My dad was the first person to shelve my artistic aspirations."

Her wry tone makes me relax, and I step inside, closing the door and putting my back to it.

So we don't wake Lillie, of course.

"You shouldn't let that happen. You're an

amazing artist. I think you should do whatever you want. Trust your instincts."

The hint of a smile is on her lips. "I trusted my instincts coming here. Then I proceeded to showcase all my poor decision-making skills."

That makes me frown. "I haven't seen you make a poor decision yet."

"I've made a couple. I made one Monday night." Her eyes meet mine, and her voice is quiet. "I should never have kissed you. I'm so sorry. It was so unprofessional."

Now it's my turn to smile. She says it like she's confessing a major sin, not a simple kiss.

Okay, that kiss was not simple.

It was fucking hot as sin, and I want to do it again and again.

If she's onboard with all the kissing, of course.

"I'm not holding it against you." Pushing off the door, I close the space between us. "I was worried when you left that night. You said something about me ruining everything? What were you talking about?"

"It wasn't fair of me to say that. Especially since it's all been me being irresponsible and acting inappropriately. You haven't done anything."

I reach out to touch the side of her cheek. "What have you done that's inappropriate?"

She takes a step back, and she's against the wall. "Nothing yet... It's more the potential is there, and I can't... mess this up. I have things I want to do, debts to pay, and I'd like to get my own place, maybe get recertified in a different field."

"I think all of that sounds great, except the part about getting your own place." My chest feels tight, and I wonder again if she's leaving us after a month. "Don't you like it here?"

"Of course! It's a beautiful house, and this room is gorgeous." She motions around the beige bedroom, which I notice she has not decorated. "You've been so generous to me. I hope I'm meeting your expectations. As a nanny, I mean."

Is she kidding me? Doesn't she see how amazing she is? How much Lillie loves her?

"You've exceeded my expectations. You're an amazing nanny. I don't know how I could've found someone any better."

A genuine smile curls her lips. "Thanks. I'm kind of still learning, but Lillie makes it easy." Her chin drops and she glances up at me with those eyes. "So do you. You're a great boss."

The way she looks up at me, standing there in that robe with her pretty hair all around her shoulders, her pink lips making me remember how soft they are when I take them... I slide my hand in my pocket, doing my best to ease the rising pressure in my dick.

"Good." I focus on her words—I'm her boss. "I should go."

"Remi, wait..." She places a hand on my arm, speaking softly. "Was that all you wanted to say? You could have said all that downstairs after dinner. Or any time, really."

I put my hand over hers, lifting it, holding it in mine. It's so delicate and fine, her nails perfectly trimmed and painted soft pink. She feels very precious to me, and I want to protect her. I want to keep her all to myself.

"I confess, I haven't been able to stop thinking about that night." Lifting her hand, I kiss her fingers then release her. "I'm sorry. I wanted to kiss you again."

She steps closer and reaches up, lightly putting her

117

hand against my scruffy cheek. "Why are you sorry?"

"I only ever want you to feel safe here."

Our eyes meet, and there's so much between us. I don't understand this pull or how fast it's grown, yet we share so much common ground. I want to hold her, but I'll never push her. "So I guess this is goodnight."

I walk to the door, but it feels like my insides are being ripped out and left behind at her feet. God, I want her so much. At the same time, I know sex will only complicate everything.

"Wait." I'm at the door when I feel her hand on me. Turning, I see her pretty pink lip is caught under her teeth. She blinks quickly before speaking fast. "A kiss goodnight is probably okay."

"Is it?"

Her shoulders rise, and her worry melts into a grin. "Probably not, but we can try one more time just to be sure, right?"

I think it's safe to say we're playing with fire, but there's no way in hell I'm saying no.

Pulling her closer, my gaze travels from her cat eyes down her soft cheeks, to her pillow lips. Reaching up, I touch my thumb to her chin, then higher, pulling her bottom lip down. "I might like kissing you too much."

Her chin lifts, and she shivers in my arms. It's sexy as fuck.

"That goes double for me."

In one fluid movement, our lips seal together then part, tongues finding each other, mouths moving in time. It's fiery and electric, currents sizzling through each of us. She whimpers, her fingers curling on my arms, and my cock is a steel rod in my jeans, begging for satisfaction.

With a groan, I chase her mouth, pulling her lips

with mine, kissing her fast and deep. My hand slides over her breast, and I feel a taut nipple through the silk fabric. I want it in my mouth, and another groan rumbles from my throat.

She sighs into my mouth, lifting her hands to my hair where her fingers curl and pull. I'm on fire, drowning in this rising tide of lust and need. My hands slide to her ass, and I lift her off the floor, placing her back to the wall. Her hips rock, and her core is right at my aching erection.

Another groan, another soft whimper. We break apart, gasping. I feel her lightly kissing my neck, then raking her teeth across my skin. *Fuck*, it feels so good. Glancing down, and I see her robe is loose. I see the curve of her small breasts, the points of her dark nipples.

"God, I want you," I groan. "So much."

"Oh, shit," she gasps. "I want you, too."

It's fire and fever and heat burning my skin. She moves, and it's pressure on my cock. I'm about to explode. Lowering my head, I claim her lips again, pulling them to mine and sucking her tongue.

Her fingers curl at my neck, and she leans into me with another moan. I want to kiss her everywhere. I want to bury my face in her breasts, in her pussy... I'm lost in a haze of everything I want to do to her when I feel pressure against my shoulders.

She's pushing against me, and I lift my head to find her eyes. "What is it?"

"I'm sorry..." She gasps, and it's more of a groan. "I'm so sorry, Remi, but we have to stop. We can't do this. You know we can't."

We're standing in front of each other breathing hard. Her chest rises fast, and I can see the swell of her breasts beneath the silk fabric as she tightens it again.

She's absolutely mouthwatering.

I place one hand on the wall beside her face. "Tell me... What's on your mind? What are you thinking about?"

She shakes her head, putting her hands on her cheeks. "It's everything we both know. I can't live here and be Lillie's nanny if we're having sex."

My body is on fire, and I'm not sure I can walk away. "You can. It'll be our secret."

"Things like that never stay a secret." Her eyes dart side to side. "Someone will find out, and it'll most likely be Eleanor. Then she'll have a field day making me look like... some kind of geisha girl."

"The geisha were Japanese. You're Korean."

"Remi—" Her chin rises, and I see the pleading in her eyes.

Still, I can't resist. I lean forward, inhaling her sweet scent, brushing her soft lips with mine.

It's not a kiss until she exhales a little groan and catches my face, pulling my mouth to hers again. It turns fast and our tongues curl and slide, but with another little groan, she pulls away from me.

"No, I can't. You have to go, Remi." Her back is to me, and she's holding her robe closed. "You have to go... or I will."

Those words change everything. They're a splash of cold water right in my face. It might be dangerous having her living here, but I can't bear the thought of this house without her.

"No... I'll go. We won't do it again."

She doesn't turn to face me, and with a heavy sigh, I open the door, taking one more look at the beautiful creature I just held in my arms before I leave.

I can't lose her. I don't know what that means, but I'm going to find out. Solving problems is what I do.

Chapter 13

Ruby

"Kissing him sober is even hotter than kissing him slightly drunk." I'm at an open-air mall in Timmons, the slightly larger suburb to the north of us.

Drew likes it because she can look for wedding dresses without all of Oakville knowing her business. I like it because it has a carousel for Lillie.

"Kissing your boss..." Drew teases as we watch the ride go around. "You'll be sleeping with him soon."

"I will not... although, he is packing some serious meat in those jeans. I swear to God."

I want to see it. I want to touch it. *I can't stop thinking about it.*

"So just get your own place and date him. You can still be Lillie's nanny."

"Can I?" I tilt my head to the side, trying to decide how I feel about that arrangement. "It seems weird for him to be paying me while I'm sleeping with him."

"Get your paychecks direct deposited." She laughs, and I crack a smile.

Then I sigh, remembering his hands on me, how easily he lifted me against the wall and devoured my mouth. How hard and massive his erection felt against my stomach. A little shiver passes through me.

"It's not a bad idea." I think about the check I

deposited this morning on my way to Drew's, thirty-five hundred dollars. It appeared in a business envelope on my dresser yesterday evening, while I was out avoiding him.

Holy shit.

"I can tell he doesn't want me to move out. I kind of suggested it, but he shut it down right away. Me living with them was part of our original deal, I guess."

"How come? Does Lillie have night terrors?"

"No... I don't know... Maybe he likes having me close?" I try to think back to our first conversation, but my thoughts have gotten so muddled when it comes to Remi now.

All I can think about are his amazing biceps, his firm chest, those sensual lips, and that massive cock I want to ride.

"He said I would be there if Lillie needed anything in the night. It makes sense, I guess. He sleeps on a whole different floor. But so far she sleeps soundly all night."

Another pass, and Lillie waves so hard, her little arm looks like it might fly off. Today she picked out a purple tutu with black and white striped knee-high socks and a long-sleeved tee with Elphaba from *Wicked* on it. She's so adorable, and every time she passes, we smile and wave back.

Warm fuzzies are in my stomach, and no matter how heavy my thoughts, she makes me smile. I'm so fucking conflicted.

"I don't want to stop being Lillie's nanny. It's not just the money. I really like that little butter bean."

I look over at my friend, and she's giving me a funny little smile. "You've gotten yourself in a real jam, my friend."

"Thanks. I appreciate your input." I shove her

arm, and she starts to laugh.

"It's going to work out. It always does." Her eyes are dancing, and despite my mental distress, I love seeing her so happy. "What do you really want, Ruby Banks? You're a grown woman. Now's your time to decide."

I think about her question. "I want to be able to take care of myself. I want to be confident in my choices." The carousel slows to a stop, and we stroll to find Lillie running to meet us. "Maybe I do want to be a part of their life, but I want to be independent first. I want to make the choice."

Drew's lips press into a half-smile. "I think that's perfect."

"Well, stop it. I don't like all this mushy stuff. Aren't we supposed to be shopping for a wedding dress?"

"Oh! I found one I really like online. I think they have something like it at Second Acts."

"Second Acts?" Lillie is holding my hand, skipping while we walk toward the pre-owned wedding dress shop. "I know you're not making celebrity-nanny money, but why are you looking at used wedding dresses? That's got to be bad luck."

We walk into the store filled with racks of ivory and white gowns, along with a rainbow assortment of bridesmaids' dresses.

"Princesses!" Lillie tosses my hand, and she's across the store burying her face in sparkly satin and tulle.

"Stop acting like your mother all of a sudden," Drew snarks.

"Bitch, you did not just say that to me," I tease right back.

"Just, no more bad luck juju." She catches my

hand and pulls me close. "The markup on all this wedding crap is outrageous. I honestly can't believe some of these prices."

"Like that's some kind of state secret." I do my best to adjust my attitude and start sliding hangers across racks.

I'll admit, there are some interesting options in here. Some don't even look like they've been worn. Lillie is in heaven twirling around the colorful bridesmaids' section, and I keep my eye on her as we shop.

"You need to do something casual with him." Drew comes from behind a rack with three dresses over her arm. "To take the pressure off and see each other in a more friend-type way."

"I'm not sure we can get much friendlier."

A sales associate appears, reaching for Drew's armload of dresses. "Would you like a room? Let me take these."

Drew follows the woman, and I'm right behind her. "I mean more as friends, less as roommates who can't keep their hands off each other."

I shrug. "Sounds reasonable. What did you have in mind?"

She goes in the room, stopping me before I can follow her. "Stay out here so you can get the full effect once it's on."

Going to the door, I watch as Lillie ducks under veils and holds her hands out. She's going to dream about this tonight.

"Gray said karaoke starts Tuesday at the Red Cat. Why don't we do that together?" The door opens, and she steps out in a fitted, sleeveless white gown. "Like old friends."

"Oh!" My breath catches, and my eyes get hot.

"You're beautiful! I'm going to cry."

Fanning my face quickly, I shake my head.

"Stop it! You're going to make me cry, and I have two more dresses to try on!"

My bestie tries on two more gowns, but the first one's the winner. We're driving back to Oakville by dinner time, and Lillie's crashed out in her booster chair in my backseat.

"So you're still coming to the wedding next month, right?" Drew's got her phone out, and I panic slightly — which my bestie doesn't miss. "Ruby! You're my maid of honor. You have to be there."

"It's just a weekend thing?" I'm really panicking because of all the parties and showers I need to get scheduled for her. If she's pregnant we can't go too crazy. Maybe a lunch?

"It's Thursday to Sunday." She shows me a wedding planner app on her phone. "Or Saturday night, I guess."

"Of course, I'll be there." We're at her house, and I give her cheeks air kisses before she hops out and takes her wedding dress inside.

Thinking a month ahead feels like a whole different world to me. In a month I'll know if I'm still working for Remi. So much can happen in a month.

Chapter 14

Remi

Mr. Remington Key, plus one, is cordially invited to Empire Investments' annual gala on… Reading the gold lettering on the folded linen invitation, I can only think one thing. I'm in.

The Empire Investments Gala is the premiere meet and greet for developers and venture capitalists in the tech world, and I have one of the fifty invitations they send every year. This is fantastic. Only one small problem. It specifically states *plus one*.

I have to bring a date. My mind immediately flies to Ruby. Will she go with me on an overnight trip to Manhattan? I've given her space since our fucking hot as shit encounter on Friday — not that I'm giving up on pursuing her. I only recognize her point. It would be difficult to engage in a romantic relationship without jeopardizing her position as Lillie's nanny, and I don't want to do anything to hurt my daughter.

Speaking of, if she went as my plus one, who would keep Lillie?

"Remington, I need to speak with you." *Eleanor.* She's both a cause and a solution for my problem.

Aren't I supposed to be the master of solving problems? Lately I have more of them than solutions.

"We're starting our second week with this young woman living in our house, and I'm just not sure how I feel about it." Her arms are crossed, and she squares off, facing me.

It's Monday afternoon, and through my open French doors, I can hear Ruby and Lillie down in their tiny garden chattering. I hear the occasional burst of laughter, and it warms my heart. It makes me want to hold onto her even tighter.

Dropping the invitation on the stack of mail beside my computer, I meet my mother-in-law at the sofa separating my workspace from the open, sitting area near the balcony doors.

"It's my house, Eleanor, and I couldn't be happier with Ruby. Did you see the paintings they did last week?"

I'm still feeling pretty proud of my little girl's first attempt at art. I'm completely knocked out by how talented Ruby is. She's really amazing.

"I did, and did you even ask if she used nontoxic paint? What if Lillie had put her paintbrush in her mouth? We already know that idiot teacher lets her eat dirt."

"I'm sure Ruby watched her closely."

I'm not, but hell, you have to give kids some credit for not being morons.

Although she did eat dirt... Because that little brat Louie wouldn't let her be a soldier. Lillie wanted to be a soldier. I wonder if it means she has an interest in the military.

"I don't think it's a good idea for her to live here with the way she looks at you." She shakes her head and inhales. "There, I said it. People are talking, and I think it's a bad idea."

"I couldn't care less about small-town gossip." Slipping my hands in my pockets, I even my tone. "I'd actually hoped you might start looking for your own

128

place. I'm sure you'd like more privacy."

Her arms drop, and she looks as if I've struck her. "I have all the privacy I need in my suite downstairs. I need to be near my granddaughter. I've lived here all her life. It's all she knows. Anyway, it'll help with these silly rumors if I'm here."

I lose the fight with my annoyance. "I don't give a shit about the rumors, and Lillie will adjust to you having your own place. It would give her somewhere to go for sleepovers, and you can spoil her all you want."

"I will not listen to that kind of language, Remington! This sounds like the influence of that young woman." Her arms are crossed again, and she steps closer, lowering her voice. "Serena North went to school with her, and it seems she's rather wild. She's dated a lot of men."

Her statement should not make me feel jealous. Ruby had a social life before I met her. She isn't a nun.

"Last I checked, dating isn't against the law."

"How do you know she's not after your money? She definitely has you in her sights. It's very obvious from the way she's always touching you."

"I haven't noticed." Has she been touching me? Not enough, if you ask me. She mostly stays away from me, which I hate.

"You would be wise to keep your head around that girl. Her kind aren't known for being the most trustworthy type of people."

"What is that supposed to mean?" My voice could cut glass. I've done my best to maintain a calm environment for Lillie, but I won't have her grandmother being a racist bitch meddling in my private life.

Her hands go up. "I'm simply saying, Remi. How

well do you know her?"

"Well enough to trust her with my daughter. Based on our first week, I think she's doing a damn good job with Lillie. I have no complaints. So what if she's a friendly person?"

She's also a kickass kisser with amazing tits.

"Friendly, ha!" She gives me a disgusted glare. "When Dr. North said how he's interested in hiring a nanny if they all look like that, Whitney Flagstaff was appalled."

It takes all my self-control not to say that old bastard had better keep his eyes to himself. Instead, I give Eleanor exactly what she's after. The truth.

"I received an invitation today to a very important business event in Manhattan next week. It's an overnight trip, and I have to take a date. I'm considering asking Ruby to go with me."

My mother-in-law's jaw drops. "Remington! I forbid it. What will people say?"

"It's a business event, and I need an escort."

"That's exactly what they'll say. She's your *escort*."

My jaw tightens. "In the literal sense. I need you to watch Lillie for me while we're gone. Provided Ruby says yes. Will you do it?"

"I will not." She straightens her shoulders, crossing her arms again. "I will not aid you in committing sin."

"You're saying you plan to live in this house and you won't watch your granddaughter while I'm out of town?"

"Not if you take that woman. I will not let you shame my daughter's memory by carrying on in this manner. What will people say?"

My throat tightens, and I literally see red.

Striding forward, I speak close to her face, my

teeth gritted. "Do not ever bring up Sandy like this to me. I have been faithful to her memory a long time, and if I choose to date someone, it's not an insult to her past... to *our* past. She will always have a special place in my heart."

The words are difficult, but as I say them, I feel calm.

Drew said the words to me almost a year ago, and I wasn't ready to hear them. Now I know them to be true. I can't die because Sandy did. I have to go on living, and I have to see what the future holds for me — if only for Lillie's sake.

Eleanor doesn't seem to agree. "If you take that woman on an overnight trip, I will not stand idly by."

"You'll be moving. I'll have my realtor begin the search for your new place today." I make a move for my phone, but she's across the room quicker than me, her voice changing to some sort of damsel in distress.

"Remington! I can't move out. I need to be near my granddaughter. She's all I have left. She's the only thing I have."

Hesitating, I cross my arms over my chest, studying her. I try to decide how much I feel I owe this woman. She did step in and help me at my lowest point. I don't want to be cruel. I'm not a monster.

At the same time...

"You will watch Lillie if Ruby agrees to go with me to the gala, and you won't say a word about it."

She closes her eyes and bows her head as if she's being martyred. "I will."

Her behavior is so over the top, but it's what I needed to hear. Now I'm ready to end this infuriating conversation. The sound of Ruby and Lillie downstairs distracts me, and I turn on my heel, leaving the room and jogging down the stairs.

As I get to the landing, I see the two of them bustling into the house. It makes me smile, and all that tension melts away.

"Dad-day!" Lillie launches into a run, and I catch her, lifting her in my arms. "My broccoli has furry little middles that look like real broccoli! But the beets just look like lettuce leaves with red stems. And Ruby showed me how to pull weeds and give them just a little bit of water. Not too much water!"

Ruby hangs at the door, but it's too much distance between us. I carry my daughter to where she's standing. Two pairs of gardening gloves are in her hands, and she looks down at them when I smile. Her cheeks turn a pretty shade of pink under my gaze.

"An artist and a gardener?" I grin, letting my eyes roam her face. "I feel like I'm getting a bargain."

She's still ready with the snark. "You're paying me way too much, but I'm worth it."

No argument here.

Lillie starts to wiggle, so I put her down. She races toward the stairs, and Ruby calls after her. "Wash your hands. No, get in the tub. You've got dirt all over you." She glances at her hands and does a little frown. "I'm kind of a mess myself."

"I'd be happy to help with cleanup."

Her eyes narrow, and she gives me a sly grin. "I bet you would, filthy boy."

It tightens my stomach and makes me laugh. "I meant with Lillie."

Damn, I really want to be alone with her again. I imagine us in the garden tub in my bathroom suite, pulling her naked and slippery onto my lap...

I've got to figure out a way to make this work.

In the meantime, I'm just starting to follow my daughter upstairs when she calls after me. "Hey, um..." She hesitates, and I stop, taking a few steps back. "You feel like doing something tomorrow night? Drew said there's this Karaoke thing at the Red Cat. Gray thought it might be fun if we all went..."

She's so awkward, it's my turn to tease. "Are you asking me out, Miss Banks?"

Her cheeks flame red. "No! It's like a friend-type thing. A big group of friends. It's not a date."

I return to where she's standing and trace a dark curl off her cheek with my finger. "Drew and Gray aren't friends. They're engaged."

She puts her hand on my chest and gives me a little push. "Yes, but you and I are just friends, so back it up, big boy."

I love it. Even with me giving her a hard time, she's ready to be feisty right back. I can't help a grin, and she looks at my face before shaking her head and walking past muttering something about a dimple.

Crossing my arms, I lean against the doorjamb watching her go. She's got the cutest little ass. I'm busted checking her out when she stops at the stairs.

"Hey!" Her eyes narrow. "Eyes up here." Two fingers point at her face, and I chuckle, following her to the stairs. "Do I get any time off?"

I hadn't really thought about it. "Sure! I mean, I guess so... as long as Lillie's covered."

"I just wanted to have lunch with Ma. It's weird not seeing her every day, and I guess yesterday at church I realized how much I miss her."

We'd all arrived at the small sanctuary together, but after Ruby took Lillie to her Sunday school class, she returned and sat with her mother. I'd wanted to move and sit beside her, but it felt rude to leave Eleanor alone. Now I'm wondering why I cared.

"You can certainly have lunch with your mom. I'll

ask Eleanor to watch Lillie." That doesn't seem to be the right answer.

"No. Don't ask Eleanor." She holds up her hand. I'm confused, but maybe she senses what's going on. Ruby is fucking smart as a whip. "What if I took Lillie with me instead? Ma would love it."

"I don't see why not."

Her lips press into a frown. "It would mess up your daddy-daughter lunch, but maybe you could do something different that day? They opened this new custard shop across from the clinic. It's supposed to be really good. I wouldn't know, because—"

"You can't have dairy. It sounds great. What day?"

She shrugs. "I was thinking Wednesday… or any day. Whatever works for you."

"Wednesday it is. And tomorrow, you and I have a date."

Her voice rings down as she jogs up the stairs. "It's not a date."

We'll see about that.

Chapter 15

Ruby

"Seems you can't do anything without causing a commotion, Ruby Banks." Drew shouts over the music blasting from the ancient jukebox as she sips her lemonade.

She's holding Gray's arm and her eyes sparkle. Everything about her glows. Her hunky hunky boyfriend—sorry, *fiancé*—is busy talking to my guest.

Remi is not my date.

"What are you talking about?" I shout back, doing my best not to blow her eardrum. "What commotion?"

"All the old church ladies are up in arms because Dr. North is interviewing nannies now. The scuttlebutt is he wants a nanny as hot as you."

She bursts out laughing, but I feel slightly ill. "What the hell is that supposed to mean? Isn't Dr. North Serena's husband?"

"Don't tell me you care what happens to that bitch Serena."

My lips twist into a frown. She's a horrible, horrible person, but it doesn't mean I want her husband bragging about hiring a sexy nanny.

"What's up?" Remi rotates around to face us, holding a tumbler of whiskey.

I kind of like that he drinks whiskey. It goes with his lead-singer vibe. I've got another Tequila Sunrise...

and I have an idea of a song I could sing...

"I was just telling Ruby about Dr. North desperately seeking a hot nanny." Drew leans forward, making a face over her drink like it's the most hilarious thing ever.

I guess it would be if I weren't the reason behind the nonsense.

Remi shifts in his seat, and one glance at his face tells me he knows exactly what she's talking about.

"You knew about this?"

"I heard something about it from Eleanor."

"Oh my God!" I throw my hands up, falling back in the seat. "Baby Jesus, deliver me from these goddamned old church ladies!"

Gray laughs. "Did you just take the Lord's name in vain in a prayer?"

Sometimes I'm so glad he's back. Right now isn't one of those times. "You should know what this is like. You were the target of their crap for a while."

"Longer than a while." He puts an arm around Drew and pulls her closer. "Now I don't really give a shit."

Drew melts into his side, and the jukebox switches off, leaving the room momentarily silent. Loud music filters through the ancient bar, and a gameshow-style announcer steps to the center of a brand-new stage.

"I can't believe they actually invested money in this place."

The guy calls out some woman named Elizabeth, and I feel Remi's arm snake around my waist. He pulls me closer and speaks low in my ear as Elizabeth launches into a pretty decent rendition of "Hips Don't Lie."

"Hey, I'm really sorry about all that bullshit with Phillip. I had no idea he'd do something so stupid."

My jaw tightens, and I know I shouldn't be mad at Remi. It's not his fault.

"Is he serious?" I look around the room, wondering who here is going to add to the rumor mill. "Or is he just taking a cheap shot at me?"

Looking over my shoulder, my eyes meet Remi's and I see real anger there. "He'd better not be doing it to hurt you. Maybe I should have a talk with him—"

Shifting around, I grasp his forearm. "Don't. Serena's been making cracks at me all my life. If this is just adult bullying, I can deal with it. The last thing I want is to play their game."

His brow lowers, and I have to say, angry, protective Remi might be the sexiest version I've seen so far. "I don't like people being shitty when it comes to you. I won't put up with it from Eleanor, and I sure as hell won't put up with it from Phillip North."

"You probably shouldn't put your arm around me like that. We're just friends, remember?"

His eyes hold mine with such intensity, I'm not sure he remembers, but it doesn't matter. Elizabeth is finished, and the Karaoke DJ calls his name. "Can we get Remi to the stage? Remi, are you still here?"

Drew squeals and claps. "I put you in! Ruby said you sing, so I put you in for Kenny Rogers."

A smile curls his lips. "You've been talking about me to Drew?"

My throat goes dry, and *holy shit*, if she put in that song…

He slips out of the booth and walks toward the stage as the piano riff that opens "She Believes in Me" rings through the bar. A few people hoot, and a few others stand to slow dance.

Remi takes the mic and walks to where I'm sitting in the booth and proceeds to sing the song directly to me. My skin hums with electricity, and I can't take my eyes off him, sexy, his voice touching my heart. I've never really paid attention to the words. Now that I hear them, I feel like I can't breathe.

He sings it so rich and perfect. His style is different from Kenny Rogers's, but it's still so good. My eyes get hot. I do believe in him... it makes me start to laugh. I'm such an idiot.

He finishes, and Drew screams like Kenny Rogers is really in the building. All I can do is smile and clap, but the room goes wild.

He does a little bow before sliding into the booth beside me and kissing my cheek. I don't even care who sees. "You're a hit."

"How did she know to pick that song?" His eyes say he knows the answer, and I just want to make out with him right here on the spot.

"I might have told her it was your favorite."

His arm goes around me again, and he speaks in my ear, giving me a shiver. "It was never my favorite until I met you."

The DJ calls out Dagwood Magee, and my head snaps to meet Drew's face. Both our mouths are wide open, and he launches into a version of Elton John's "I Guess That's Why They Call it the Blues."

Gray starts to laugh. "Biggest Elton John fan I've ever known."

Drew pushes his shoulder, and he slides out, taking her hand. They proceed to slow dance in front of the table, and Remi looks at me, a question in his eyes.

Inhaling deeply, I consider it for a hot minute. "We'd better not. People are already talking about us, and you have to think about Lillie."

"I think about Lillie a lot." He smooths a curl off

my cheek and tucks it behind my ear. I love when he does that. "I want to think about you, too."

The song ends, and Remi gives me a little squeeze. "I'll get us another round."

Gray claps his hand, and they take off together toward the bar. Drew scoots around to me, and she's glued to my side.

"I loooove Remi!" She's bouncing on the red vinyl. "You have to date him now."

"What the hell? You just agreed with me I can't date him because it would be too risky with Lillie involved."

"Yeah, but I'm rethinking that position." She takes another sip of lemonade, and she's so giddy, I'm wondering if it's spiked. No, my bestie would never take a chance with her baby. "Lillie's getting older, and that voice!" She falls back clutching her chest.

"His voice is amazing." I polish off my tequila, remembering when he sang in my ear. *Panty-melter!* "Either way, I'm screwed with the monster-in-law. She pretty much hates me."

"Oh, fuck her! Who do you know that has a good mother-in-law?"

"I don't know many people with in-laws, but I've heard good ones exist."

"It's not a sign of compatibility. She's not even related to him. If anything, it shows what a great guy he is that he takes care of her like he does. I heard he pays all her bills."

Inhaling deeply, I nod. "It's true. He's pretty patient with her, too." My mind slowly connects the dots. "I wonder if that's the problem. Like maybe she feels threatened by me?"

"Now who's a great therapist?" Drew just loves being right about my dead-end career path. "It's like in that rich Asians movie—she's playing chicken with you."

Our eyes meet, and my insides are buzzing. "I can't let her win."

"You know what to do!" Drew snaps her fingers in a Z. "Bok Bok, Bitch! You're a badass chicken."

The buzzing in my stomach gives way to a laugh. I shake my head, puzzling over this possibility. "Remi always stands up for me to her. He really lets me take the lead with Lillie's care." Which I'm getting better at. "It makes total sense."

I feel so blind. Of course, she hates me. I'm crowding her territory.

Drew puts her hand over mine on the table. "He sounds pretty close to perfect."

I flip my hand over and give hers a squeeze. "It's a super complicated situation."

"Doesn't sound so complicated to me."

Dagwood walks with the guys to the table, and I jump up to meet them. "Didn't know you had such a decent voice, Fontleroy," he says to Remi. "Too bad you sang a pussy song."

Gray snorts a laugh, but I punch Dag on the arm. "Dagwood! That's his favorite Kenny Rogers song."

"Ow, don't hit me, Ruby Roo! That is not his favorite Kenny Rogers song." He turns to Remi, who's smirking into his glass. "I'm sorry. Unless you're gay, man. Nothing wrong with that, but you should let the ladies know. It's not cool to lead them on." He makes a face and hooks his thumb in my direction.

I grab that thumb in my fist. "He is not gay. And stop calling me that." Turning to my date, I touch Remi's arm. "It's your favorite song, right?"

His lips press into a smile, and I can see he's trying not to laugh.

"Wait..." I look from Remi to Dag to Gray. "It's not... Why would you tell me it's your favorite?"

Dagwood's loud voice answers me. "Because chicks dig it. Gah! Keep up, girl!"

My mouth hangs open. "Is that true?"

Remi looks sheepish. "Sorry, babe."

Drew bursts out laughing. "Oh my God, you're hilarious! It worked. I'm pretty sure every woman in this bar is in love with you since you sang it."

"Every woman?" Gray puts his arm around her shoulders.

"Almost every woman," she adds, rising on her tiptoes to kiss him.

I pretend to be mad. "You lied to me."

"It was just a tiny lie." He puts his arms around my waist, and I don't even stop him. "You were so pretty in the moonlight. I wanted to sing it to you."

He's grinning, and I'm clearly not mad. I'm clearly buzzing letting him hold me this way out in public. "So what is your favorite Kenny Rogers song?"

"I don't really have one." He reads my face and quickly adds, "but 'The Gambler' is pretty great."

"Are you just saying that because I did?" I step out of his embrace and cross my arms.

"No. It's a great song. Know when to hold 'em."

"Know when to fold 'em!" Dagwood sings the rest of the chorus loudly before hopping out of the booth. "I'm putting you in. The whole bar wants to sing that song."

"Hang on." They're both walking to the DJ booth, and I sit in the seat beside my bestie.

She leans forward and puts her chin on my shoulder. "I really like seeing you so happy."

A knot is in my throat, and I can't argue with her. "He might be kind of perfect."

"Ruby?" A male voice pulls me out of my thoughts, and I look up to see Henry Pak standing in front of me. "I thought that was you. How are you?"

"Henry, hi!" I stand and give him a hug.

My mom's one attempt to rescue me from the dating apps was a Korean (of course) pediatric surgeon, who interned with my dad in Charleston.

"I haven't seen you in... a year?" Henry is very nice, very polite. Too bad his ears make me wonder if he can fly.

"You look amazing." He smiles and touches my elbow. "How's your mom?"

"Great—she's doing really great. Still working at the church..." I try to step out of his reach, but the booth blocks me. "I'm having lunch with her tomorrow. I can tell her you said hi. Are you still living in Charleston?"

"For now." He nods, pointing to my hand. "Can I buy you a drink?"

"I've got her covered." Remi's voice is hard, and his arm goes around my waist.

"Oh, hey." I don't know why I suddenly feel nervous. "Henry Pak, this is Remington Key."

I motion between them, but neither makes a move to shake hands.

Okay.

"Henry's a pediatric surgeon in Charleston."

Henry adopts a proprietary tone. "We dated a few times last year."

"Just like... one or two times. Right?" I'm doing my best to salvage this. Thankfully, I'm saved by the DJ calling Remi's name. It's not a busy night at the Red Cat.

Glancing up, I see his jaw is clenched. The guys are staring each other down, and I consider waving a white napkin between them. Instead, I speak close to his ear.

"Remi, you're up. Are you still singing 'The Gambler' for me?"

It breaks the staring match, and his eyes flicker to mine. "Yes." He's not smiling, but he kisses my cheek. "Be right back."

The whole house is dark, and it's after midnight when we get home.

"We should've asked Eleanor to take Lillie to preschool." Remi whispers, leading me across the grand foyer to the stairs.

He's been slightly distant ever since our encounter with Henry. Still, he brought the house down with "The Gambler." Dagwood was right—everybody sang along, but Remi's smooth voice sealed the deal.

We're holding hands as he leads me past the second floor up to my suite. "You don't have to walk me to my room."

Butterflies are beating their wings like crazy in my stomach, and my throat is tight. I wonder if he's going to kiss me. I really want him to.

He stops in front of my door and faces me. "It's the closest I can get to taking you home, seeing as you live here."

I can't stand his formal manner after we had so much fun tonight.

Putting my hand on his chest, I clear my throat, choosing my words. "You know, I had a life before I met you."

"Eleanor mentioned you dated some." His expression is stony, and I don't like knowing Eleanor is talking about me to him.

Still, I own my past. "I dated a lot. Henry was one

of the many fish I threw back."

"I don't like thinking of you out there."

"I'm here now." My voice is quiet, soothing.

His is not. "Yes, you are."

Reaching up, he cups my cheeks in his strong hands, and his mouth covers mine, pushing my lips apart and plunging in his tongue. It's insistent, demanding. My back is pressed to the door, and he kisses me as if he's claiming what's his. It's fucking hot as hell, and I feel the heat all the way to my panties.

A little whimper escapes my throat, and it's like fuel to the fire. His hands go to my waist, ripping my silk blouse out of my skirt.

"Oh," I gasp as his palms smooth over the bare skin of my sides, rising higher to the band of my bra.

His lips are on mine again, and I hold his cheeks, doing my best to keep up with his kisses. His mouth moves quickly, pulling my lips, nipping my jaw. He's desperate, starving, but so am I. I want him so much. Lifting his head, he looks deep into my eyes.

I nod so slowly, but it's all he needs. With a fast jerk, my shirt is open, revealing my black lace bra. The demi-cups only reach the tops of my areolas, and they rise and fall on every breath.

"You're so beautiful." He roughly cups my breasts with both hands, lifting them together.

I squirm against the heat zipping through my body. My back is against the door, and I'm burning up inside as he hooks his thumbs in the cups and jerks them down, exposing my tight nipples.

"Remi," I whisper, but he doesn't look up. He lowers his head to give one a firm suck. The other he pinches between his fingertips.

My knees nearly give out, and my panties are drenched. "Oh, god." All my good intentions are flying out the window. "We can't have sex out here."

Once more his mouth finds mine, and I kiss him back with as much ferocity, wrapping my arms around his neck. His hand finds the doorknob behind me and turns it. We both stagger into my room, but he rotates me, putting my back against the wall again.

Stepping back, he looks at me, eyes dark and stormy. I'm standing with my shirt torn open, my breasts spilling over my bra, breathing like I've just run a marathon. His gaze is like a rough caress, sliding over my sizzling skin.

"You are so fucking sexy." Reaching out, he cups my breast, sliding his thumb across my nipple. A soft noise hiccups from my throat, and his eyes flare with lust. "I want to taste you. I want you all over my face, coming and screaming my name."

Oh, shit.

I can't even answer before he drops to his knees and shoves my skirt up to my waist.

He murmurs a *yes*, when he sees I'm wearing thigh-high black pantyhose. Large hands grip my legs, lifting me as if I weigh nothing, opening me to him, and jerking my thong to the side of my bare pussy. "Beautiful."

"Oh, god," I gasp at the first pass of his warm tongue over my sensitive clit.

My knees melt when he does it again, then again, circling and sucking. Another noise trembles from my throat as heat surges low in my pelvis. God, it feels so good.

I reach down, fisting my hand in his thick hair as the pleasure tightens between my legs. His movements are quicker, his light stubble scuffing the charged skin of my inner thighs. My head drops back and my hips rotate in time with his movements. *I'm going to come so hard...*

"Remi..." It's a cry as he plunges a thumb into me, still licking and sucking. "Remi!" My cry is even louder.

The pressure grows tighter and tighter, my thighs flex, and with one more firm suck, one more slow lick, I shatter, moaning and rocking against his expert mouth.

My hips buck, and my back arches. Then I bend forward, the waves of orgasm shuddering through my entire body, centering between my legs.

He doesn't stop, tasting me as if I'm the most delicious thing he's ever had. Until at last I'm begging. "I can't... it's too much."

Lowering me gently to my wobbly feet, he sits back and looks up at me. A satisfied smile is on his lips. "You're perfect."

Rising slowly, he holds my face in one hand, lifting my chin. Our eyes melt together, and he leans down to kiss me. His other hand palms my breast again, sliding over my erect nipple.

I taste myself on his lips. I feel the massive bulge in his pants, pressing against my stomach. It's wanton and erotic, and he kisses a line across my cheek to my ear. "Here is right where I intend to keep you."

I can't speak. I'm wrecked from that amazing orgasm, but he steps back, opening the door again. "Goodnight, Ruby. Sleep well."

The door closes sharply, and he's gone, leaving me in the center of my room, my mind blown, and my clothes disheveled.

Chapter 16

Remi

As soon as I get to my room, I go straight to my shower.

Flicking on the water, I strip out of my jeans and boxer briefs. My shirt is over my head as the steam starts to rise. I could barely walk downstairs from the erection in my pants. My cock aches from wanting release. It's like a giant redwood in my fist, and I pull it steadily as the water flashes off my skin.

In my mind's eye, I see her bucking, her long hair spilling over her breasts, rising and falling in that bra as she panted for me. God, she's so beautiful, pure ivory and jet black with those pink lips falling open, her small hands fisting my hair.

"Yes..." The orgasm rises in my ass, my balls tighten. I remember how she looked when I ripped up her skirt. Sheer hose ending in lace bands at the tops of her thighs, her bare pussy.

I can still taste her on my lips. I can still smell her on my skin. She came so beautifully, just like I wanted — shuddering and crying my name.

My beautiful Ruby. I will have her. I will plunge into her depths, feel those legs wrapped around my waist.

"Fuck, yeah," I whisper as the streams of come wash down the drain. I brace myself through the pulses of orgasm. My eyes are closed, and she is the only thing I see.

Holding on a moment longer, the hot water splashes off the back of my neck. I lift my chin and let it wash down my face.

I didn't want to take her tonight. She said she couldn't sleep with me and be Lillie's nanny. I don't agree, but I won't give her a reason to quit. I can't have her deciding to leave me. I need her here.

But when that Henry Pak showed up, and I saw him talking to her, touching her arm. My jaw tightens at the memory. That motherfucker acted like he knew something I didn't, like he'd been with her... I might have gone a little crazy thinking about it.

Or maybe it was Eleanor's words in my brain.

It's not fair, I know. Ruby is a grown woman. She didn't even know me before two weeks ago. She's gorgeous and fun and full of life. She isn't the type to sit at home. Hell, I probably wouldn't be as into her if she were.

One thing's for sure—I was not going to leave the possibility of her going to bed tonight thinking of that guy. I only want her thinking of me. I want my lips haunting her dreams.

Snatching up the washcloth, I quickly get clean and shut off the water.

The last thing I see as I fall asleep is Ruby's smile. I grin thinking about how she is with Lillie, how she is with Drew. She's sweet and good, and I've got to convince her to go with me to New York.

The sun streams through the blinds, waking me, and I throw back the covers, jerking my jeans over my hips and snatching my shirt off my chair. I button it quickly as I run down the stairs to the kitchen.

Last time I kissed Ruby, I didn't see her for nearly a week. I'll be damned if that happens again. My stomach is tight, but as soon as I round the corner, my daughter's voice slows my pace.

"Daddy!" She bounces in her stool at the bar, and I walk over to kiss her little head.

"What's for breakfast, princess?" I look around the kitchen, and Ruby has her back turned, facing the coffee machine.

"Ruby made me a pear." Her little face is scrunched. "She put cottage cheese in the middle."

I do my best not to laugh. "Do you like it?"

"I didn't... then she put honey on it." She still seems unsure.

"I can make you toast with peanut butter if you want." Ruby speaks softly, as if she's trying not to be noticed.

Like I could possibly miss her looking amazing in my kitchen in black jeans and a long-sleeved striped sweater. Her hair is in two low ponytails on each side of her head.

"You need to eat your fruit, Lillian. And cottage cheese is full of calcium and protein." Eleanor is at the table with a cup and saucer and a newspaper spread in front of her. "I didn't think you'd be down so early, Remington. I heard you come in after midnight."

Why does she talk to me like I'm her teenage son?

"I had to see my best girl before she left for school." Leaning down, I kiss Lillie's cheek then I go to the fridge where Ruby is holding a carton of soy half and half. "Did you sleep well last night?"

I imagine pulling her into my arms and kissing her good morning. The heat between us is palpable.

She keeps her gaze on her coffee preparations. "I did, actually. I was very relaxed."

A grin splits my cheeks. She's being playful, and I love it. "Are you still going to your mother's for lunch?"

Our eyes meet, and I feel a charge, but she blinks away fast. "If that's still okay?"

"I think it's great." Eleanor is watching us like a hawk, so I go to the coffee machine. "We're not having lunch today, Lils. You're going with Ruby to her mom's house."

My daughter's little brow furrows, but before she can decide she's not happy about it, I add. "You and I are going to get ice cream at Dipper's instead."

She inhales a little gasp and claps her hands. "Yay! Daddy's taking me to Dipper's!"

"Like everyone in the room didn't just hear me." I go over and tickle her, and she shrieks so loud I stop at once. "Too loud."

"Remington, don't tickle her. She'll wet her pants."

"I will not!" Lillie shouts even louder. "I'm not a baby."

Eleanor abandons her post at the table to attend to her granddaughter. I take advantage of her momentary distraction to touch Ruby's arm lightly.

"Hey." My voice is soft. "I'd like to talk to you if that's okay. Maybe after you drop Lillie at school?"

Her lips press together, and she hesitates. "I have to take care of a few things for Drew's shower on Saturday. When you get back with Lillie?"

"Sure." Sliding my hand down, I brush my fingers across hers. I'm addicted to the rush of heat between us. It tightens my stomach. "Have fun today." Man, I wish I could kiss her.

"Thanks," she whispers before turning to my daughter. "Time to go, Lil."

Lillie runs to grab her coat and snack bag, and

they head for the door. I lean against the bar watching them go as I sip my coffee. Ruby holds her hand, and Lillie skips every other step. She's singing some Disney song I vaguely recognize, and I can't help thinking how great they look together.

I set my coffee on the bar and notice Eleanor watching the whole scene play out with a scowl. I don't have time for this.

I set my cup in the sink and give her a nod. "I'd better get to work."

She doesn't even respond.

Chapter 17

Ruby

"Then you press the edges together like this, and it's done." Ma guides Lillie's small fingers along the edge of her dumpling while I work on my own.

"I made a dumpling!" Lillie holds it up to me, and I smile.

"It's called *mandu*." I give her a little hip bump. "And you're a natural. I couldn't make mandu that good until I was five."

Lillie's little mouth quirks, and she leans closer. "You're not like Tiana."

"Who is Tiana?" Ma collects our crescents into her steamer and places it over the boiling water.

"It's a Disney princess." I walk over to watch her mixing soy sauce, rice wine vinegar, sesame oil, scallions, and garlic for the sauce. She makes a separate batch with red pepper flakes for us. "Lillie, you can play in my room if you want. Just don't turn up the K-pop too loud."

Her hazel eyes widen, and she takes off running to my old bedroom. She reminds me so much of her dad. I watch after her remembering his smile this morning. Just as fast, my mind drifts to his face last night, eyes heated and possessive. He kissed me like he would never let me go, then he dropped to his knees and blew my mind.

"Why is your face so pink? What are you thinking?" Ma's voice is scolding, and I clear my mind.

"Nothing! I was just thinking how cute she is. She looks a lot like her dad."

"You must be professional with that man. He is your boss." She gives me a stern glare, and I can't argue.

"I agree. I've turned over a new leaf, and I'm being very serious." *Seriously in lust.*

Her voice drops, becoming more urgent. "People at church are talking about sexy nannies. Are you having sex with him?"

"No!" I hop up on the counter, wondering if oral sex is technically sex. "I told you I couldn't live in his house if I did that. I'd have to get my own place."

"Good. You must be careful. That man is not like us. He is not Korean." She lifts the lid on her bamboo steamer and turns the dumplings with chopsticks.

I just can't even. "Why should I be careful? Dad wasn't Korean, and it didn't stop you from marrying him."

"I should have listened to my mother." She takes a bowl of kimchee out of the refrigerator.

That makes me remember. "I saw Henry Pak last night. He said to tell you hi."

"You should go out with Henry again. He's a good Korean doctor."

"Who looks like Dumbo." She makes a scolding noise, but I let it pass. "So what did your mother have to say?" She looks confused, and I lean closer. "The part you should have listened to."

Her eyes close, and she shakes her head. "She said I should not have married outside our community."

This intrigues me. Ma has never dared to speak ill of my late father. "Are you saying she didn't want you to marry Dad?"

"Your father was a very good man, but it is a lot of work to be married. It was very difficult at times."

I can't say *no shit* or she'll lose her shit.

She's quiet, thinking, then she does a sharp nod. "I'm not saying bad things about your father, but it's good for you to know."

"So why did you? Marry him, I mean." She puts one of the dumplings on a small plate and cuts it in half.

I watch as she tests it, and I pick up the other half to test it as well. It's delicious.

She hasn't answered me, but when her dark eyes flicker to mine, she can't stop her smile. Ma doesn't show her soft side very often, so I always jump on it when she does.

"You thought he was hot." I point my chopsticks at her and start to laugh. "Dad was Mr. Handsome American Doctor and you couldn't resist."

"He was very handsome, and I should have resisted."

"Why?" I hop off the counter, legitimately curious. "I mean, he was hard on me, but—"

"Your father wanted you to be the best. He had very high standards." Her voice is stern again, and she arranges large butter lettuce leaves on a platter. "He was no harder than a good Korean father would have been."

She uses a wide ladle to spoon the dumplings onto the platter, and I watch as she sprinkles the pale beige skins with bright orange fish eggs.

"So what's the problem?"

She shakes her head, carrying it all to the table. "He did not respect our traditions. He wanted his home to be completely American. He did not like the grace, the politeness."

He said we were all push-overs. I remember that very well. *Submissive*, is what he called it. Ma called it good manners. If I didn't know how tough she could be, I might have agreed with him. As it is, I know her "good manners" made for a very peaceful home.

"I don't think Remi would oppose other cultural influences in his home." She gives me a hard look, but I know I'm right. "Anyway, this is a silly conversation. I'm not even dating him, and you're acting like he proposed to me."

"The way to a man's heart is through his stomach."

I huff a laugh. "Then you have nothing to worry about."

"It is also through his children."

When we get back to the house, I find Eleanor in the living room, digging in one of the cabinets under the enormous flat screen television. I don't want to stop, but she sees us before we can make a dash up the stairs.

"Hello, girls." She stands up, holding a long, brown bottle. "How was lunch?"

"I made a dumpling. It's called mangoos, and Ruby's mom made a dessert that had beans and fruit mixed together!" Lillie's talking fast, which I know means she's excited.

Eleanor doesn't seem so impressed. "That sounds very exotic."

Her attention returns to the bottle she's holding, and I can tell she wants me to ask about it. With a sigh, I decide to be a peacemaker.

"What's that, Eleanor?" I can play her game, but I can't keep my voice from sounding like a robot.

She looks up at me with a knowing smile. "I found this Tawny Port from Prager Winery in the cabinet. Sandy and Remi got it for me when they traveled to Napa on their honeymoon."

My throat tightens, and I have to hand it to her. She got me.

I'll be damned if I let her know it, though. "That's really cool. You never opened it?"

"No. It's a very rare wine… Just like theirs was a very rare love." She sighs like she's being so innocent. "We should open it and enjoy it after dinner tonight before it passes it's prime."

My lips press together, and my stomach hurts, thinking of how that will go. Not that I want to replace Lillie's mom, not at all. I don't want Remi to be sad. I don't want things to be strange between us.

"After Sandy died, he said he'd never love again." Eleanor's tone is wistful.

An ache is in my throat, and I don't know why my silly eyes heat. "Never is a long time. Remi was twenty-six when she died?"

"They both were." Her eyes aren't on me.

I sound weak, but I think about my therapy training. "Grief recovery isn't about forgetting the past. It's about remembering with joy, not pain."

She continues like it's not tearing up my heart. "I wonder if Remi will even remember that trip."

"His honeymoon? I'm sure it's something he'll always remember." I'm ready to go to my room now.

"He seems to be forgetting a lot of things these days." She gives me a pointed glare, but I don't want to fight this battle. Ever.

"I'm sure it will always be very special to him."

Remi cuts us off just as I'm leaving the living room. "Hey!"

That dimple is in his cheek, and he looks genuinely glad to see me.

It makes me want to cry.

Which is a ridiculous response to seeing him after hearing his mother-in-law talking about his honeymoon. Remi and I are not serious. I shouldn't feel anything about Eleanor dragging out old tokens of his past life.

His brow furrows when he sees my face. "Everything okay? Where's Lillie?"

"Everything's fine." I manage a smile, but his expression isn't buying it.

"Daddy!" Lillie comes running inside from the patio. "Are we going to Dipper's now?"

"Sure, honeybun. Ruby, want to come with us?"

I shake my head. "It's your special time, remember?"

"You can go, Ruby!" Lillie grabs my hand. "You don't have to eat the ice cream. You can have a cookie."

Remi turns to his mother in law. "Eleanor? Would you like to join us?"

"Oh, no." She waves a hand in front of her face. "You go and have fun. I'm just doing a little cleaning."

Is that what it's called now?

"Then we'll be back in what? An hour?" He looks at me, and the dimple is back.

I almost sigh. He's so good looking. "An hour should be plenty of time."

Lillie grabs his hand and takes off running toward the door.

Chapter 18

Remi

Ruby waits in the park across the street while Lillie and I get our ice cream.

My daughter is on her tiptoes pointing at the chocolate-dipped waffle cones. "You sure you want a cone, peanut? It'll drip all over you."

"I want a cone!" She pumps her little fist over her head like a cheer.

That does it. "Two swirl cones, please."

As soon as the girl passes them to us, I grab an extra set of napkins and my daughter's hand. We walk across the street to the town square, where Ruby is sitting on an iron bench in front of the gazebo... with that fucking Henry Pak again.

What the hell? Does he live here now?

I catch the end of Ruby's sentence as we approach. "How soon are you looking to move?"

Good, maybe he's planning to go back to Korea.

"We're closing on the condo tomorrow. Depending on the contractor, it's possible I could be here full time by the end of the month."

"That's great." I can't tell if Ruby really thinks it's great or not.

When she sees me, her expression changes. She shifts in her chair and looks worried.

"Remi!" Her voice is too high. "You remember

Henry Pak. You met him last night?"

Thankfully, my hands are full with my daughter's hand in one and an ice cream cone in the other. I'm not interested in shaking this guy's hand.

I nod. "How's it going?"

"Ah, yes." He smiles, but I can tell he's about as glad to see me as I am to see him. "You're Ruby's boss, right? The tech guy?"

It's tech billionaire, asshole. "She's living in my house now."

Ruby's eyebrows shoot up. "I'm the nanny. I share a floor with this little girl right here." She reaches for Lillie, who is completely oblivious.

My daughter crawls onto Ruby's lap, focused entirely on licking her ice cream as it tries to melt all over her hand and arm and striped sack dress.

"Here, I have extra napkins." I hold them out, and Ruby takes them, quickly catching the chocolate drops.

"Last time we talked, you were working with Drew at the Friends Care Clinic." Henry's brow furrows as he watches her. "What happened with that?"

Like it's any of his business. "I made her an offer she couldn't refuse."

Her lips press into a frown, and she cuts her eyes at me. "Actually… it's not as easy as you think to build a client list. You know how tiny Oakville is."

Henry nods. "I can relate to that dilemma. As a physician, I was lucky to work with your father and other prominent men in Charleston. It fast-tracked my career."

I don't like the way he says *physician* like he invented the lightbulb or the internal combustion engine or air.

Ruby jumps in with some story about her dad I

don't know, and they both laugh. It's annoying as fuck the way he's sitting beside her, talking to her.

"Daddy! You're dripping!" Lillie points at my ice cream, and I just barely catch a drip of vanilla before it hits my slacks.

"Oh, no! Here." Ruby hands me a napkin and smiles. "I think custard melts quicker than regular ice cream."

"Thanks." Taking the napkin from her, I have a thought.

I step over behind Dr. Henry Pak and pretend to be looking at something over Ruby's shoulder. At the same time, I drag my tongue slowly over the swirl cone. Ruby is half-way through answering one of Henry's stupid questions when her eyes land on mine and her voice trails off.

I give the cone another, slower lick, flickering my tongue along the side, and my eyes fix on hers. Her pretty pink lips part as her jaw drops, and her cheeks flame bright red.

Her response makes me grin. She remembers where my face was last night. And how loudly it made her scream my name.

"Ruby?" Henry leans forward. "You okay? You seem a bit flushed."

She's more than flushed, fucknut. She's mine.

"Sorry!" She blinks fast, looking at him again. "What did you say?"

"I said you wouldn't have to be a babysitter if you were with me." He grins widely, and I'm ready to punch him. "Once I move in, I'll send you my number. Since you're in Eagleton Manor now, you could just walk over."

Like hell she will. I jump in at this point. "You know, I'd really like to see those condos. They're supposed to be nice. Not as nice as the houses, of course, but maybe we could walk over together, Ruby."

Henry leans back to look at me, annoyance all over his face. Get used to it, pal. Better yet, how about you flap those ears and fly on back to Charleston.

Ruby stands, helping Lillie to her feet and cleaning her up. "Why don't we just see how it goes once you're all settled?"

Henry stands beside her. "I'll give you a call. Is your number still the same?"

"Uh... yeah, it is." She smiles, and I'm two seconds from putting my arm around her and telling this guy to delete it from his contacts. Ruby keeps talking. "In the meantime, I'd better get back to work. Good to see you, Henry!"

Her pretty smile is too sweet, and Henry takes it as encouragement. Why are guys so clueless? She's not into you, pal.

"Have a great afternoon. Good to see you again, Key."

"Yeah, good." I put my hand on Ruby's arm, and lead her and my daughter away from our unwelcome intruder.

Once we're several steps away, Lillie takes off running ahead of us to watch a guy twisting long, colorful balloons into animal shapes.

"You were rude to Henry." Her voice is quiet, but sharp. I kind of love it.

"I don't like that guy." I toss the ice cream in a trash bin as we pass. "I don't want Lillie around him."

Ruby stops walking and makes an astonished face. "He's a well-respected pediatric surgeon. I think he won an award last year."

My voice is level, calm. "Award for being the

biggest dumbass. He can't even tell you're not interested in him." Her jaw drops, and our eyes hold each other's. Several seconds pass, and she doesn't have a comeback. "I stand by my statement."

"There's nothing wrong with Henry."

It's the best she can do. "He needs to keep looking. You threw him back, remember?"

"I should never have told you that."

Several seconds pass as we watch the fellow making giraffes and dogs. It reminds me a little of Central Park, and I decide there's no time like the present.

"I've been meaning to ask you... I have a very important business function next week in New York. It's an overnight trip... I'd like you to come with me."

Again, I've stumped her. I kind of like knowing I have this power over her.

"We'll be attending a gala for tech developers and investors like me," I continue. "So you'll need a formal dress. I can help you with the expense if you need—"

She finds her voice. "I can afford a formal dress. But what about Lillie?" Her eyes dart forward to where my daughter is jumping up and down and asking for a unicorn.

"Eleanor has agreed to take care of her while we're gone."

"I don't know about this." She exhales, looking down and crossing her arms. "I can't date you, Remi. You're my boss."

"You can think of it as more of a work function." Bullshit. It's a total fucking date.

My girl is too smart for that.

My girl? What?

I kind of like the way it sounds, though.

Dark eyes slant up at me, and she's so pretty.

163

"How is it a work function?"

"I have to take a plus one." I shrug, adopting a very professional tone. "I don't have the time or the inclination to find some woman to go with me. Your salary is dependent on my business being successful, so you'll go with me. And we'll have a nice time."

"Will we be staying in the same room?"

"No." *Technically.* "I booked the penthouse suite at the Four Seasons We'll each have our own rooms."

"In the same, bigger room? I don't think so."

I like that she's apparently considering it. "How is it different from our current arrangement?"

"A floor and a mother-in-law." We take a few more steps. "And a little girl."

I'm standing just behind her shoulder, and I trace a finger up the back of her arm, thinking how soft her skin is. "None of that made a difference last night."

Goosebumps break out on her skin, but her gaze is focused straight ahead, on my daughter. "You're not helping your case."

My tone changes to coaxing. "Come on, Ruby. It'll be fun, and I can't think of anyone else I'd rather have with me."

Turning, she looks up at me. "Why?"

For a beat, I'm taken aback. "Because I like talking to you… because you're funny and smart." Because you'll look amazing on my arm as we meet potential clients and intimidate the competition.

Her lips press into a line. "How is it you don't have a date? You're easy to talk to, funny, and smart."

"I don't know. I guess I've been too focused on my work, on Lillie."

What I don't say is no one interested me before I met her. I don't want to go back to that lonely existence. At the same time, I'm not interested in meeting someone new. I only want to be with her. She completes a part of me I didn't know had been yearning for completion. She loves my daughter, she fills my house with light... She's kind of perfect.

"Look, Daddy! Ruby, he made me a colorful unicorn!" Lillie comes running back to us waving a white, lavender, pink, and yellow balloon horse over her head.

Ruby squats down to greet her, admiring the latex creation. "That's amazing! Did he make it just for you?"

Lillie nods dramatically, and Ruby tweaks her nose before standing and taking her hand. She catches my gaze and does a little chin lift. "I'll think about it and let you know."

"Let me know tonight."

Chapter 19

Ruby

Lillie's in her bedroom playing with her dolls, and I scoop up my phone tapping out a quick text. *Help. Need help. Emergency. 911!*

The gray bubble floats a second before Drew's reply appears. *OMG! Are you okay? Did you crash the car?*

I'm already tapping out my reply. *Remi asked me to go to NYC with him. Overnight. Penthouse. 4 Seasons!!!*

More gray dots. I'm chewing my lip like crazy. My heart is beating out of my chest, and all I can think about is me in a formal gown, Remi in a tux, dancing at a ball at the Four Seasons Hotel... It's straight out of a Disney movie.

Are you at the hospital? Are you bleeding? Don't text 911 unless you're injured. You almost made me go into labor.

I exhale a little growl. *You can't go into labor at six weeks. Would you focus please? He wants me to give him an answer tonight. I can't... can I?*

Drew is taking too long to reply. I stand and pace my room, looking out the French doors down at the lake. My stomach is in knots. After last night, I'm not sure what will happen if we're alone together again. As much as my brain says I can make it one short month, my body is on overdrive when we're together.

Today at the park was a prime example. He knew what he was doing, licking that cone and watching me with those eyes. My panties almost melted right off. Sitting here now, I can't even remember what Henry said to me.

Drew's text finally appears, and it's one word. *Go.*

All that, and just one word? I tap back quickly. *Everyone will know. Everyone will be talking.*

She replies just as fast. *You only live once. And everybody's already talking. Go.*

"Ruby!" Lillie's voice cuts through my mental meltdown. She prances in the room holding her pink Lottie doll. "Gigi says it's time to eat dinner."

Tapping quickly, I say goodbye with a reminder. *The shower is Saturday noon at my mom's. Can you make it?*

Yep. Can't wait to hear the latest hot nanny gossip.

Good grief. She's teasing, but who knew when I said yes to this job it was going to turn into some kind of twisted soap opera? More like one of those telenovelas.

"Let's go then." I take Lillie's hand and square my shoulders.

I feel like I'm heading into battle.

"Grass-fed buffalo filet, flown in from Montana just for you, ma'am." The female server, who I now know is named Tessa, puts plates in front of us, and Jake, her helper, slices Lillie's as usual.

"It wasn't for me." Eleanor pretends to be appalled. "This steak is for Mr. Key. He loves a good ribeye, and it's been weeks since we've had red meat."

She motions to Tessa, who disappears into the

kitchen again.

Lillie pokes a slice with her fork then looks up with wide eyes. "It's bleeding."

Eleanor is unaffected by her granddaughter's horror. "Your meat is cooked medium rare, Lillian. Take one bite. It's the perfect cut prepared the perfect way. Don't you think, Remington?"

Remi quickly cuts a piece and puts it in his mouth. "It's delicious. Thanks, Eleanor."

"Is that all you have to say?" She laughs, and puts her hand on her chest. "I'll have to import Kobe beef to impress you next time."

I watch as Lillie pushes her meat into a pile on the side of her plate before dipping a scoop of whipped mashed potatoes with her fork. I'd be worried about her being hungry, but she had a good lunch at Ma's and a late snack today.

I take a bite of buffalo, and it's pretty darn good. "You know, I read they massage those Kobe cows with Sake and give them beer to make them eat. It sounds great, but some say it's inhumane."

"I guess you would know." Eleanor doesn't even look at me before taking a sip of wine.

"How would Ruby know?" Remi's voice has an edge in it. It makes me uncomfortable, and I don't know why I decided to share that tidbit of knowledge.

"Oh, Asians know Asian practices—"

"Ruby's American." The way he says it fills me with a weird mixture of pride and defensiveness.

I'm not ashamed of my heritage, at the same time, Kobe beef comes from Japanese Black cattle. Once again with feeling, *I'm not Japanese.*

"Oh of course she is." Eleanor dismisses the topic with a wave of her hand as Tessa returns to the room carrying that fucking bottle of port. "Remi, look what I found today in the bookcase. It's that Tawny Port from the Prager Winery. Remember this?"

My throat is so tight, I'm sure I won't be able to eat another bite. I have no idea what's about to happen, but I sneak a glance at Remi.

"I do remember." His voice is soft, and his expression is happy with a little sadness around the eyes. "It was a special trip."

"It was your honeymoon. I'll never forget when you got back, how happy you both were. Sandy said we had to save this a few years. I think we should have it now before it goes past its prime."

"After dinner." Remi takes another bite of steak, seeming to recover. "I miss being on the West coast. Seattle has a wine region as reputable as California's. I wouldn't mind taking a trip back home and scoping it out."

Eleanor's face goes from smug to startled. "You're not thinking of moving back there? But it's so far away. How would I see Lillian?"

"I want chicken," Lillie whines, and I can't help thinking *Bok bok, bitch!*

I fight it, because it'll make me laugh, and it's definitely not the time for laughter. Eleanor dug up that old memento to take us down a difficult memory lane, and guess what? Backfire!

Still, the last thing I want is to appear frivolous or insensitive.

"I'm sure we'd figure it out." Remi doesn't seem upset at all. He seems really healthy.

"My tummy hurts." Lillie starts to whine, and I say a silent prayer of thanks.

"You should not have had ice cream so close to dinner." I don't know who Eleanor is scolding, but I put my napkin beside my plate.

"I can take her up and give her a bath. She's had a busy day. I'm sure she's tired."

"Thank you." Remi's eyes meet mine, and my insides warm at the emotion I see in them.

I know from my work how complex his situation is, and the last thing I would ever do is hold his feelings against him. I want to tell him to take his time. I'm here to help. Instead, I take his daughter's hand.

Eleanor's loud voice makes me pause. "Don't you want to try the port?"

I'd like to try shoving it up your butt.

I do not say that. I pause and smile. "I don't really care for fortified wine, but thank you."

Lillie gives me a pull, and I follow her up the stairs, away from whatever scene Eleanor thought she was putting together.

If she thinks she's going to pit me against the memory of Lillie's mother, she's wrong. As much as my feelings for Remi are growing, as much chemistry as we share, I'm not a monster. I don't expect anything from him.

I'm here to do a job, and that's my primary focus now. I'm almost through week two. Two more weeks, and I'll have made it through the month.

Chapter 20

Remi

Stopping by my daughter's room after dinner, I hear her voice coming from the tub.

"Henry's ears stick out. He looks like Gus Gus in *Cinderella*." Water splashes, and I change my mind about interrupting. I'd like to hear how this conversation goes.

Ruby's voice is gentle. "People can't help things like ears and noses, so it's not nice to point out if they're big or shaped funny."

"I like Gus Gus. He saves Cinderella with the key from her wicked stepmother's pocket. Even though Lucifer tries to eat him."

More water sounds. I imagine Ruby's rinsing her hair with a cup. "Henry does look a little like Gus Gus. But he's not fat."

I cover a silent laugh with my hand, and they continue stirring the water. It sounds like Lillie's playing. "What's *evolve* mean?" My daughter's tone is sweetly curious.

"Where did you hear that word?"

"Henry said it."

"You should probably call him Dr. Pak. You should get out before you turn into a prune."

"What is it?"

"Evolve?" Ruby exhales. "It means to grow and

change. To learn from experience."

"You sounded like you don't like it here. Do you like it here?" Noises of standing, stepping out of the tub, send me from the door into the hallway. I don't mean to eavesdrop, but I have to hear Ruby's answer.

"I like you." Ruby carries her into the bedroom, and I can see from the doorway Lillie's wrapped in a hooded towel. "I like your pretty house and my pretty room. I like our garden."

No mention of me. My jaw clenches, and I think about what happened at dinner. Ruby was eager to get away when Eleanor brought out the port.

"Are you going to go out with Henry?" Ruby pauses in scrubbing my daughter's head with the towel. I realize I'm holding my breath.

"I don't know."

Her answer pisses me off more than it probably should.

Or hell, maybe it pisses me off the right amount? Go out with Henry Pak? Leave here? After what we've shared? Turning on my heel, I jog down to my office. Adrenaline is pumping in my veins as I pace in front of my desk, and I know I'm not getting any work done tonight. Not with all these thoughts racing in my mind.

Leaving my work station, I storm down to my bedroom and strip off my slacks and work shirt. I go to the dresser and take out a tee and some nylon jogging pants. In less than five minutes I'm out the door, running down the circle driveway and out to the path leading past our house and through this expansive neighborhood, around the lake.

Every lot in Eagleton Heights is two acres. It makes for a nice, long path for walkers and joggers. I loop past the condos, where I now know Dr. Pak is setting up residence. Without even thinking I pop the bird at the new construction before circling around to where I started.

My legs burn with exertion, and I'm covered in a sheen of sweat when I arrive back at the house. I drop my hoodie in a basket in the laundry room and strip off my sweaty tee. I don't feel like going upstairs for a new one. Luckily a stack of folded clothes sits on the drier, and I grab a white undershirt from it.

I didn't eat much after Eleanor dragged out that port. I don't know what kind of reaction she expected me to have, but I'm pretty sure from her response it wasn't what she got. My feelings about those days are only good.

I never believed I would get here, but five years out, I look back on my honeymoon and the short time I had with my wife as cherished memories. A blessed time, followed by one of the darkest times of my life.

When I was in therapy, Drew said I would eventually get to this place of peace with the past, and a desire for a future. I didn't believe her, but now it seems she was right. Those memories will always live in my heart, and I hope I'm blessed enough to have more to come.

My stomach rumbles, and I walk to the refrigerator. Eleanor keeps us on a relatively healthy diet, so I'm not expecting to find much in the way of snacks. Thinking about it more, I decide it's time to take back this portion of my life as well. I want some fucking snacks in this goddamn house.

I grin, remembering how Ruby made pigs in blankets her first day here. They were delicious, and it sends my mind along a trail of all the ways she's different from the women my mother-in-law associates with, different from Sandy's old friends, the women I see when I take Lillie to preschool.

Ruby is fiercely independent, and she has her own unique style. She's not a follower. She's not a member of the herd. She doesn't seem to want anything from me other than honest work, and she's amazing with my daughter.

A soft noise behind me draws my attention, and when I see her, emotion hits me hard in the chest. My feelings for her have grown so strong over the past week and a half. I don't want her to date Henry. I want her to stay here with me.

"What are you doing in here?" Her voice is soft, a little flustered, but I can tell she's trying to tease me.

She's standing there in cotton shorts and a thin tee with "Dream Big" printed on the front. A robe hangs from her shoulders, but it's open. I watch as her eyes travel over me fast, her cheeks blushing pink.

"You blush easily."

"Do I?" Her voice is soft, and she grins, her cheeks growing pinker. "I never did before. I didn't mean to catch you in your underwear."

Glancing down, I see the wife beater I'm wearing doesn't cover much. I'm sweaty, my hair's a mess, and I'm standing barefoot in the kitchen. "I just got back from a run. I thought everyone had gone to bed."

"Lillie's in bed." She comes closer. "I don't know where Eleanor is."

Lifting my chin, I return to the refrigerator, where I'm holding the door open. "I just needed a little something more to help me sleep. I was thinking about Lillie's leftovers, wishing we had something like cookies or pigs in blankets."

She almost laughs. "Sorry about that. Didn't mean to contaminate Lillie with my horrible food choices."

"You should have a baking day, make cookies."

Her voice turns sassy. "Are you saying you want

176

my cookies?"

"I'll eat your cookies." I give her a wink, meaning it in every way.

She snorts a laugh, and it makes me smile. I love when she plays with me. Returning to the fridge, I take out a plastic container of what looks like cantaloupe. When I open it, it smells like alcohol.

"Hm." I study the salmon-colored fruit. "This might be bad. I'm going to need you to taste it for me."

"I don't think so. That's not my job." She does a hop, and she's sitting on the bar.

Perfect. I step between her legs, lifting out a cube. "You're saying you won't taste this to be sure it won't hurt me?"

Holding it up, I lightly trace the corner across her full bottom lip. She pulls her head back. "It smells like it's fermented."

"Will you nurse me if I get sick?" I pop it in my mouth, imagining her in a sexy nurse outfit. It makes my dick twitch. "Tastes okay."

"I wouldn't eat too much of it."

Stepping to the fridge again, I find a smaller container of strawberries and take it out. "How about this?" I hold a slice of strawberry to her lips. "Don't you like strawberries?"

"Yes and no—the seeds get stuck in my teeth."

Parting my lips, I watch as her mouth opens slightly. Her pink tongue slips out and tastes the fruit before she pulls it between her white teeth.

I have a full-on semi at the sight, and I put the other half in my mouth. "It's juicy and sweet, just like you."

"Remi…" Her voice is a warning, but my hands go to her thighs.

I slide them higher as I lean closer, possession

running hot in my veins. "I don't like you talking to Henry Pak. I don't want you going to his condo when he's moved in. I don't want him calling you."

Her eyebrows rise, and her hands grip my wrists, stopping my progress. I'm ready to devour her like that fruit, and I'm pretty sure she sees it in my eyes.

"That's not your business." Her voice is low, thick, and her breath is a little faster.

"I can make it my business."

"How?" Her brow quirks, but her grip on my wrists loosens.

"I don't want Lillie around him."

"Henry's polite, he's a doctor, he's Korean..." Her lips twist into a cute frown. "He's just the type of guy my mother would love."

"Now I really don't like him." That makes her laugh. "Besides, you don't like polite men. I can tell."

Her eyes narrow. "How can you tell?"

"I watch and learn. Figuring out what you like has become my favorite pastime." My hands start to move again, but she catches my wrists.

Her chin lifts, and when our eyes meet, it's electric, like always. "What are you saying?"

I'm not sure exactly. "You're important to me... I care about what you're doing. It matters in a way I didn't expect."

"I really need to find my own place."

Those words are a slice to my stomach. "I don't want you to move out." Leaning forward, our breath mingles. "Then I wouldn't be able to kiss you whenever I want."

"Not here. Someone might see us." It's a heavy whisper, but she leans closer, meeting my mouth.

Her lips part, and our tongues entwine. She's sweet like the strawberries and a little salty, which I guess is from me. Her small hands cup my jaw, sliding her thumbs lightly along my cheeks. Our mouths move faster, and I pull her closer so her core is against my waist, hitting the top of my cock. *Fuck me it feels so good.*

"You taste so sweet." My lips travel to her cheek, higher to her ear, and she exhales a soft moan. "You smell so good." I inhale the flowery scent of her hair.

"Remi," she speaks my name on a breath, and I move my hand to the top of her thigh, higher into her shorts, sliding my thumb along the damp center of her panties.

She moans, and I close my mouth over hers again, kissing and chasing her tongue. I loop my fingers inside the thin lace until they're slipping inside her pussy.

Another soft noise, and her hips begin to rock in time with my fingers sliding up and down her wet folds, touching her gently, then more insistently, massaging that little spot as she whimpers and sucks on my lips.

All at once, she stops and moves away. "We can't do this."

She catches my hand, taking it out of her pants and hopping off the bar. Her back is to me, and I watch as she brings her hands to her cheeks, her shoulders rising and falling with her rapid breaths.

I rake my hand through my hair. "I'm sorry. I shouldn't have done that. Forgive me."

Pain is in my chest, and the last thing I want is to drive her away. I've dreamt of her moans, how she says my name when she comes, since I buried my face between her thighs. She's like a drug to me now, and I want to hear those sounds again and again. I want her to want me as much as I want her. I can't stand the thought of someone else having her, touching her that way.

"You don't have to apologize. I like it. Too much."
It's what I want to hear, but she doesn't turn to me.

I want to pull her into my arms and hold her close, taste those sweet lips again. I want to ask her if she's decided about New York... but I decide maybe I'd better not go there with the scent of her still all over my fingers.

"I'd better go to bed now."

With that, she leaves me standing in the kitchen with a tent in my pants.

Chapter 21

Ruby

"So? Are you going to New York with Remi?" Drew sits on her feet on my mom's couch.

Her bridal shower is small, but it's what she wanted—just our closest friends, Dotty Magee, and a few girls from Drew's church group. They're in the kitchen helping Ma with the platters of cake and cookies. I'm on the couch, surrounded by torn wrapping paper, sexy lingerie, photo albums and frames, with the book listing who gave what on my lap.

"Shush!" I hold my hand in front of her lips. "If Ma hears you, she'll put me in a convent."

"Too late for that." Drew leans back, beaming. "Well? What did you tell him?"

My lips press into a frown. "I haven't told him anything yet."

I think about our hot make-out session in the kitchen, his fingers in my panties nearly making me come. It makes me hot all over, and I clear my throat.

Again, I'd spent the last two days doing my best to stay out of sight. It didn't matter. He would find me, and every time we'd look at each other, it was blazing hot. Any time our hands would brush, whether I was handing him a plate or taking care of his daughter, it was sparks of lightning.

181

His possessiveness, the way he talks about Henry… I hate admitting it, but I love it.

Drew's watching me with a knowing light in her eyes. "I take it karaoke night didn't move you back to the friend zone?"

"God, no. That was a total backfire." I put the book on the coffee table and start packing Drew's gifts in their boxes.

It's all I can do to keep my mind from flying to his tongue inside me after that night of singing. *Jesus.* My thighs squeeze at the memory.

"Well, I don't blame you." Drew helps me clean up the mess. "His voice is like chocolate ribbons of pure sex. And with those eyes and that dimple…"

She sighs, and I straighten, putting my hands on my hips. "Aren't you supposed to be in love with someone else?"

"For you! I'm appreciating him for you." She laughs. "I'm so happy you've finally found someone. I swear, I thought you might end up with Ralph after all."

"Good god, Andrea! Don't even say those words." That makes her laugh more.

"Is living with him your only reason for not diving headfirst into this love fest? Because I'll help you find an apartment. Heck, with the money you're making, you could buy one of those new condos in Eagleton Manor."

"Remi would just love that." My sarcastic tone makes her frown, so I explain. "Remember Henry Pak?"

"Oh…" She makes a sympathetic face. "He has those ears."

"Yeah, well, I saw him at the park again, and he said he just bought a condo in Eagleton Manor."

"That's cool. He seems like he'd make a great neighbor. If you had an emergency, he'd be right over."

"Remi pretty much forbade me from speaking to him. He says he doesn't want Lillie around him either."

Drew's jaw drops. "What happened?"

"I went out with him. Twice. Apparently, that's enough to make poor Henry a leper."

My bestie squeals. "That does it. I'm going to find you a place of your own. I can't stand you two being apart one more day! And you're going with him to New York. Don't make me call and tell him myself."

My stomach is tingly and hot, and I know I'm going to do it. "I have to buy a formal dress."

"You can totally afford a formal dress. I'll help you pick it out." I think about my check that appeared on my dresser again while I was out with Lillie.

"It's such a great job, but I still don't know how I can take money from him and go out with him."

"You take care of his daughter, right?" Drew adopts a very scientific tone. "You're providing a service anyone else would get paid for. Why shouldn't you?"

Chewing on my lip, I do my best to see it her way. "I guess you're right. I don't know why it makes me feel so icky."

"If he doesn't have a problem with it, neither should you. Of course, once you're married, it'll all be common property."

"And now you've soared off into crazy town." She's still laughing as our friends return to the room, chatting with my mom. "Let's just take this one step at a time."

Pastor Hibbert's sermon is about the appearance of evil. He reads the text from the Bible, and I feel four sets of eyes boring into the back of my head.

How did I let the jealous bitches get to me?

One glance to my left answers that question.

After dropping Lillie off at Sunday school, Ma was tied up helping her ladies' group organize another Senior outreach. Drew texted me that she was tired and wouldn't be at church this morning. That left me with only one option—sitting with Remi and Eleanor.

I suppose I could have sat by myself, but my goal had been to sneak in on the other side of Eleanor so the monster-in-law would be between Remi and me. But when Remi saw me slipping in the end of the pew, he maneuvered everything so I was at his side.

I won't lie, I love having him beside me, holding the hymnal for us, making sure I have everything I need. I love feeling the warmth of his body now that we're sitting beside each other. I've always been attracted to men like Remi, experienced, controlled, demanding—which I'm sure is more of my childhood coming out.

Still, after song service, when we're instructed to greet the Body of Christ around us, the minute I turn, Serena North turns her back on me, as does Anita Flagstaff and her steely-haired old crone of a mother.

It's one thing for those bitches to act like they don't know me when we pass in the halls at preschool, but honestly, we're in church. I feel like saying out loud, "You're even acting this way in God's house?"

But I don't want to give Eleanor any more ammunition, and Ma would probably say I'm acting out. I'm not entirely sure Drew would back me up on calling people out after song service. She probably would, but I guess I have more self-control than that.

The only "Christian" in the group who enthusiastically shook my hand was Dr. Phillip North, that skeevy old creeper. I'm pretty sure I heard Remi growling under his breath.

Now we're being regaled about how we should guard our appearance against accusations of impropriety. I'm ready to walk out. Instead, I think about what Drew said. I'm providing a service that anyone else would expect to be paid for. I signed a contract, for goodness sake. There's no reason I should feel awkward about going out with Remi.

It helps Drew and I spent yesterday afternoon researching rentals in and around Oakville. We found a sweet little house in the newer part of Oakville Estates, actually within walking distance of Eagleton Heights. It's just a small, one-bedroom home with one and a half bathrooms. Still, the rent is totally affordable, even without the crazy salary Remi is paying me, and it's available now.

A little digging revealed Dagwood's aunt Marsha owns the house, and she's super sweet. She said she'd take a deposit to hold it, and I could move in as soon as I'm ready. The water, utilities, everything is on. It's just waiting for me.

That just leaves me to figure out how to tell my boss.

Pastor Hibbert tells us all to bow our heads for prayer, and Remi reaches over to hold my hand. We don't lace fingers, but still... it's a public display of affection. A knot is in my throat, and I can't help wondering if Eleanor sees. The last thing I want to do is pull my hand away, and when I steal a glance, it's like a shot straight to my core when I meet Remi's eyes.

He smiles, that dimple peeks out, and my heart is

off to the races. I smile back, and he gives my hand a squeeze before letting it go with the Amen.

We're back at the house, lunch finished, and Eleanor and Lillie are down for naps when I make my way to his office on the second floor. It's empty when I tap on his open door, but when I see his shadow on the balcony, I go to where he's standing looking at the lake.

"Knock knock." I pretend to tap on the French doors. "I hope I'm not disturbing you."

He's still in his slacks from earlier, but his coat is gone. I see his tie is gone as well when he turns his back to the lake. He crosses his arms in that white button-down and gives me his irresistible, dimpled grin.

Panties officially ignited.

"You never disturb me." His sleeves are rolled up, so I can see the lines on his forearms. He's just too delicious for words. "What's on your mind?"

"Everyone's napping, so I figured it's a good time to talk."

"I'm not sure if I like the sound of that or not." His smile fades a notch, but he still has me captured in his gaze.

Blinking away, I go to stand beside him on the balcony, facing the lake. "I think I'm overdue to give you an answer about New York."

"Ah, yes." He turns to face the lake beside me, placing his hands on the iron railing. "Have you made a decision?"

My thoughts are a cyclone in my head. I have my concerns, aided by what my mother would say, the preschool bitches, and even Pastor Hibbert this morning in church, battling against Drew's encouragement.

Ringing over it all like a bell is this longing in my heart to know Remi better. I can't pass up what could be a life-changing chance with a man who might turn into someone very special. It's the one thing Drew said that cut through the noise.

"I've thought about it, and I decided yes. I'll go with you."

His shoulders drop as if he were holding his breath, and his smile kicks up to a hundred watts. It sends a kaleidoscope of butterflies swirling madly through my insides, and I have to grab the reins before I forget the rest of what I need to say.

"On one condition."

His smile doesn't dim, but his brow furrows, and damn him for looking so damn good. "What might that be?"

"I'm not staying with you in the penthouse suite. I'll only go if I have my own room..."

"Done." He cuts me off before I've finished.

"On a separate floor. I can make my own reservation and pay for it—"

"I already said you're not paying for your room. This is a business trip you wouldn't be taking if I didn't need you there with me."

"I still don't think you really need me. You never have." My mind travels to Eleanor's words on my very first day in this house.

Stepping closer, he puts his hands on my arms, and I can barely hold his gaze, it's so full of emotion. "You have no idea how much you're needed."

His voice is low and close, and I feel the tension radiating in my spine, the push-pull between what I want so badly and what I feel I have to do, at least for now, to maintain my reputation. *Thank God Drew helped me find that house.*

"Just so you understand, we're traveling as friends."

"Whatever makes you comfortable." He leans down and kisses my cheek, and goosebumps fly down my arms. "Thank you for going with me."

I'm pretty sure everything's about to change.

Chapter 22

Remi

I watch as my daughter hugs Ruby like her life depends on it.

On the one hand, it makes me sad—not because she didn't get as upset about me leaving—but she was a newborn when her mother died. I wonder if she still feels a sense of loss or abandonment.

"Who's going to make me penny cakes?" Lillie's hazel eyes are round and full of tears. She blinks and a drop hits her cheek.

Ruby pushes a golden curl behind her little ear and wipes the tear with her thumb. "It's only two days, Lil. I'll be back on Thursday, and I'll make you penny cakes for lunch."

My daughter nods slowly, pitifully. "I guess."

"Hey, I know." Ruby's voice takes on an excited tone. "Which monster did you meet this week? Last week was white monster number three, right? *Tres*?"

Lillie's voice is pouty. "Yellow monster number three."

"That's right!" Ruby is working hard to keep the enthusiasm alive. "And who is it this week?"

Lilly shrugs, but Ruby holds her middle, giving her a tug. "Come on, I know we were busy packing and getting ready last night, but tell me his name."

Hazel eyes are fixed on Ruby's collar. Her rosebud

lips quirk, and she tries not to smile. Ruby gives her another little squeeze, and she relents. "Purple monster number four."

"Purple?" Ruby's eyes go wide, and I'm kind of loving everything that's happening right now. "Do you know purple is my favorite color? I can't wait to hear all about purple monster number four. I wonder what his Spanish name might be."

"Cuatro."

"Cuatro... I like that name. Do you?"

Lillie shrugs and puts her arms around Ruby's neck again. "I miss you now."

Ruby holds her close, kissing her cheek. "I miss you too, butter bean. We'll do something special when I get back, just you and me."

"Good heavens, it's not like she's joining the Foreign Legion." Eleanor appears in the grand foyer, hands on her hips. "Lillian, come with me. We have to go to school now."

Ruby gives my daughter one last squeeze, and they both make grunting noises. After that, she takes her grandmother's hand and follows her out to the waiting Crown Vic.

When Ruby turns to me, I see tears in her eyes. "I never know what she's going to do." She breathes a laugh and wipes her eyes with her palms, looking up at the ceiling. "It's only a two-day trip."

It tugs at my chest, and damn, I didn't think I could care for this woman more. Is she crying over leaving my daughter at home with her grandmother?

I slide an arm around her waist and hold out a handkerchief. Thanks to my old-fashioned mother, I always have one in my pocket. "You realize Eleanor has been taking care of her since she was born. All the way up until you arrived... just two and half weeks ago."

She laughs a little more, touching the white cloth to her cheeks. "I know. I'm such a goose." She hiccups a little breath. "I just..."

Her voice trails off, and she doesn't finish her thought.

"What?"

She shakes her head, but I want to know. "Eleanor doesn't listen to her."

"It seems like she does."

"No, she's just pushy. She waits for Lillie to finish speaking, then she tells her what to do. There's a difference. Even little kids know it."

I can't take it anymore. I reach forward and pull her into a hug. Her arms go around my waist, and I hold her against my chest. She takes a deep breath, and I hope she's not still crying.

My lips are right at her ear when I speak. "I love that you're so worried about my daughter." She nods against my shoulder. "Now, no more crying. Lillie is going to be fine. We're going to have a fun trip, and you'll see my daughter again in two days."

Releasing her, I catch her watery eyes. They melt into that sweet smile I love... followed quickly by her snarky sass. "You're not going to miss her at all? Did your sentimental chip get lost?"

I huff a laugh, grabbing her suitcase and hanging bag, and carrying them out to the waiting limousine. "I will miss my daughter, even though she didn't seem too upset about telling me goodbye. At the same time, I know she'll be fine while I'm away."

Her eyes slant over to me. "You're hurt she didn't cry over you leaving?"

"If the tables were turned, I suppose I'd be more upset over you being gone, too."

"Are you flirting with me, Remington?"

"Always."

That makes her laugh, and I'm glad to see we've moved past the water works.

The limo drops us at the terminal for the private jet service. A few cars are parked in the lot, but we're the only ones flying out this morning.

"Wow." Ruby's eyes are round as she follows me up the short flight of stairs into the Lear 60. "Do you own this?" She's speaking just above a whisper as we pass through the oval door and walk down the short aisle separating seats with tables in the center.

"No." I sit in one of the seats toward the back and motion for her to join me. "I charter it for short flights. It's not really worth the upkeep to own a jet, with as little as I travel."

She sits beside me in the plush, cream leather chair. A small sofa is behind us, but this plane doesn't have a bed. Our flight is barely over an hour.

"I've never been on a private jet before." She's still speaking low, tilting her face toward me as the flight attendant puts glasses of champagne in front of us.

"Welcome aboard, Mr. Key, Miss. Banks. We'll be taking off momentarily. If you would, please fasten your seatbelts, and I'll let you know when it's safe to move about the cabin."

"Thanks, Grace." Taking the glass of champagne, I hold it to Ruby's. "Here's to a successful business trip."

She clinks my glass and takes a sip. "Mm... that's delicious."

Our seatbelts are fastened, and we're in the air in less than fifteen minutes. Grace comes through and tells us it's safe to move around. We only take off our seatbelts, and I rotate in my chair to face my companion.

Ruby's like a kid in a candy store, looking around, touching everything. It's hits me like a renewed thrill. I remember a time when all this was new to me, too.

"Why do they always give you champagne on private jets?"

"I thought you'd never been on one."

Her nose wrinkles as she takes another sip. "I've seen it in the movies. Is it to celebrate being so rich?"

Shrugging, I sip my own sparkling beverage. "More likely to celebrate not having to stand for hours in the TSA line then be forced to sit in a cramped seat next to a potentially annoying neighbor."

She nods. "I can get onboard with that. What's our schedule like in New York?"

"We arrive in Manhattan after noon then we'll take a car to the hotel. The gala is tomorrow night at eight."

"What do we do between now and then?"

"I'm meeting one of my investment advisers tonight for drinks. His name is Stephen Hastings. I'd really like it if you'd join me, but you don't have to… if you have something else in mind you'd prefer."

"I'll join you." She scoots closer, biting her lip. "I've never been to New York."

"You haven't?" That changes things. Reaching out, I tug her lip free from her teeth with my thumb, thinking about kissing her. Based on the look she gives me, she seems to be thinking the same thing. "Then I think we should spend a little time being tourists."

A huge smile splits her cheeks, and it's like I've won the fucking lottery. "You'll do that for me?"

"I'd love to do that with you. What do you want to see?"

"Oh man, I want to see everything." She leans back in her chair, taking another sip of champagne.

"The Statue of Liberty, the Empire State building, Central Park, Wall Street, Time's Square, Broadway, the Guggenheim museum, the Met, the Brooklyn bridge, Soho, the Village…"

I start to laugh. "We can't do all of that, but we can make a plan and see how much we can fit in."

Reaching down, I clasp her hand in mine, threading our fingers. I'm gratified when she doesn't pull away. In fact, she seems very comfortable holding my hand up here, thousands of feet above the world.

Her face is turned toward the window, and she seems far off in thought.

"What are you thinking?" I lift her hand, studying her fingers entwined with mine.

She shakes her head, dark hair sliding around her shoulders. "It's silly."

I give her hand a tug. "Tell me."

Turning to me, her eyes hold so much emotion. "I'll never forget this."

In that moment, I never want to let her go. Placing my lips against her fingers, I speak softly. "I'm glad I'm here to share it with you."

The limo drops us at the Four Seasons, and I tip the driver as the bellhop collects our bags to send up to our rooms. As requested, Ruby is on the fifty-first floor, while I'm in the penthouse, one floor up.

Standing on my balcony, I grab the house phone and call her room. "Come up and see my view of Central Park."

"You're just showing off." Her voice is sassy, and I don't like us being apart.

"You might recall my original plan was to share this with you. Bring a few things in case you decide to stay."

"How many times do I have to tell you—"

"Sorry, bad connection."

"It's a landline."

"Hurry up, I'm hungry." *Thirsty, is more like it.*

I grin, hanging up and thinking about the next forty-eight hours. I put her name on the guest list for this room and gave her a key so she wouldn't have any trouble accessing my suite. Five minutes later, she's walking through my door.

"This is amazing." She flops on the leather divan beside the sofa facing the balcony where I stand. "It's like a whole house up here."

"It's half the top floor. The other half is a separate suite." Inspecting her hands, I frown. "You didn't bring a bag."

"I'm not staying in your room, Remi."

We'll see about that. "Are you hungry? I've been craving a cheeseburger all week."

She laughs loudly. "A cheeseburger? What would Eleanor say?"

"I don't give a fuck."

Out on the street, we fall into the speed race of Manhattan foot traffic.

I grab her hand and keep her close. "We're in a pretty touristy part of the city, right in Midtown."

"Near Rockefeller Center!"

"Right." We meander through the crowd, dodging sightseers who stop in the middle of the sidewalk. "We can head down toward the Village and see Soho after we eat. That'll take two things off your list."

She does a little excited skip. "Can we go to Magnolia Bakery and get cupcakes?"

"We can do as much as we have time to do."

Traffic is a nightmare, but we manage to get all the way to Whitman's in the East Village. A short wait, and we're digging into two Juicy Lucys. Pimento cheese spills out, and Ruby squeals, wiping her chin.

"I can't eat all of this." She leans forward, and I wipe a spot of mustard off her cheek.

"Get a go box. We can eat it tonight after we meet Stephen."

"You're not cheating too bad. It says, 'fresh local ingredients.'" She takes another bite of cheeseburger.

"I'm pretty sure there's nothing healthy about this lunch."

It's perfect, and as soon as we're done, we're out on the street again, leftovers in hand. We come out of Alphabet City and walk over to the East River, facing Brooklyn. The sun is high overhead, and a light breeze ripples across the water. We continue walking south until we reach a set of park benches facing the water. A large bridge is in the background.

"Is that the Brooklyn Bridge?" She takes my hand and leads me to sit.

"Williamsburg." I sit beside her, putting my arm around her shoulders. "Brooklyn is further south."

"Is this the one from the movie?"

"That's Queensboro. It's further north."

She laughs and shakes her head. "I'm all mixed up."

"It's okay. I know the way." Reaching for her hand, I lace our fingers again, loving this day, the time we're spending together. "I'm really glad you came with me."

"I'm having an amazing time."

I like that again, she doesn't pull away. She leans her head against her hand and studies me. "How do you know so much about New York? I thought you grew up in Seattle."

"My mother loved it here. She always wanted to

live in the city." A pinch of sadness is in my stomach. "My father hated the city. It's too noisy, too crowded. You have to have a reservation at every restaurant. If you do get a table, the service is terrible… "

"He sounds like a lot of fun." The sarcasm in her voice makes me laugh.

"He was the proverbial dark cloud. I never want to be like him." Exhaling deeply, I look out at a barge slowly passing.

Ruby gives my hand a squeeze. "I told you. You're nothing like him. I don't know your mom, but it sounds like you're much more like her. You like to have fun, and so far, you've shown me all the cool parts of the city."

Standing, I pull her to her feet. Melancholy is not a mood I want to have on this trip. "We're only getting started."

By the time we stumble back into the hotel lobby, it's after five, and we've strolled through SoHo, wandered up to Washington Square Park to see the arch, continued northeast to Gramercy Park, past the Flatiron building until we hit Korea Town just before the Empire State building.

"I feel like I'm walking on my ankles." Ruby is hanging off my arm, and I give her a bump.

"We've got to meet Stephen at seven. Take a quick shower and change."

She does a little whine. "Where are we meeting him and do I have to walk?"

"It's seven blocks to the Top of the Rock. Since you're new in town, I thought you'd like to see the view." Her adorable pouty face makes me grin. "Do this and I'll order cupcakes from Magnolia Bakery and give you a foot massage after."

"Deal!"

Chapter 23

Ruby

My head is spinning from all the sights. I'm not sure I've ever been this tired, but my heart is beating out of my chest, and I'm exhilarated.

Taking the white beaded cocktail dress out of the closet, I slip it over my freshly washed body and turn side to side, inspecting myself in the mirror. These shoes aren't made for walking, but I can make it seven blocks… I hope. I have a black wrap over my shoulders with a huge scarlet bow, and my hair is styled in a low bun with tendrils hanging around my face.

When we meet in the lobby, Remi is dressed in dark pants and a charcoal jacket with a green tie that brings out the green in his eyes. They blaze to life when he sees me, and my stomach flips.

The more time we spend together, talking and getting to know each other, the harder this pull between us is to fight. Once again, he takes my hand, threading our fingers. All day, walking up and down the city streets, he kept my hand firmly in his, my body pulled close against his side. I love it.

The streets are just as busy at night as they are during the day, and I totally get why they call it the city that never sleeps. All day I've been trying to be very Carrie Bradshaw, but I'm afraid I'm more Kimmie Schmidt. The city is so huge and alive and full of sights, I've been running around with my mouth open, gazing skyward like a stereotypical tourist.

At the Top of the Rock, the view is stunning. I only have a moment to see it before Remi leads me to the bar, where a tall guy with light brown hair and intense blue eyes stands to meet us.

"Remington." The man I assume is Stephen clasps his hand, and they do a bro hug.

"Stephen, meet Ruby, my assistant."

I'm his assistant now? "How do you do?" I smile, and Stephen leans back, eyeing me up and down.

"Not bad." His voice is strong, snobbish, and completely arrogant. Remi punches him on the arm, and he shakes it off. "I meant to say I'm not doing bad. You seem to be doing quite well yourself."

"What's that supposed to mean?" I've found after growing up with my dad, I'm not easily intimidated by overgrown jerks.

"Remi has never had an assistant. I wouldn't expect him to have one like you."

"Like me?" I smile. "Is that a compliment?"

Remi leans forward, speaking in a low voice that's loud enough for us all to hear. "Stephen likes to think he can figure everyone out in the first five minutes."

"I'm not wrong." He waves to the bartender. "Whiskey up, vodka, and..." He gives me another glance. "Tequila?"

"Sunrise." I lift my chin, unintimidated. "You're pretty good at guessing drinks. What am I like? Or do you need a few more minutes?"

Stephen turns his back to the bar and squints. "Stubborn... smart." His eyes graze from my head to my toes quickly. "You're very beautiful, and most dangerous of all. Ambitious."

Our drinks are set in front of us, and Remi puts his arm around my shoulders. "Okay, that's enough flattery."

"You're not really his assistant." Stephen grins, taking a sip of vodka. I don't have time to answer before he turns to Remi. "I see Oakville's working out after all. I couldn't figure out why you stayed all those years. Why not move back to Seattle?"

Remi shrugs, sipping his whiskey. "I can't tell you how many times I've considered it. Last summer I had one foot out the door... But I found a reason to stay."

My heart sinks at the thought of Remi leaving Oakville. I quietly sip my cocktail, and Stephen winks at me. "I suppose we have you to thank for that."

"Actually, we just met a few weeks ago."

Stephen's eyebrow quirks. "Remi has always been the lucky one." He turns back to my boss. "Let's talk about tomorrow night. Stellan will be there. I suggest you make a point to get to him first. His secure communications app is the talk of the industry. It's going to be big."

They spend the next several minutes discussing Remi's business at the gala. I'm intrigued because I've been at the house half a month, and I've learned very little about what he does, other than investing in new tech.

Their conversation is partly confusing to me, partly fascinating. Remi's watching a new surveillance app he wants to procure and pour money into with the goal of selling it to the government for military use. Stephen, I learn, is like a spy, keeping tabs on other investors looking at the same developers as Remi.

"What's new with you?" Remi finishes his second whiskey, and I lean forward slightly, curious about the answer to this question.

Stephen is cocky and arrogant, but I can tell he cares about his friend. I can also tell he's incredibly smart.

"I'm working on something a little closer to home." He places his empty tumbler on the bar and signals for the check. "Two things, actually. The first has more immediate use. An app that tracks prescriptions by patient driver's license or tax identification, similar to the way the government tracks gun sales—"

"Hopefully not as sloppily," Remi quips.

"Nothing I do is ever sloppy." Stephen's eyebrow arches. "The second is more dependent on current events, politics. It's something companies can use to facilitate healthcare enrollments across state lines. Similar to how car insurers work."

"Both healthcare related." The bill is paid, and Remi takes my hand as we walk toward the exit. "It always goes back to healthcare."

He says it like it's some facet of Stephen's personality only the two of them know.

"It's simply the biggest problem we have in this country. It needs a solution, and I'm prepared to develop some."

"So you're developing them yourself?"

"Oh, I'll farm out the coding. Unless I get bored."

No one speaks as we ride the elevator to the first floor. I'm thinking about Stephen being so interested in healthcare and wondering why that's the case when he breaks the silence, turning to me. "My apologies for monopolizing the evening, Miss Banks."

"No way, I found it fascinating. I've been wanting to know more about how Remi makes all his money." I give him a wink.

Stephen lifts his chin as if he won a bet. "So I was right. Not an assistant."

Remi chuckles, but I'm tired of feeling like the butt

of his friend's jokes. "You know, I thought I was pretty good at figuring people out, too, but I realize I'm not always right."

Stephen pats my arm. "It's a skill mastered by meeting lots and lots of people."

I frown, pretending to be troubled. "Actually, I think I just made an honest mistake. I had you pegged as a conceited asshole the moment I saw you. Now I realize you're simply an engineer."

He laughs out loud. "You're absolutely right, I am. Although I also pretty much hate everyone... Except Remington. And possibly you."

We're out on the sidewalk facing Radio City Music Hall saying our goodbyes, when Stephen grips his friend's shoulder and points at me. "Hang onto her. She's smart."

Remi's arm slides around my waist, and my heart beats a little faster. "I intend to."

We have a spectacular view of the Empire State Building from the balcony of the penthouse suite. I'm holding a glass of Beaujolais, watching the lights flicker all around this amazing place when Remi walks up behind me, placing his hand on my lower back. It sends a humming sensation through my body. I love being here with him, learning about his world.

"I've gotta say, you're the first girl I've met to stand up to Stephen like that." The pride in his voice fills me with warm satisfaction. "I know many who've wanted to say the things you did, but never do."

"If you'd met my dad, you'd understand." Turning, I lean against the rail, admiring the way the light shines in his eyes, the way that dimple teases me when he smiles.

Remi's holding a glass of the red wine, and he's so

perfectly elegant. "I remember you said your dad made you question your choices. You didn't say he made you strong."

Tilting my head to the side, I think about this. "I guess I didn't really realize it until just now."

"Silver lining?" His voice is gentle. "You're not afraid of anything."

"That's not true." I'm terrified of my feelings for him.

I've dated so many guys, and I've never felt this way about any of them. It's like Remington Key holds my breath in his hands, and it scares me to death.

"What scares you?" He grins, caging me between his arms. We're facing each other with my back to the balcony, his strong arms around me, his warm scent capturing my senses.

Circling a finger around the button on his shirt, I think about my words. "Earlier, when Stephen asked you if you'd ever move back to Seattle... Would you?"

His brow furrows, and I can see he's considering his answer. I love that even in this moment, with us so close, he hits pause to give me a serious response. No off the cuff answer. He's listening to me, thinking, as if everything he says to me is important.

I want to reach up and trace my finger along his forehead, move that curl off his brow. He looks down at me, and my heart beats faster. "Would you ever consider leaving Oakville?"

Exhaling a laugh through my nose, I relent. "When I was young, all I wanted was to leave Oakville. I thought it was a hick town with small-minded people."

Remi takes the wine glass out of my hand and sets it with his on the glass table beside us. Then he turns back, enclosing me in his arms. I love being surrounded by him.

"I think I hear a but coming."

"Everyone I know has a big butt," I tease.

He grins. "Well?"

I take a deep inhale of his cedar and leather scent, of soap and Remi. "Now I realize how much I love my friends and being near my mom, even though she drives me crazy." His expression doesn't change, and I add, "It made me sad to hear you'd thought of leaving."

Leaning forward, he traces his nose along the line of my hair, just at my ear, rising higher to my temple. "I haven't thought of leaving once in the last eighteen days."

His words are warm and sensual. My eyes close as electricity skates down my arms, as my panties flood with heat. "Has it been eighteen days?"

"Tomorrow will be nineteen." It's a low rumble I feel all the way to my core.

"Is that a good thing?"

Warm lips touch my forehead, my nose. His eyes capture mine. "I think it's a very good thing. Do you?"

Lifting my chin, I kiss his scruffy jaw. "I think it's amazing."

Our mouths meet in a sensual kiss. Warm lips cover mine, our tongues curl in a primitive dance. Leaning down, he lifts me into his arms, and I don't even try to fight. I wrap my arms around his neck, kissing his cheek, moving up to his temple as he carries me through the suite to his bedroom in the back.

Lowering me to my feet, he puts his hands on my shoulders, tracing his thumbs along the lines of my sleeveless dress. "I want to make love to you now. Is that okay?"

My stomach is hot and clenching, I nod before the words are out. "Yes, please."

Hot eyes darken. He frames my face with one hand, his thumb on my chin, lifting it. Our mouths collide, and he parts my lips, plunging his tongue inside to find mine.

A little whimper aches from my throat. I'm chasing him, holding his face as his mouth moves down to my jaw, to my neck. My entire body is on fire as his beard scuffs my skin.

"I've dreamed of this every night since you came." It's a rough confession. It curls my toes.

Large hands are on my thighs, rising higher, lifting the hem of my dress until he reaches the center.

"Oh yes," my chin dips, and I kiss his neck, his cheek, struggling to touch every part of him with my mouth.

Long fingers curl between my thighs, ripping my panties aside and diving between my folds. "You're so wet," he groans against my neck.

His hand is gone, and I'm acutely aware of its absence. He's behind me now, grasping the zipper on my dress and pulling it down. My white dress falls in a puddle at my feet, and I reach behind me for his neck. He holds my waist, sliding his hands over my ribs, higher to cup my breasts.

"I love your body." Kissing my neck, he pulls the skin between his teeth, and my knees go liquid. "You're so beautiful. Look at you."

My eyes blink open, and I see us in the mirror across the room. I'm standing, my dark hair wild and falling all around my shoulders. I'm still in my heels, but otherwise, I'm only wearing my black lace bra and panties. Behind me, Remi's face is in my hair.

His darkened eyes sear into mine, full of hunger, lust, and longing. I watch as his hand spreads out over my stomach, sliding lower until it dips into the top of my panties. He watches the progress of his fingers, dipping between my thighs, searching for that little spot that makes me scream his name.

My eyes are fixed on his hand, spreading me, touching, probing, until he finds it, and my body starts to quiver. "Remi…" It's a hoarse whisper.

His face is beside my ear. "Say my name again. I want to hear you saying my name as you come apart."

His hand moves faster between my legs. I'm hypnotized by the movements, focused entirely on the surges of pleasure streaking through my body from my thighs to the arches of my feet. I feel his erection at my back, and I reach behind me, sliding my hand up and down the bulge in his pants.

"Fuck yeah," he whispers into my hair, and my orgasm tightens in my lower stomach.

The pressure grows hotter, his hand moves faster. My gaze is full of him holding me, one hand inside my bra, kneading my breast, the other massaging my clit.

I feel the orgasm start to flutter, tighter, tighter in my pelvis, and my head falls back as it breaks through me. "Remi!" I gasp his name, bending my knees as my thighs shudder.

His arm becomes a steel band around my ribs, holding me up as he gingerly touches my clit, stroking it through the last waves of orgasm.

"Oh, yes," I'm trembling, riding his hand, my pussy tightening between my legs, longing for that ache to be filled.

Without a word, he walks us to the bed, guiding me forward until my hands are flat on the mattress. My ass is up, and I look over my shoulder as I arch my back. I want to see that cock I've only felt time after time.

His lids are heavy as he goes to the nightstand,

reaching into the drawer for a condom.

"Compliments of the hotel?" I tease.

He's too focused to grin. "I put some in the drawer. Just in case."

I haven't moved. It all happens so quickly. I watch as he unfastens his slacks, letting them fall to the floor as he steps out and makes his way to me. My eyes are hot and straining. I want to see, but I don't want to move.

Once he's back behind me, he drops to his knees, jerking my panties from my waist to the ground and burying his face in my ass.

"Oh shit!" I gasp, my knees giving out as he kisses me, licking his tongue into my core and sucking me at the same time. "Remi, oh…"

His tongue is back on my clit, his cheeks scuffing the electric skin of my inner thighs. I'm crying out and rising onto my toes as waves of orgasm flare to life inside me again. My pussy is clenching, grasping, begging.

He's back on his feet again, and I hear him rip the foil, rolling the condom on quickly. I'm fisting the bedspread when his tip nudges at my entrance. He moves my legs wider with his thighs, and in one swift plunge, he's inside me, all the way to the hilt.

We both groan loudly. My back arches, and he catches me around the waist, holding me to his chest as he starts to pump. He's thrusting fast, relentless, focused. I hear his breathing in my ear, ragged and desperate.

"Ruby… yes… fuck, yes." His mouth is at my neck, and he holds my shoulders, my waist, leaning us forward as he drives harder.

My hands shoot out to hold the bedspread. He's over my back, forcing us faster and deeper to climax.

Lights flash behind my squeezed eyes. It's fireworks and irresistible need. It's something I've only read about but never experienced. I lift one leg, putting my knee on the bed, and it sends him even deeper. We both cry out, and he thrusts one, two, three more times before holding steady, holding my ass against his pelvis, as he erupts with a loud, ragged shout.

I feel his dick pulsing, filling the condom. I feel his chest against my back, slick with sweat. I feel his heart beating hard against my skin.

It's the most amazing thing I've ever experienced.

He's blown my mind. Again.

Then he says my name.

Chapter 24

Remi

Being inside Ruby is like diving into warm, crystal clear waters in a private cove surrounded by jasmine and roses.

Her hair swirls around us like glossy silk, and her body is so sexy. Her hips rock and sway when I touch her, and she rides my hand, threading her fingers in my hair chanting my name. It's incredible. My cock is so hard and aching, when I finally get it inside her tight little pussy, I almost blow my load in two pumps. Steadying my thoughts, I'm able to crest the overwhelming wave of pleasure.

Still, the way her body moves with mine, it's all nearly more than I can handle. Her scent is all over me. I had to taste her one more time, get her right to the edge, because this first time won't last long. We've been building to this for weeks.

When we finally reach that cliff together, I'm holding her to my chest as we dive together, white light blinding me, the orgasm snaking up my legs, pulsing into her.

"Ruby." I say her name like a prayer, kissing her face, the side of her cheek, her hair.

My heart is beating out of my chest, and I'm warm in her depths. I don't want to pull out. I only want to hold her.

Reaching carefully between us, I grasp the condom, tying it off quickly before depositing it in the small trash under the desk. Just as fast, I catch her hand, leading her to the bed. Sliding back the blankets, I guide us through the silky sheets into each other's arms.

Her panties are long gone, and she unfastens her sexy bra before snuggling in beside me. "I really like that bra." I wrap my arm around her, holding her close.

She grins, tossing it to the side. "I thought you might."

My grip tightens on her. "What happened to not sleeping in my room?"

"We're not asleep yet." That teasing glint is in her eyes, but I pull her small body tighter to mine.

"You're not going anywhere tonight."

She starts to laugh. "You're kidnapping me?"

Rolling us onto her back, I look down into her sweet face, her dancing eyes, and white smile. "More like... holding you hostage."

Her chin lifts, and I meet her halfway, pulling her lips between mine, parting them and sweeping my tongue to find hers. It's heaven. It's more than I thought it might be. We finish with short nips, light touches. I bend down and trace her chin with my mouth.

Dropping beside her on the bed, I have one arm behind her neck. The other traces the skin of her flat stomach. "I've been thinking about what you said before we left Oakville."

She turns onto her stomach facing me, her arms bent over her breasts, hands tucked beneath her cheek. She smiles, and her nose crinkles adorably. "I said a lot of things before we left Oakville."

Reaching out, I move a dark wave off her ivory cheek. "I don't want us to be friends."

Her eyebrows rise, but that smile sparkles in her gaze. "You don't?"

"No."

"Hm…" She nods, doing her best to make a serious face. "So we're not friends anymore. Interesting."

"We are not." Leaning closer, I kiss her jaw. "I plan to do very naughty things with you. Things friends would never do."

Her shoulder rises, and she makes a little noise. "Very unfriendly kisses?"

"Very unfriendly kisses, touches." My hand slides down to her waist, over the curve of her ass.

I'm ready to explore her body with my mouth again when a loud knock sounds on the door and we both jump. She sits up, holding the sheet over her breasts.

"What the—" I slide to the edge of the bed, snatching a robe off the hook on the wall.

"It's our cupcakes!" She hops out of the bed as well, grabbing the other robe and pulling it over her naked body.

Sure enough, it's our order. We move from snuggled in a cocoon of afterglow to sitting in the middle of the floor in the living room, a pink box of confections between us. We ordered the "I Cupcake New York" dozen, a collection of red velvet, chocolate, and vanilla cakes with assorted decorations.

"Look at this one." Her eyes are wide as she lifts a white cupcake with pink frosting and a candy daisy on top. "It's the Carrie cupcake."

I grab a standard chocolate with chocolate frosting. "We should bring a few of these back for

Lillie."

"Yes!" She tries to clap with her hands full of cake. "She'll love it."

"I really love how much you care for her." I've thought it so many times, but it's the first time I've said it out loud.

"She's an amazing kid. She's sweet and smart... and she's goofy like you."

"I'm not goofy." Happiness tightens my chest. It's so easy to laugh when I'm with her. It's been so long since I could laugh this way.

"You like to tease and have fun." She takes a bite of her pink cupcake and falls onto her side. "Oh my wow! This is the best thing I've ever tasted!"

I have to confess, her orgasmic cries have my dick twitching. "If you keep making those noises, I'm going to have to fuck you again."

Her eyes widen, and she pulls her lip between her teeth as a naughty grin spreads across her cheeks. I watch as she slowly lifts the cupcake to her mouth. Her pink tongue slips out to take a lick, and she moans, closing her eyes. It's fucking sexy as hell.

"It's sooo good."

That does it. I toss my cupcake back into the box and crawl across the floor to her. She squeals and tries to get away, but I'm too fast. I catch her ankle, then I'm on top of her, holding her hands out to the sides.

"You're a tease, Ruby Banks." Leaning down, I cover her mouth with mine, kissing her quickly before lifting up again to meet her gaze.

"I'm very sweet." Her voice is sultry.

"You're delicious." I kiss her jaw. "Everywhere."

A pretty flush stains her neck. I lean down to kiss her skin, my cock growing harder as I make my way lower, into the loosened wrap of her robe.

"Do you want me to taste you?" I speak against her body, moving the cloth aside with my nose so her tight little nipples are exposed.

"Yes." The word slips out on a hot exhale, and I pull her breast into my mouth, sucking and biting gently.

Her body moves beneath me, and I push my thigh between her legs, spreading them wider. We're both in only bath robes, and my dick is hard on her thigh. She whimpers, moving her hips around to center me above her core.

"I have to get a condom." My voice is strained as I kiss her shoulder, making my way up to her neck, behind her ear.

"Oh!" Her back arches, and I know I've found an erogenous zone. "Remi, just the tip."

Fuck. I don't know if I have the self-control for it. My dick is aching for her body, for release. Still, I move higher, covering her mouth with mine as I tease her with the tip of my cock.

"Ruby," I groan. She's hot and clenching, and the sensation is almost unbearable.

I almost come.

I'm off her at once, headed to the bedroom to retrieve another condom from the nightstand. I'm taking it out as I return to the room, kneeling beside her as I start to roll it on.

"So big..." She reaches out, stopping me as she wraps her fingers around my shaft, pulling and watching me, leaning forward and putting her soft lips around the head.

"Ruby." It's a sacred whisper as I watch her pull me into her mouth, grasping the base with her hand and meeting it as she licks around the shaft like an ice cream cone.

Ice cream… I remember teasing her in the park…

My head drops back, and I'm lost in the flex of orgasm tensing my lower belly. She's pumping me, and my hips move forward to meet her mouth. I'm so close. I'm riding her sucks, following her rhythm, but I want to be inside her.

"Wait." My voice is a rasp, and I gently nudge her aside so I can roll on the condom.

Then scooping my hands through her hair, under her arms, I lift her to my lap, positioning her so she's straddling my cock, which is pointed to the ceiling.

She reaches between us and positions the head then drops completely, sending me balls deep into her clenching core.

"Oh, fuck," I cough, holding her body.

I'm still sitting on my knees, and she rises again, only to drop all the way once more, sending me impossibly deep. My eyes roll back in my head, and I swear to all that's fucking holy it's the best thing I've ever felt.

She rides me like a champ. Her breasts bounce at my chin, and I dip down to pull one into my mouth, feeling her clenching and pulling me deeper inside her.

"So good," I groan, trailing my fingers lightly along the sides of her ass.

Her head tilts back, and the ends of her hair tease my fingers. She grinds against me, and I grab her hips, digging my fingers into her skin and holding her so I'm buried so deep, moving her up and down as she moans.

Sweat trickles down my chest. My hair sticks to my forehead, and I can't hold out any longer. With a shout I break, orgasm pulsing through my cock into her. She wraps her arms around my shoulders, still rocking her hips until I hear her gasp. I feel the cascade of spasms around me as she comes.

We're holding each other through the cyclone of sensation, as our bodies rise and fall on waves of ecstasy. Our rapid breathing synchronizes as we float, holding each other as we come down, satisfied and happy.

Ruby's head tilts to the side on my shoulder, and her lips graze my neck. "That was amazing." It's a happy whisper, and I smile.

Catching her under the ass, I slowly stand, carrying her in my arms to the bed. It's late, and I quickly dispose of the condom before easing us to the center of the king-sized mattress, where we drift to sleep, our bodies entwined.

When I open my eyes again, it's after noon. I haven't slept so long or so soundly in years. Rolling onto my back, I consider the gorgeous creature in my bed. She's wild and sweet, sexy and sensual. I can't get enough of her, and *fuck me...* I remember sometime in the early hours, in the darkness, pulling her to me and sinking into her depths. It was a hot as fuck quickie, and I realize with a jolt I didn't use a condom.

She was still asleep with her back to my chest, my arms around her waist. I wasn't fully awake myself, but it was perfect as fuck. My morning wood arose, and it was like a guided missile.

Shit. We haven't discussed our sexual histories, although mine has been nonexistent since Sandy. I literally buried myself in work, neglecting everything, including my personal needs.

That drought has ended.

Ruby awakens parts of me that have long been dormant, and now that I've had her, now that my body is awake, I'm like a starving man. I can't get enough of her.

Still…

She makes a noise and stretches, and I swear, I've got a rail spike between my legs. I'm ready to pin her to the mattress and go to town. I slide away so I don't poke her with my dick, and she rolls slowly onto her stomach then turns her face to the side, towards me.

A sleepy smile curls her lips, and she bends her elbow, putting her fingers over her mouth. "Good morning."

My stomach floods with heat fueled partly by lust, but even more by pure affection. Her eyes have captured me from the start, but now when I look in them I see her soul, her strength, her independence.

I want more. I told her last night I don't want to be friends. I want to make her mine, but I fear she'll run. She's told me so many times we can't do this. I know she only caved because we're here. It's a special time. What happens in New York stays in New York.

Regardless, I don't think I can stay at arm's distance. Now that I'm inside her gates, I want her to want me. I want her to come to me and say *make me yours…*

And I'll do it.

"Good morning." I smile, and she blinks slowly, studying me with those wise eyes.

"I had this dream… It was early in the morning and something hard poked me in the ass. Then it moved higher between my legs…" Her teasing eyes narrow, and my stomach tightens.

"Yeah… I'm sorry. Pretty sure I was still asleep."

"We didn't use a condom." Her lips press together.

"You don't have to worry. I can assure you I haven't had any sexual partners since Sandy, and even then—"

"I'm not worried. I'm pretty sure I was complicit in the poking."

The memory is hazy, but I do recall her sweet little ass arching into my pelvis. It didn't take much to glide into her slippery core. As rakish as that may be.

"I'll do whatever you need to set your mind at ease. Testing—"

"No." She shakes her head, her eyes traveling around my face. "I've always been very careful. I'm on the pill. We should be safe."

The way she says the word, makes me wonder if she's thinking the same thing I am. We're venturing into dangerous territory. Sleeping together takes us to a whole new level.

I don't want those worries clouding this time.

I want to own it. "Are you hungry? It's too late for breakfast, but if you're in the mood for another cheeseburger..."

She starts to laugh and pushes into a sitting position, her back facing me. She has the most beautiful back, long and elegant with black waves sweeping down almost to her ass.

"I'm going to have to start jogging with you if I keep eating cheeseburgers." I watch as she disappears into the bathroom.

"You're welcome to join me anytime." She's welcome into every part of my life.

I roll onto my back, staring at the ceiling tiles as I envision all the ways she could fit into my world.

Chapter 25

Ruby

More running around the city follows cheeseburgers at the Shake Shack.

As much as I hated it, I insisted we cut today short. Listening to Stephen and Remi talk last night, I realized the gala is a pretty massive deal for Remi's business. He needs to be alert, and I want to look amazing standing at his side... Not like I'm dying of foot pain after running all over Manhattan.

Standing in front of the closet in my room, I slide my fingers down the silk skirt of my dress. The bodice is held up by a network of straps that goes around my neck and crisscrosses over my bare back down to my waist. I can't wear a bra, but Ma helped me take it up so the triangle top is held securely over my breasts, and we added a few darts at the waist to keep it from being too poufy.

The result is it stays close around my torso then opens up into a stunning waterfall of thick ivory silk. It's stunning and seductive, and I close my eyes as I imagine being in Remi's arms tonight, his hands sliding over my exposed skin.

So much warmth floods my body when I think of him, of last night, of this morning. Being with him was so much more than I expected—and I'd fantasized a lot. He's seductive and possessive, but at the same time, he's attentive and curious, delicate and demanding.

He didn't just make love to my body. He made love to my mind. He didn't simply chase his own orgasm, letting me work mine out on my own. It was as if he studied my touch, followed the experience of our bodies moving together, savored my kisses.

Even this morning was hot, grinding out a quickie. He just grabbed me and took it, and I rode along, basking in the heat of primitive desire.

Like the drop of black in the bright white, a thread of fear trickles through my chest. We can't possibly go back to the way we were before we came here. Not only do I have to get my own place, I'm not sure I can even work for him anymore. *Can I?*

I don't want to think about this now. I will ignore the twist of fear and focus on this enchanted evening. Anyway, Drew has the solution—direct deposit!

Exhaling through a nervous laugh, I swallow the tightness in my throat and do a little spin, holding my hands over the rich satin rippling to the floor. Negative thoughts aren't allowed here. Tonight I'll let the fantasy play out.

I'll be the princess at the ball with the gorgeous prince. I'll exult in the way he looks at me as if his eyes can't get enough. I'll be beautiful for him and we'll dance and swirl through the clouds.

My feelings and our problematic reality can stay in Oakville.

Tonight, it's all about the dream.

Remi wanders through the hotel bar looking toe-curlingly handsome in his black tux. I sent a message for him to meet me here, and I came down ten minutes early so I could have a drink and be at the bar when he appeared.

My dress is one of those high-low numbers, so sitting in the chair puts my crossed legs on full display. My hair hangs in thick waves down my back, and I watch as his brow furrows, as he scans the faces.

The muscle in his jaw moves attractively. He likes being in control, and I've tilted him off balance. It makes me smile a little as I watch him. Frustration tightens his expression. *I'm right here, sexy prince…*

When his eyes finally land on mine, his expression melts into hot desire and a thrill surges through my stomach. This is so much better than meeting in my room.

His gaze is fixed on me as he closes the space between us. "You like playing games, Miss Banks."

The tone in his voice has my body humming, and when he touches my back, I can't help a shiver. "It's not a game, Mr. Key. I wanted to have a glass of wine before we left for the gala."

His eyes flicker to the glass of Pinot Gris on the bar in front of me. "No tequila tonight?"

"Maybe later. I figured we should start out a little more sophisticated."

"Don't get too formal on me."

Slipping out of my chair, my heels bring me closer to his eye level. His hands are on my waist, his fingers toying with the bare skin of my back. I'm surrounded by his warmth, the earthy scent of his cologne. It's heady and exhilarating.

I straighten his black bowtie, leaning closer to kiss his jaw. "Being formal can be a fun change."

A naughty smile curls his lips, that sexy dimple teasing me. "I should have already told you you're beautiful. I look forward to getting you out of this dress after the party."

"Then let's get the party started."

A limo takes us to the gala... Actually, we abandon the car in a long line of limos when we arrive. Remi holds my hand, leading me up the carpeted stairs. He's obviously distracted by what's to come. His phone lights up several times as we walk, and while I'm not trying to look, I see Stephen's name at the top of the screen.

My hand is in the crook of his arm as we enter the convention hall, and I feel like a queen. It's an elaborate space. The floors are marble, and the windows soar to the roof, allowing breathtaking views of the city. Chandeliers like icicle waterfalls are dotted throughout, and music floats in the air. I can tell it's a live jazz band, but I can't see it through the throng of men and women in formal attire.

Everyone appears very important and focused. I do my best to keep my shoulders straight and my chin up... like Remington Key's date should be. He's as important and connected as all these people, and I don't want to let him down.

Leaning against his shoulder, I whisper. "Are you nervous or excited? Personally, I'm scared to death."

He chuckles softly. "You have nothing to be afraid of. I'm afraid of all the men who'll try to steal you from me."

"You don't have to worry. I'm not going anywhere." My stomach squeezes.

The words are out so fast, so automatic. I can't believe I just said them out loud.

The smile in Remi's profile eases my anxiety. "Stephen said he's waiting at the east bar. If you don't mind, I'll take you to him while I track down Stellan and secure his business."

"Why is Stephen here? Is he an investor or a developer?"

"Neither and both." Remi stops to shake an older man's hand.

I wait as they exchange brief small talk, then we're moving again. I can tell Remi's focused on finding this tech guy Stellan.

"So Stephen is both?" I pick up where we left off before Mr. Old Guy interrupted us.

"Stephen likes to be the idea guy, start with his own inspiration then decide whether he wants to create it all himself or hire someone else to do the work. Then he and I and a small group of investors fund the final product."

"He sounds really smart."

"He's the smartest guy I know—and trust me, he's the first to say it. Stephen's got a big brain, a big ego, and a big bank account."

Squinting my eye up at him, I tease. "I take it he doesn't play well with others."

Again, I get that partial laugh. "Not in the slightest."

We're finally through the hall, and I see Stephen leaning with one elbow on a high-top table. He's also in a tux, and his blue eyes are intense.

He's actually very handsome, and I wonder why he doesn't have a plus one tonight. I think I can guess. No one tells Stephen Hastings what to do.

Reaching for my arm, he passes me a glass of white wine as he moves me from Remi's side to his. "Stellan's just across the room by the bar. If you go now, I think you'll have him all to yourself."

I'm impressed by how slick that handoff was. Remi seems less eager to ditch me, which smooths my ruffled feathers.

Turning to face me, he touches my arm. "I don't expect this to take very long. Will you be okay hanging with this asshole for a few minutes? I promise to make it up to you."

Pressing my lips into a smile, I step forward to kiss his cheek. "Break a leg."

His hands catch my waist, holding me before I return to Stephen's side. "Thank you for being here."

He speaks into my ear before giving me a quick kiss that lights a fire all through my insides.

When he releases me, he grips Stephen's arm. "Keep an eye on her."

"She'll be safe as the crown jewels."

With that he's gone, and I turn to face the piercing blue eyes of my guard. "I see you've graduated from assistant to… something more fun."

Heat floods my cheeks, and I wish my face didn't betray how flustered I get. "I was never his assistant."

"You don't say." Stephen's voice sounds bored. I slant my eyes at him, and he takes a sip of what I assume is vodka. "So you slept with him."

He catches me mid-sip, and I almost choke on my wine. "You don't beat around the bush, do you?"

"What's the point?" He half-heartedly pats me on the back. It's okay. I'm not coughing much. "We're all adults here. Don't act like you're shocked."

"I'm not shocked." I shrug my shoulder. "I guess I'm used to people being a little subtler with their digs."

"It wasn't a dig." He eyes me up and down. "I appreciate you bringing him out of retirement. Remi was too young to lay down and die like he almost did."

"I really don't know what you mean." My voice is quiet as I take a sip of wine. It pains my heart to think of Remi wanting to die. "We've only known each other about a month. Less than a month, actually."

"So how'd you meet? Are you in tech?"

Inwardly, I cringe. I'm not sure how this confession is going to play out. "He hired me to be the nanny." That sounds wrong. "To be Lillie's nanny."

Stephen chortles… yes, he literally chortles. "Classic. Remington's sleeping with the nanny."

The way he says it irritates me — probably because it's the way I expect everyone to say it. "I only took the job to help him out. He was having some sort of conflict with his mother-in-law. It was very frustrating to him."

"Eleanor." Stephen nods, taking another sip. "Dragon lady." My eyes narrow, and I try to decide if I'm offended. He doesn't give me the chance. "Oh, please. Everyone's so ready to get their panties in a knot these days. Eleanor's not even Asian, but you know what I mean when I say it."

I do know what he means.

"She can be a bit much." My mind returns home briefly. "I'm going to have to resign. I don't see how we can go back to having a platonic relationship."

He turns, putting both elbows on the table. "In my experience, there's no putting that genie back in the bottle. What will you do if you're not Lillie's nanny? Do you have another position waiting in the wings?"

Finishing my wine, I shake my head. "I have a master's in social work. Before I started with Remi, I was a therapist at the clinic in town."

"So you'll go back to shrinking heads?"

"That's not technically what I did. It's not really what I want to do again. The idea was I'd figure it out while I worked for him."

"Did you?"

I swallow the knot in my throat. "I got a little distracted."

Confessing my lack of direction makes me feel

irresponsible, guilty. The crowd is growing thicker, but through the bodies, I see my prince making his way toward us. His entire demeanor has changed. His eyes are bright, and a victorious smile is on his lips. Just the sight of him sweeps the dark feelings away.

"Good luck with whatever you decide, Miss Banks. I hope it works out for you." Stephen leans down and air-kisses at my temple. "Thank you again for bringing my boy back from the dead."

He leaves me to meet Remi in a handshake. "How'd it go?"

"I got him." He passes Stephen and catches me around the waist, lifting me in a squeeze that turns into a spin. "You're my good luck charm. It's time to celebrate."

Leave it to Remi to find a karaoke bar in walking distance of the gala. I'm sitting in a round vinyl booth in a dim-lit, brick-walled cellar, and he's onstage belting out "She Believes in Me."

He's singing it with gusto, clutching his chest and going down on one knee for the final words, and I can't stop laughing. It helps I've had several more glasses of wine.

Stephen is across from me grimacing, and when Remi returns to the table, he complains loudly. "That song is the musical equivalent of a Lifetime movie."

"It's Ruby's favorite Kenny Rogers song." He slides in beside me, kissing me long and hard on the mouth.

He even pushes my lips apart and goes for a little tongue action, which elicits more groaning from our companion.

"Time to call it a night." Stephen stands, tossing some bills on the table and pointing at Remi. "I remember when you could hold your liquor."

"I'm holding my liquor." Remi grabs me by the waist and hoists me out of the booth. "You're right, though. We have an early flight tomorrow. Time to head back to the hotel and get busy."

"Oh my God," I gasp a laugh.

"Good work tonight." Stephen grasps him by the shoulder. "Glad to have you back in the game."

They clasp hands, and we say goodnight, heading out to hail a cab. Remi dismissed the limo when we took off on foot to the hall. It takes a little time to maneuver the traffic all the way to Midtown, and I wish I'd worn walking shoes.

It's a lie. I love these heels and this dress and Remi in a tux. I feel like a true Cinderella.

In the elevator, Remi holds me by the waist. "You're sleeping over at my place again. Don't argue with me." He gives me a little tug, and I grin.

"Okay, but don't get used to it. Starting tomorrow, it's back to business. You're my boss. I'm Lillie's nanny."

"You know, banging the hot nanny is a very popular male fantasy." He leans in to kiss my neck.

His breath tickles my skin, sending goosebumps flying down my arms. "Are you saying that's why you hired me?"

"Not exactly."

The bell rings, and we stumble out at the top floor. He clasps my hand, leading me across the marble tiles and into the elaborate suite. He's fiddling with his phone, and we're out on the balcony as music begins to play over the speakers hidden in the eaves.

Reaching out, he takes my hands and pulls me into a slow dance.

My face is right at his cheek. "Not exactly means

partly."

Exhaling, he kisses my temple. "I was attracted to you the first time I ever saw you."

"That night in the bar?"

"That day on the church lawn when Drew introduced us. Lillie was squirming all over me, and you took one look and walked away."

He extends his arm, moving me away from him in an impromptu dance, still holding my hand.

"I told you that wasn't me."

A sexy smile curls his lips, and have I mentioned how much I love that dimple?

"It was you." He pulls me back into his arms, looking deep into my eyes. "Oakville isn't big enough for two insanely sexy, smart, stubborn, irresistible, half-Korean beauties like you. Why deny it?"

"I was in a really bad head space back then." My voice is quiet, and he rocks us side to side in time with the song. "I was using these silly dating apps, and they kept matching me with losers. I was pretty miserable. Way too far up my own butt."

"I'd like to be far up your butt."

My eyes widen. "Hello!"

We both start to laugh, but just as fast, his brow lowers. His face grows playfully stern, possessive. "I won't lie and say I'm happy to hear about you dating other guys—"

"Trust me, the dates didn't last very long. I usually sneaked out."

"Good." Leaning down, he kisses my lips. "So to answer your question, attraction might have had a little to do with your job offer."

My hands are on his neck, and I gaze into his eyes. Here, on the balcony overlooking all of Manhattan, under a sky filled with stars, I'm sure I've found something money can't buy.

"Don't think for one minute attraction had nothing to do with me saying yes." Rising on my toes, I meet his mouth, lips parted, tongues curling together.

His fingers tug on the strings holding my dress up, and I allow him to lead me into the suite, into the bedroom, into another night of heaven in his arms.

Chapter 26

Remi

My daughter climbs Ruby like a tree as soon as we walk through the door. I'd be hurt, but watching Ruby scoop her up and carry her into the house fills me with such calm.

I don't even mind being left alone to manage our luggage. I shake my head, grinning as I tip the limo driver and throw our hanging bags over my shoulder.

Eleanor meets me in the foyer with a stern expression as always. "I trust you had a successful trip?"

"More than successful. I landed the developer I was after and got leads on two more." It has me feeling generous. "Thank you for keeping an eye on Lillie while I was away."

"She's my granddaughter." She says it as if it's an unwritten decree. "I'll do anything to keep her safe and be sure she's cared for."

"Good to know." I have all the bags, and it doesn't take long to have them deposited where they belong.

Dropping off Ruby's things in her room, I hear her and Lillie in my daughter's bedroom chattering as if they're old friends who've been separated for months.

"There's a new girl?" Ruby's voice is surprised.

"Yes, and Louie tried to make her eat dirt just like he did me." My daughter is very adult sounding—full of righteous indignation. "I marched over there, and in my most serious voice, I told him, 'You'd better watch it, Mister.'"

"Then what happened?" Ruby sounds on the edge of her seat. I put my hand over my mouth so I don't laugh.

"Bunny came with me and we played Mulan the rest of recess."

"I see."

Peeking my head in, I smile when I see them both in the middle of Lillie's princess bed. "I hate to interrupt the party, but are we having penny cakes for lunch?"

"Daddy!" Lillie takes off running to me, and I scoop her up in my arms. "Penny cakes! Penny cakes!"

She pumps her little hand in the air like it's a football game and I just scored the winning touchdown.

The rest of the day passes so fast. Even dinner with Eleanor doesn't feel like a chore.

Perhaps I'm different, or maybe I'm seeing Ruby differently. She does her best to avoid conflict with Lillie's grandmother, to compliment the dishes, and to guide my daughter's manners, then she exits the scene as soon as possible. Eleanor doesn't appear miffed when I tell her goodnight, which is a relief.

The temperatures are falling outside. The days are getting shorter, and the house is so quiet with everyone in their rooms. After spending a few hours at my desk following up with Stellan and the two potentials, I'm lying in my bed alone, wishing we were back in that penthouse suite. I glance at the clock, and It's almost eleven.

Turning onto my stomach, I try to quell the heat smoldering inside me. Fire is in my belly, and it feels like it's radiating through my pelvis, up my spine, and to my brain.

I can't sleep like this.

I have to find her. I need to touch her face, kiss her one more time.

Just to tell her goodnight.

Ruby said she can't sleep with me here in this house, with me as her boss. I have to respect her wishes.

In my mind, I assure myself I won't push her to do more than she's comfortable with as I climb the stairs to the third floor, quietly padding in my bare feet to her room.

A light shines from under her door, and I rest my forehead against the wood straining my ears to hear any noise. I'm breathing so fast, I only hear myself. My shoulders rise and fall rapidly. In my fevered haste to get here, I didn't even think to grab a shirt. I'm only wearing pajama pants.

This doesn't look good for my "no pressure" approach.

I brace my palm against the door, trying to convince myself I'm okay with simply knowing she's there, knowing this thin parcel of wood separates me from the woman I suddenly can't seem to live without.

I'm midway through my pep-talk when the door opens in front of me. A soft gasp draws my eyes upwards. Ruby stands there in her short green robe. Her hair is tied in a low ponytail, and it hangs in shining waves over her shoulder, down her breast. Her face is fresh, as it always is before bed. She's so fucking beautiful.

"Remi?" Her voice is breathless, rushed. "I thought I heard a noise. I—"

"I didn't mean to disturb you." I imagine what I must look like standing here, feverish, driven, going out of my mind with need for her. "I was in bed, and I couldn't stop thinking about you. I..."

I can't finish that sentence.

I want to kiss her beautiful body. I want to put my hands all over her and sink my cock deep between her thighs. I want to relive the two nights I spent in heaven less than twenty-four hours ago. I can't stop thinking how much I need her.

But I can't violate her wishes.

"I should go."

"Wait..." She steps forward, placing her hand on my bare chest, and it's almost too much. I capture her in my arms, pulling her against me.

Her mouth finds mine, and our lips part, our tongues unite, chasing. Hands are everywhere, grabbing, pushing clothes aside. We're ravenous, kissing, biting, sucking every bit of skin we can find. Through the fog of desire, I close the door, fumbling with her in my arms to the bed.

Her robe is gone, leaving only a thin scrap of cotton between her beautiful breasts and me. It's torn like a tissue. She pushes at the waist of my pants, and I pause to shove them off impatiently before joining her in the bed.

We're under the blankets, and I pull her naked body flush against mine. We both groan as we slide together. I kiss her shoulder, moving to her center. I run my teeth along her collar bone before dipping lower to capture a hardened nipple between my lips.

She moans, and I can't get enough of the taste, the feel, the smell of her body.

Her fingers are in my hair, threading and drawing me closer to her. Her legs part, and I roll her onto her back, moving between them. My arms are under her shoulder blades, holding her firmly against my chest, and I lift my chin, finding her eyes.

They're hooded, and she nods, leaning up to meet my lips as I rise higher, thrusting deep and burying myself to the hilt in her hot, slippery depths. Again we groan as our bodies unite. We're wild, grasping and holding, rocking together so fast. Her hips rise to meet mine, and our mouths fuse.

I've lost track of time, place, everything except the sensation of her body around me, pulling, milking, the growing orgasm tightening in my pelvis. She arches up, moaning and scratching her fingernails down my skin, and I can't hold back. I'm pulsing and filling her, holding her as my only anchor to this world.

My heart beats frantically, and I blink my eyes open slowly, regaining my bearings, realizing I probably left her behind that time.

"Are you okay?" I'm propped on my elbows, holding my weight from crushing her.

Her hands touch my cheeks, and she smiles. "I'm pretty sure that's the first time I've been devoured."

She's absolutely gorgeous, and I start to laugh. She laughs, and I slip out of her. She makes a little pouty face, and I move to my side, gathering her to me.

"I'm pretty sure that's the first time I've gone crazy wanting to devour someone."

Her finger circles lightly on my chest. "I was going a little crazy myself. I couldn't decide if it would make me a total slut if I showed up at your door. Then I couldn't decide if I cared."

"You can always show up at my door. I will never judge you."

She laughs again, burying her face in my chest and inhaling deeply. "You smell so good."

I take a deep breath at the top of her hair—fresh roses and jasmine. "I love the scent of you all around me."

"We might have a problem, Mr. Key."

"I can't see a single problem anywhere."

We lie together in the darkness, me tracing my fingers along the soft skin of her back, her tracing her finger along the line of my bicep. After a while our breathing slows, and I start to fall asleep. The last thing I remember is the press of her lips against my skin. It's possible I'm dreaming, but it seems like she agrees with me.

Not a problem in sight...

"Lillie, No! Oh my God—NO!" The scream snaps me out of the most divine slumber.

Ruby jumps off my chest and starts grabbing clothes. For a moment, I can't get my bearings. Then it hits me like a sledgehammer. I slept all night in Ruby's bedroom, naked in her bed, and now Eleanor is screaming.

Her voice is coming from down the hall where Lillie's room is.

"Shit!" I fall out of bed, searching for my clothes.

Ruby is wearing a tee and jerking pink sweatpants over her naked body as she yells. "Eleanor! What's wrong? What's happening?"

She flies out of the room, and I follow her, quickly shoving my legs into my pajama pants, panic rising faster than my breath.

I'm nearly blind by the time I burst into my daughter's room, and what I see there almost sends me slamming to the wall.

Lillie is sitting in her bed crying. Her face, her arms, her sheets, her entire bed is covered in splatters of deep red liquid. It looks like blood.

"Jesus, what happened? Lillie?" I try to get to her.

My daughter is wailing and Eleanor is ripping back blankets and sheets. The scene is utter chaos.

"Lillie!" Eleanor stands over her, grasping her arms and searching her body for wounds. Lillie's face is beet read, and she's bawling.

Ruby pushes right in the middle of the melee, snatching my daughter's arm from her grandmother. Then she does the unthinkable. She lifts it to her face and touches it with her tongue.

"Ruby, no!" I shout watching her taste what looks like blood. My throat closes, and I think I might vomit.

"It's okay!" Ruby holds up her hands, her face melting into relief. Lillie is still crying, but Ruby scoops her out of the messy bed. "It's ketchup! It's only ketchup."

"Ketchup?" I collapse against the wall trying to get my heart started again.

"Thank the Lord… Lillian Alexandra, you almost gave me a heart attack!"

The sheets are a red-stained mess, and only then do I notice the three little white foil packets in the middle of the nightmare. *Fucking ketchup?*

"I don't understand." My voice is ragged. I feel like I've run a marathon. "How did she get them—"

Unfortunately, it's at that very moment Eleanor sees what I'm wearing and seems to connect the dots. "Were you just…" She looks from me to the door then back at me again. "Did you just come from Ruby's bedroom?"

"Eleanor, I can explain."

"No." Her hands go up in a halting motion, and she shakes her head violently. "No no no. This will not go on in my presence."

"If you'll just let me explain." Actually, I'm not sure what I'm explaining. It's my fucking house.

239

Her rant continues. "I will not live this way, Remington. I draw the line here. I will not live in a house of sin. If this is what goes on, we are going to have to find another deal. You cannot have sex with an employee."

I hope the noise of the running faucet drowns out what she's saying. Eleanor is ranting and storming around the room with her hands in the air.

Just then the water shuts off, and I hear Ruby speaking gently. "Stop crying now. Use that cloth and wash all the ketchup off your face. I'll be back to wash your hair."

She enters the room and goes to the dresser. She doesn't even look at Eleanor, who's now glaring holes in her back as if she were the Whore of Babylon.

"I'll wash her hair then start these sheets first thing in the morning. She can sleep with me tonight." Ruby holds up little girl panties and a nightgown. "Good thing we had a waterproof mattress cover on the bed. I'm afraid we'll probably have to toss these. Ketchup stains never wash out…"

Her voice dies when she finally looks up and sees Eleanor's glaring eyes about to pop out of her head.

Ruby looks from her to me. "What's happening now?"

To her credit, my mother in law steps closer and lowers her voice. "Was Remington sleeping in your bedroom just now?"

Ruby's mouth drops open, and her cheeks blaze red.

I've had enough of the theatrics. "That's really none of your business. What Ruby and I do on our own time is our concern."

Lillie's grandmother stiffens her back, tugging on the front of her robe. "Ruby is your employee. She lives in this house. I will not have this… this… *fornication* going on just steps from my granddaughter."

"Jesus, take the wheel." Ruby exhales, putting her hands on her forehead. Her eyes squeeze shut, and she shakes her head rapidly. "You know what? You're right, Eleanor. You're absolutely right."

"Wait, what?" I step forward, not liking this turn of events one bit. "Ruby, what are you saying?"

"I was going to tell you in New York, but we were having such a good time—"

My shoulders are tight. "Tell me what?"

"I put a deposit on a house. It's right near the entrance of Oakville Estates, walking distance from here. Not that I would walk. Dagwood Magee's aunt actually owns it, and she said I could move in as soon as I'm ready."

"You're moving out?" I feel my control slipping.

"Good." Eleanor crosses her arms. "I'll help you pack."

"That won't be necessary." Ruby's eyes are fire until she turns to me.

When her eyes meet mine, they change to pleading. "I can't stay here, Remi. You know I'm right."

She steps closer, putting her hand on my arm, and I'm ready to argue until I hear my daughter sniffling from the bathroom.

"We'll talk about this tomorrow." My tone is firm. "After you take Lillie to preschool."

Eleanor starts to speak, but I shoot her a look that says *don't you dare.*

Her chin lifts, and she wraps her robe tighter around her body before stalking from the room as if she has a reason to be offended.

"Eleanor." I call after her, and she pauses in the

hallway outside the door. "I'll secure you a place in Eagleton Manor tomorrow. I want you out of my house by the end of the day."

Her lips part as if she's about to say something. I only shut Lillie's door in her face.

Chapter 27

Ruby

I don't expect to get much sleep after snuggling Lillie into bed with me. She sniffled all through her bath, and now with her little head resting on my chest, I can still feel her crying.

"Stop crying now, Lil." My voice is soothing and I pick at her damp curls with my fingertips. "You just scared us. That's all. It looked like you were bleeding."

"I just wanted to squeeze them. I didn't know they would pop." Her little body tenses against me, and her chin dips. "Gigi thinks I'm a bad girl."

I don't say what I'm thinking. *Gigi thinks everybody's a bad girl.*

Instead I give her a little hug. "She does not. She's your grandmother. She thinks you poop roses."

That turns the tears into giggles, at least for a moment. "Daddy won't get me a puppy now. I'm not re-sponsible."

She says the word slowly, as if she's sounding it out, and my lips press into a frown. "I think your daddy might have forgotten about the puppy. I'll remind him to think about it tomorrow."

"No! Don't remind him tomorrow. Wait til Saturday."

I suppose when you're four, one day makes a big difference. Too bad it's not that way for grown-ups.

"Okay, I'll wait. Now you have school tomorrow. We need to sleep."

She's quiet, and I continue playing with her soft curls, tracing my finger along her arm. My heart hurts thinking what I have to do. It's the first time in the three weeks I've been here she's actually needed me in the night. Now I have to leave her.

I can't help feeling like I'm abandoning her to the Wicked Witch of the West. Only... I guess the witch has been evicted. I wonder if Remi realizes what he's done. I fall asleep with a frown on my face, and by morning, Lillie's foot is under my chin, and I'm lying diagonally in the bed.

It's hard to believe I started the night blissed out in Remi's arms.

"Come on, butter bean. Time to get moving." I pick up the sleeping Lillie and carry her to her bedroom.

She lets out a little whine, but I get her started brushing her teeth. Then I lay out a cute little sack dress and leggings on her bare mattress. No sign of ketchup anywhere. Remi must have carried all the sheets downstairs after I took her to bed.

When we arrive in the kitchen, Lillie and I are both dressed for the day, and I'm surprised to see a plate of scrambled eggs, bacon, and toast waiting on the bar. Glancing around, I don't see anyone in the living room or the patio. I can't imagine Eleanor did this. She was shooting fire from her nostrils last night. *Dragon lady...* Stephen was right.

I scoop breakfast onto a plate for Lillie and put a mug in the Keurig before walking down the narrow hall to the laundry room. "Eat up, Lil. I'll just check on your sheets."

Rounding the corner, I almost bump straight into

Remi, who's holding a bottle of Spray and Wash and looking confused.

"Hey! Did you make breakfast?" I don't know why I feel awkward around him. After all we've shared, you'd think I'd start being comfortable.

Maybe the problem is all we've shared.

"Yeah, is it still warm? I wasn't sure how much sleep you got after last night." He seems worried, like it's not my job to take care of Lillie.

"I managed to get a few more hours. You?"

"Nah, I was pretty much done for after that." He returns to the bottle. "You said the sheets were probably ruined. I'm afraid you might be right. I treated them with this last night, but I can't tell if it's making much of a difference."

"Don't tell me you know your way around a laundry room." Teasing helps me relax a little.

I step around him to look at the white sheets covered in tiny drawings of a mermaid princess riding a unicorn.

"I'd hate for her to lose these. Do you remember where you got them? Maybe I could order her some more."

"No clue. I can check with Eleanor."

Glancing up at the clock, I pat his shoulder. "Let me know. I've got to take off or she'll be late for school. Just leave these. I'll tend to them when I get back. Maybe bleach will work."

Lillie is buckled in her booster chair in the backseat, and she sings all the way to school. I glance at her happy face in the mirror and shake my head thinking how quickly trouble is forgotten when you're four. I bypass the car line like always, parking instead in the lot and sweeping her out of the backseat.

Today I'm wearing a calf-length tweed skirt with a

black tee that says "What's Your Dream?" in white on the front. My hair is wrapped in a messy, low bun, and I carry Lillie's backpack along with my square leather purse on my arm. *Executive nanny.*

I'm surprised to see a cluster of moms in the hall outside Terry's class today. It's Friday, and I try to remember if the kids have a party I forgot... I don't remember anything, but it is the first day I've been here since Monday.

Shit. I chew my lip, hoping I haven't forgotten to bring something.

"Well, look who's back from the big city." Serena's voice is sharp as glass, but I don't acknowledge her.

Leaning down, I give Lillie a hug and a kiss before sending her into class. "Say hi to purple monster number four for me."

She takes off running. I hang her little backpack on a hook inside the door and give her teacher a wave before heading back into the hall where the bitch patrol is waiting.

Serena stands expectantly after her jab. I don't know what she's getting at with her statement or how she even knows where I was, and I'm not interested in finding out.

"Good morning, Serena." I speak quickly, doing my best to make my way around them and not engage.

"I noticed Eleanor bringing Lillie to school these last few days. I thought you'd finally turned in your resignation. Seems I was wrong." Her tone is like nails on a chalkboard. "Seems somebody got herself a promotion."

"I accompanied Remi on a business trip, not that it's any of your concern. He needed a plus one."

"Is that what they're calling it these days?" Anita Flagstaff places her hand on her chest—I'm sure to put her Birkin bag on full display. "Seems not too long ago they simply called it an escort."

"I suppose it's the same deal. He pays her. She provides the service." Serena turns her back to me, but she's speaking loud enough for me to hear. "If Phillip thinks he's hiring a nanny like *that*, he's got another thing coming."

Sarcasm drips from her tone when she says the words, and a bitter taste fills my mouth. My throat goes dry, and I'm worried I might gag. For the first time, instead of blushing beet red, I feel the blood rushing from my face, as if a spotlight was shined straight on me, and I was standing in front of them all butt naked.

I don't speak. I simply walk fast toward the door.

Serena calls after me, something about how changing names and labels doesn't change the meaning. I walk faster. My vision blurs, but I order myself not to cry. I will not let her get to me ever again.

Driving home, I can barely see the road for the tears blurring my vision. First Eleanor, now those bitches. God, it's all over the whole fucking town. Everyone knows I went with him to New York. How can I possibly deny what's happening between us? Clearly the monster-in-law isn't keeping her big mouth shut.

Leaving Lillie stabs at my heart like knives, but somehow, the thought of leaving Remi hurts even worse. Pain radiates across my shoulder blades, and I almost have to pull over. I'm so close to the house or I would.

Lifting my cell, I tap Marsha Magee's number. She answers at once, and I quickly work out the details of moving into her small rental house this weekend.

My next call is to Drew.

"Hey, Cinderella! How'd it go at the ball? I want to hear all about it. Don't leave out a single detail."

I blink and rivers of tears coat my cheeks. I swallow, but my voice wavers. "You think Gray might be able to help me move this weekend? I need a truck."

Drew's tone changes at once. "Ruby! Are you okay? It sounds like you're crying. What happened? Talk to me."

"I will. I just can't do it right now." Blinking up to the sky, I try to get control of myself. "I just need you to help me get settled, help me get my bed and furniture from Ma's. Then I'll tell you everything."

"We'll be there."

Chapter 28

Remi

Ruby takes longer than I expect to get home. I'm pacing in my office, chewing my thumb when I hear the front door open. Dashing out onto the landing, my stomach tightens when I see her face. She looks different, like she's been crying.

"Ruby?" She blinks up at me as if I startled her, and I gentle my tone. "Hey, sorry. Would you mind coming up here for a minute?"

She's dressed in business attire, a green leather purse on her arm, and she hurries up the stairs, looking so professional. Taking care of my daughter is demanding and important work. Still, I can't help knowing Ruby could do anything she wants. She's smart and capable and so pretty.

When she enters the large space, I motion for her to follow me to where a sofa and chairs are arranged. I envisioned this being a conference area of sorts, should I have any potential clients to the house.

She doesn't waste any time. "Remi, we need to talk."

"First." I take the long business envelope off my desk. "It's the first time I've been able to give this to you in person and thank you. After last night—"

"What..." Her voice fades out as she takes the envelope and looks inside.

I'm standing back feeling pretty proud of myself. "I included a little extra to cover our trip to New York. I know you had to buy a dress and shoes... I'm sure there were expenses."

"You added... cash." The color drains from her face, and my feelings of pride fade along with it. "New York was just a business trip to you?"

A knot is in my throat, and I feel like I've misread something. "No... I mean, yes, it was a business trip, but—"

She interrupts me talking fast. "If anything, I would've expected you to pay me less for this week, considering we spent three days..." Her voice breaks off. "Doing what? What were we doing, Remi?"

Her eyes flash anger at me, but I see tears gathering in them. It's like a knife plunged straight into my heart. Stepping forward, I try to gather her into my arms.

"No!" She pushes me away hard. "What was it? I want to know."

She's trembling and I don't know what to say. New York started as a business trip... Hell, it was always because of business, but having her with me gave me the strength to believe again. She believes in me, and it makes me believe in myself.

She brought me back to life.

I try to find the right words to say. My insides are a hot mess of feelings and thoughts and details I have to sort out. It's all a tangle in my head, and I realize now I've taken too long to answer her question.

Her hand goes up, and she pushes me away. "I don't have time for any more men and their games. I'm sick of it. I'm sick of you."

She throws the envelope at me, and I scoop it up, chasing after her, up the stairs to the third floor.

"Ruby, wait. I didn't mean to insult you." I follow her down the hall, and she's moving fucking fast. "We talked about all of this before you came here, and you were fine with it. Hell, you seemed happy with the arrangement."

"Yeah, I was." She jerks open the drawers of her dresser and starts taking out her clothes. She tosses them on the bed and goes the closet, where she pulls out her suitcase.

"What are you doing?"

"I'm moving out. We discussed this last night."

"Like hell we did." Anger blazes in my chest, and I snatch the suitcase off her bed. "You're not going anywhere."

Her anger is back, flashing in her eyes. "Give me my suitcase."

I relent and put it on her bed again. She immediately resumes throwing clothes in it.

"Why are you doing this? Aren't you happy here?" It feels like a childish question, but I'm so fucking confused. I thought things were going great — better than great. I thought she cared about me. I thought she and I were on the verge of becoming something more.

"Am I happy here?" She stops slamming her clothes in the black case. "I was. Until people like Eleanor started calling me a whore. Until Serena North basically called me a high-class hooker in front of everybody at the preschool today."

Fire roars in my chest. I didn't know it was possible to feel this level of rage. "What did she say to you?" My jaw is clenched, and the words are more of a growl.

"Stop." Ruby holds up her hands. "I would argue with them if I had a leg to stand on. As it is..." She shakes her head. "I've turned into exactly what they think I am."

"You are nothing of the sort." My voice is still growly. "I'll shut every one of their stupid mouths. I'll—"

"Remi…" Her voice is just below a shout. "Don't you see they're right?"

"I do not see they're right. I don't give a damn about those women or what they say or think."

"But I do."

I'm stunned by her quiet confession. "You do? But… Why?"

I'm confused and grasping at anything. I feel like my world is crumbling, and her mind is completely made up. I feel like she's slammed an invisible door in my face and nothing I can say or do will get her to let me in.

I can't make her stay, and it's ripping out my heart. It's tearing up my insides. I need her.

She resumes filling her suitcase, only slower. "I don't care as much about *me* or my reputation. I care about my mom and how hard she works taking care of the seniors at church. I care about Lillie and the kids at preschool repeating what their parents say to her, or talking behind her back. She might not understand it now, but one day she will." Ruby's breath hiccups, and my heart breaks. "I care about you and what people say about you."

"Fuck what they say." I can't stand this. "What can I do?"

"Nothing." She puts the last of her folded clothes in the suitcase. "I'm moving out. That's it."

"You signed a contract. As Lillie's nanny, you're contractually obligated to live in this house." I say it mostly as a joke, as a way to lighten the soul-crushing pain in my chest.

"I have to resign as Lillie's nanny."

"No..." It's the final straw. I feel like she's bringing me to my knees. "Lillie loves you."

Her hands cover her face, and she nods quickly as her shoulders shake. When she speaks, her voice goes high. "I know."

I can't stand it anymore. I close the space between us, pulling her into my arms. "You can't leave us. You have to stay."

Her hands are on my arms at once, moving them away and stepping out of my embrace. "I'm sorry." She clears her throat, getting her voice under control. "I'll explain to her why I have to go."

"What will you say?"

"I don't know. I'll think of something."

"Ruby, please. Tell me what I can do to fix this."

Her chin lifts, and her dark eyes meet mine. They're so open and vulnerable, so deep and soulful. It breaks my heart. I wait for her to say anything, to tell me what she wants.

She waits a moment longer. Then she breaks our gaze.

"I'll pick up Lillie from school. You can let Eleanor know I won't be having dinner here tonight."

Chapter 29

Ruby

Life has a funny way of changing our plans.

Lillie had only been home five minutes before she went to the bathroom and immediately started wailing. I'd intended to tell her what was happening over lunch, now I'm in her pink bathroom holding her in my arms.

"Ruby!" She's sobbing, and I cover my mouth and nose at the stench.

"Oh! Oh no." It's the best I've got.

Her little leggings and white undies are on the bathroom floor soiled.

"My butt threw up." Her voice is so small and weak.

I grab the shower curtain, ripping it open again. "It's okay, baby. It's going to be okay."

My heart breaks a little bit when I see how miserable she is, knowing she had a shitty night's sleep last night and knowing what's coming. What I have to tell her.

It'll have to wait.

"Here." I help her wipe, feeling the fever radiating off her little body.

I quickly strip off my skirt and lift her into my arms, stepping into the shower as I hold her against my chest. Her little arms are around my neck, and she whimpers softly.

The water is warm and soothing, and I let it wash the filth away, using a washcloth to help with the bits I can't see.

I stroke her hair as we stand under the spray. "It's going to be okay, baby. Everything's going to be okay."

We stay in the water about a minute longer as I make sure I've gotten all the dirt off her bottom. Then I shut it off and grab a fluffy towel off the rack. Standing her in front of me, I dry her gently. Her hands are on my shoulders, and her eyes are closed. She's flushed and feverish, and I wrap her up tight before carrying her into her bedroom.

She's dressed and tucked in her bed, and I quickly gather her dirty things in the towel I used to dry her. I dash to my room and change clothes then start another load of laundry before I grab the ibuprofen, saltines, sprite, and a banana.

I'm just guessing over here.

When I make it back to her bedroom, she's lying on her side, her big eyes hollow and tired. I help her up and give her a dose of children's ibuprofen for the fever. Then I climb in beside her, cuddling her against my chest.

"Are any of your other friends feeling bad today?"

"Bunny wasn't at school." Her voice is slow and weak. "Louie said she has a bug. I thought he made her eat dirt when I wasn't around. She lives by his house."

"I think Louie meant she had a virus. Some people call viruses bugs. I don't know why."

Lillie sniffs and scrubs her face on my shirt.

"I was thinking about the ketchups today," I start. She makes a little noise and tucks her head closer to me, hiding her eyes. "They make these things called stress balls. You squeeze them when you feel stressed out, and it's supposed to make you feel better. It might be a great alternative to those packets. What do you think? Want me to get you one?"

She's quiet a minute. "What's stress?"

"It's bad feelings you get when you can't control things. Or maybe too many things are happening at the same time, and you feel overwhelmed."

Again she's quiet, thinking. "I don't like to feel stress."

"Nobody does. It's like those dolls with the beady eyes. They always stress me out." I exaggerate my tone, hoping to cheer her up.

"Or Veggie Tales."

"Yeah…" I'm encouraged she's playing along. The ibuprofen must be working. "Or Thomas the Tank Engine. Talk about beady eyes!"

She starts to giggle. "Or Gigi's clock when it says ten."

I confess, I'm stumped by that one. "What happens when it says ten?"

"It has all those eyes."

Ah… it's a digital clock. Interesting. "You have a vivid imagination, Lil. I'll be sure and never get you an American Girl doll."

She snorts and I turn on the television, finding a princess movie on Netflix. Halfway through, she's getting droopy. She wraps a little arm around my waist and yawns. "I wish I had eyes like you. I think you're beautiful."

Leaning down, I kiss her button nose. "I think you're beautiful. Sleep now angel."

She's asleep curled against my side, and I'm watching the second half of *Mulan* when a soft tapping sounds on the door. I look up to see Remi peeking his head in. His expression is worried or maybe anxious.

"How's she doing?"

"Her fever broke. I think it's just a twenty-four-hour virus." He nods, and I have an idea. "Do you happen to have an extra stress ball?"

Those dark brows furrow over his pretty eyes, and inwardly I sigh. He's so handsome.

"I might. Why?"

"I think the reason she likes to play with ketchup packets is the same reason you like squeezing a stress ball. It's soothing."

He exhales, dropping his chin. "She scared the shit out of me this morning. This whole day has been just one hit after another."

"Tell me about it." I look down at the little angel holding my waist. Her face is so peaceful.

My eyes are still on her when Remi touches my shoulder. Our eyes meet, and his are anguished. "Don't go, Ruby..." It's a tortured whisper, and my heart jumps in my chest. "She needs you."

Then it fizzles right back down again.

She needs me.

Say you need me, Remi... You.

Say you'll make me yours...

I swallow that emotion away. "Not living here doesn't mean I won't see her anymore."

His brow furrows, and he scrubs his eyes with his fingertips. "Will you at least stay on as her nanny until I can find a replacement?"

The idea of being replaced should not offend me. "What's wrong with Eleanor?"

She started this whole thing, after all.

"I don't want her involved. I don't like how she treated you. I don't like how she treated either of us."

Lifting my chin, I give him a nod. "I'll help with Lillie until you find someone."

258

"Thanks." His expression is dark and he stands slowly, leaning down to kiss his daughter before he leaves.

He pauses on the way up, hovering with his lips just over mine. My heart beats painfully hard in my chest. I hold my breath until he stands completely. Without another word, he goes to the door and leaves us.

I lean back on the pillows as the tears streak down my cheeks.

Chapter 30

Remi

It's a punch in the chest to see Ruby holding my daughter so sweetly, taking care of her when she's sick, making her laugh and slowly helping her regain her strength.

I might not be sure of her feelings for me, but I know she loves Lillie.

It takes her less than half an hour to clear her things out of her room. My daughter follows her whining the whole time, but Ruby assures her repeatedly she's not far away. She'll be back every day to drive her to school and to spend the afternoons.

My daughter's tears are like salt in my already bleeding insides. Everything about this is wrong, but short of tying Ruby up with ropes, I don't know how to make her stay.

Before she walks out, I put my hand on her shoulder. "I took out the extra cash for New York." I give her the business envelope, and she looks at it a few moments. "You did the work as Lillie's nanny. You deserve to be paid."

Her lips press together and she nods, taking the envelope from me. "I'll be here Monday morning to take her to preschool."

"I can take her in the mornings. What if you pick her up and stay with her during the afternoons until dinner?"

She lifts her chin and our eyes meet. Our chemistry is still alive, but it's tantalizing pain, like the promise of something I desperately want held just out of reach.

"I'm doing half the work. You should adjust my pay to reflect that."

"Whatever makes you comfortable."

It's our last exchange before she's gone. I scoop up my daughter, and she lays her head on my shoulder, squeezing the striped stress ball I found in one of my drawers.

"Feeling stressed-out, peanut?"

"Why did Ruby have to go?"

"She felt like it would be better for all of us if she didn't live here anymore."

Lillie lifts her head and looks me in the eyes. "I don't think it's better for me if she's not here anymore. Do you think it's better?"

"No, princess. I don't think it's better at all."

My daughter wiggles to get down, and I set her on her feet. She walks slowly with her little shoulders slumped to the patio, and I climb the flight of stairs to my office with the same posture. This big ole house feels too huge, too empty now.

Eleanor left on Friday. I would feel guilty about it, but she moved quickly into the condo I secured for her. I almost feel like she expected it. Or she welcomed it. I don't really care.

I've communicated briefly with her on her requests to see Lillie. I'm furious at her, but I don't want to hurt my daughter. So far, I agreed she can pick Lillie up for church tomorrow morning. I don't feel much like attending.

Standing in front of my computer I see unread

emails from Stellan. A few more emails wait from Stephen and a rising entrepreneur he thinks I should meet. I hover my mouse over them and think about work and why I'm doing all of this.

All these feelings and things I want to say to Ruby churn in my stomach. It all came to a head this past week.

She's not interested in my money. She's not interested in what I can give her. She likes me for me, and we have so much fun together. She makes me feel alive. I feel like I can trust her—not to mention how much I love seeing her with my daughter.

Picking up my phone, I tap the face of my old friend.

"Hastings here." He speaks through an exhale.

"I have a situation and I need a sounding board."

"Something happen with Stellan?" A tone enters his voice. "That kid was totally onboard the last time I talked to him. If you did something to piss him off—"

"It's not about Stellan. It's… personal."

"I don't do personal."

"You'll do it for me. I'm pissed and I'm tired and I feel fucking powerless."

"You are never powerless. If something appears out of your control, you need to step back and reframe the situation." He speaks like some old guru. "Unless it's a woman. Then you're probably powerless."

"Ruby left me."

He's quiet a beat. "And?"

"That's it. She packed up all her things and moved out this morning. Just like that." I'm pacing my office, snatching up a stress ball and squeezing the shit out of it.

"Did she say why?"

"Some bitches at the preschool made a crack about

her attending the gala with me. It made her feel like I was paying her… for her time."

Stephen doesn't need to know everything.

"You *were* paying her for her time. Her time spent with *your daughter*."

The distinction makes me cringe. I played right into their stupid accusations putting the extra cash in with her check. I thought I was being generous. Now I realize how it made her feel.

He makes an impatient growl. "Do you care about this woman or not?"

It's such a straightforward question. I step back, walking to the balcony, looking down over the patio where she spent so many afternoons with Lillie. Every day, I'd step outside and watch them paint or work in the garden or sing songs or just blow bubbles. It soothed my soul to know she was there. It was like a part of me that was missing had been found.

"Yes." It's so easy. "It didn't matter. I asked her to stay, and she still left."

"Did you tell her you wanted her to stay?"

Now I make the impatient growl. "It's the same thing. I asked her to stay."

"It is not the same thing, and I'm sure you framed it as being for Lillie."

"Of course, I mentioned Lillie." Remorse flashes in my neck. How could she not understand how much I wanted her to stay?

A long sigh fills my ear. "If you want her to stay, tell her. If you care about her, ask her on a date, propose to her. Marry the girl. Whatever is in your heart. Just stop making it harder than it is."

"That's what she said."

"What?"

I can't help it. It's so easy.

"Thanks, man. I owe you."

"Damn straight you do. Now go fucking get her and stop wasting my time."

"Fuck off. I have a woman to claim."

He chuckles and we disconnect the phone. I'm a problem-solver. Why didn't I figure this out before now? Rubbing my chin, I'm stumped. What do I do with Lillie?

Chapter 31

Ruby

Drew sits beside me on the bed rubbing my back.

After unpacking all my things last night, I opened a bottle of wine, drank most of it, then crawled beneath my covers and fell asleep. I opened my eyes a few times once the sun came up, but all I want to do is stay under the covers and cry.

"He tried to pay me extra for New York. In *cash*." I sniff, my chest squeezing with the ache of a broken heart.

"He didn't say it meant more to him?" Drew is wearing church clothes, leaning against my headboard while I stay under the covers.

"He didn't say anything," I wail.

"Men are bastards." She shoves a tissue under the blanket, and I take it to blow my nose. "Not you, honey."

The way she says it makes me crawl a little higher and peep out. I see Grayson leaning against the doorjamb looking down. His hand is in his pocket, and he looks like something out of a men's magazine.

"I didn't know Gray was here."

"We came straight over from church. Your mom was worried about you when you didn't show up today."

"I couldn't sit in church with those bitches." I sit

up, wrapping my comforter around my shoulders. "They pretty much flat out called me a hooker."

"Don't even think about those women." Drew pulls me into a hug. "You're going to come work for me now."

Shaking my head, I blow my nose again. "I can't go back to the clinic. I feel like such a failure. I was supposed to be getting financially independent. I was supposed to be finding out who I am. Instead I fell in love with him." More tears fill my eyes. "I'm such an idiot."

"To be fair, you were kind of already into him when you took the job." She reaches for the box of Puffs and hands me another one.

"You're always so logical." My nose makes a loud honk when I blow it. "It's why you're a better therapist than me."

"I thought you said being a good therapist made me a doormat." Her blue eyes narrow, and my stomach plunges like a rock.

"I was so wrong to say that. I take it back. You're the best friend a person could ever have. I'm so lucky to have you." I throw my arms around her shoulders, and when she hugs me back, I start to cry again.

"Okay, we're getting out of the house now. Come on." She grabs my arms and drags me to the side of the bed.

"I can't go out looking like this."

"Then let's head to the showers."

She's holding my arm, and I let her drag me out of bed, past the longsuffering Gray. "I have beer in the fridge if you want one. I bought all the alcohol so I could get good and drunk last night."

"Is this what you were drinking?" He holds up a mostly full bottle of red wine.

I frown, looking around my bedroom. "Is that all I drank?"

He starts to chuckle. "Take it easy, lightweight."

Pushing off the door, he goes into the kitchen. I follow Drew into my bathroom.

The rental house is actually pretty cute. It's a perfect square with the bedroom and dining area separated by a full bathroom. The living room is adjacent to my bedroom and the kitchen is attached to it. It has nice flow and an open floor plan.

It's just so lonely.

"It's so quiet here at night." Drew's in the bathroom with me, and I sit on the closed toilet watching as she turns on the shower, testing the temperature through the curtain. "I miss people. I'm not used to living alone."

"You've been in this house less than twenty-four hours. How do you even know?"

"I should get a pet. A puppy… Lillie would love that! I'll take her with me to get one tomorrow."

Drew steps back and takes my hand. "Get up. The water's ready. I'm going to send Gray home. Can you give me a ride?"

"Sure." I nod, stepping into the warm spray.

I'm showered, lightly made up, and my hair's brushed as we walk through the craft store.

"First, we can get started fixing up your little house. What color should we paint it?"

"You can't paint anything. You're pregnant." I'm pushing a cart past stretched canvases and acrylics.

It sends my mind traveling back a month ago to something I read on the Internet. "Since I already have my master's and my license, I only need a few classes to add Art Therapy to my list of services."

Drew stops in the aisle. "Could you do it in a

group setting?"

"I don't see why not." I pull two canvases off the rack and put them in my cart. Next I pick up a few different tubes of maroon paint, holding them together in the light.

I select the darker one, then I take a white, brown, and navy tube from the bin. "In the meantime, I want to start painting again. I have something in mind."

"See?" Drew is right beside me, giving me a squeeze. "You just needed to get out of that bed and start moving around. You already know who you are and what you want. It's just about doing it."

Nodding, I steer the cart to the checkout area. I still feel like a heavy weight is sitting on my chest, making it difficult to breathe.

"I'll see about getting registered for those courses tonight."

Drew and I also swing by the grocery store, we check in with my mother, and it's late when I'm alone again in my little house. I'm standing in front of the stove in my sweats and a cropped sweatshirt with my hair in a high ponytail.

I imagine I look like Barbie's Asian best friend Midge, confused in front of the stove because she doesn't know how to cook.

If only I had Barbie money.

And Barbie perks.

"Then I'd have a chef." I hold my phone reading the recipe for Black Bean Breakfast Bowl.

It sounds simple enough. A can of black beans, scrambled eggs, avocado slices, and salsa. How hard can that be? Hell, even Eleanor might approve of this dinner.

Setting my phone down, I crack the first egg imitating Tessa's voice. "Free range chicken eggs and organic black beans." Picking up the can, I don't see organic anywhere on the Bush's label. "Oh, well, Jake. I guess we'll have to hope for the best with these avocados."

As I drain the beans, my mind drifts to those dinners, Remi sitting across the table in his blazer and tee. He was always so handsome, so refined. Lillie usually said something funny about the meal or had some silly story from preschool. Pain twists in my stomach as I think about how much I miss them.

My eyes are misty, and I'm cracking Egg 2 when a rapid knock on my door makes me squeal and toss it across the counter. It falls with a splat on the floor, and I spin, putting my back to the counter and scanning the kitchen quickly for anything I can use as a weapon.

I snatch a carving knife out of the drawer. Ma gave it to me because it needs sharpening, but that doesn't stop it from looking scary.

Tiptoeing to the front door, my heart is beating out of my chest. Why am I so freaked out by someone knocking on my door at night? I'm in freakin' Oakville. Nothing ever happens here. This is what happens when I watch serial killer documentaries on Netflix.

I put my shoulder to the wall right beside the door and sneak a peek through the shade. My breath catches, and I drop the knife when I see Remi standing there.

He's steps from the door on the porch, and his hand is behind his neck. He looks like he might have jogged over here. He's all sweaty and sexy, and my mind flies to that night in the kitchen when he kissed me.

Grab the reins, Ruby.

Turning the lock, I open the door for him, scooting the knife out of sight with my foot. "Remi? What are you doing here?"

More importantly, who's watching Lillie?

His pretty eyes lighten when he sees me, and he takes a half-step forward. "Hey." His voice is slightly breathless and so sexy. "Sorry for just barging over. I was thinking I should have texted first or something. I hope I didn't scare you."

"Oh, no. Why should I be scared in Oakville?" I do a fake chuckle. So fake.

"I was just thinking about yesterday and Friday and how everything went down." He clears his throat. "So much shit was happening from the gala to the ketchup scare to the moving out business. I think we had a massive miscommunication."

I shift on my bare feet, crossing my arms at my waist. Remi's eyes flicker down to my breasts, and the way his lips press together makes my panties hot. It's like he's thinking about kissing me... And my whole entire body wants that to happen. *Yes, please.*

"A miscommunication?" I focus my brain.

"I'm sorry for not realizing how that extra money made you feel. In no way did I think of it as any sort of payment for your time... I just wanted to do something nice for you."

His eyes are pained, and I can tell he's struggling with getting this right. It melts my heart to see him so sincere.

"Apology accepted." My voice is quiet, and I give him a little smile.

"Ruby..." He steps forward on that nugget of encouragement. "I came here to ask you... Would you consider going out with me?"

"Like on a date?"

"Yes. Go to dinner with me."

I rub my forehead, trying to think. "I don't know if

that's a good idea."

His expression collapses, and I see something like frustration and anger bubbling beneath the surface. It's a teensy bit scary and a whole lot sexy.

"Why not?"

"First, don't shout at me... Second, why do you think I moved out?"

"I didn't shout." His jaw is clenched, and he's a little growly. "I thought you moved out so we could date without people making rude insinuations — because you care what these assholes think, and I don't."

Okay.

"I moved out because too many lines were getting crossed. Things were getting muddled, and you have a little girl to consider."

He exhales deeply and turns, looking out at the street a moment before turning back to me. "So you're saying you won't date me while you're Lillie's nanny?"

"I don't think it's a good idea."

"Is that a no? Is that really what you want, Ruby?" The crack in his voice breaks my heart.

"Not really... I just. I think it's too soon to have this conversation. I think we need to give it some time." My hand is on my stomach, and I instinctively rub the pain there. "When I started you said you needed to focus on your work. Maybe we both need to take a step back and think about what we really want."

His arms drop, and he pivots toward the street. "I have to go. I was just out jogging, and I needed to say these things. I wanted to be sure you know how I feel."

"Who's watching Lillie?"

"Eleanor's at the house. I expect she'll want to leave when I get back."

Nodding, I swallow the lump in my throat. "I'll

see you tomorrow."

"Afternoon." He does a little wave and jogs off into the night.

I stand and watch him go until I can't see him anymore. Then I slowly close the door and pick up the knife. I'm not in the mood for black beans anymore.

Chapter 32

Ruby

I pick up Lillie in the car line for the first time ever since I've been her nanny. Not because I don't want to face the Mean Moms—I'm not that big of a wuss—but because I got a text from Drew as I was leaving the house.

Dotty's neighbor has free puppies. Miniature Schnoodles!

Just reading the word makes my insides feel happy. I can't resist texting back, **Bless you! Now, Miniature whats?**

Her reply is the laugh-crying emoji, and I'm bouncing in my seat waiting for Lillie. I called the school and asked them to send her to the car line, and while I'm waiting, I shoot a quick text to Remi. *Important errand to run. Taking Lillie with me. Exciting day!*

Remi texts me back with the okay just as the back door opens and Lillie climbs in with all her things. She looks a little sleepy, and I reach back to hold her hand.

"How are you doing, butter bean? Feeling tired?" She does a little shrug, and I can't stand it anymore. "Want to go look at some puppies with me?"

That changes everything. "For me?"

"What if..." I turn the car toward Dotty's house. "What if I get a puppy for you, and it lives at my house?"

She presses her little lips together looking to the side. "Would I get to see it every day?"

"Yes! You could see it every day after school. We can go to my house and play with it, and maybe, if your daddy says it's okay, we can take it to your house sometimes too."

"Okay!" She starts bouncing in her seat. "Let's get a puppy!"

"It gets even better." We're pulling into Dotty's driveway, and I kill the engine, giving her my most excited look. "These puppies are called Miniature Schnoodles!"

Her little mouth drops open. "What?"

"Let's go see them!"

She jumps out of her booster seat, and I grab her hand. We both take off jogging across the lawn to knock on the door.

It's pretty much love at first sight when we see the box of three apricot puppies with their curly coats and happy little faces. Lillie tries to hold all three at once. She squeals and sits down, and one starts licking her face while the other grabs her pigtail and plays with it like a chew toy. Finally, she gives up and lays flat on her back as the puppies jump all over her.

Janet stands back grinning with her arms crossed. "You taking all three of them?"

That makes me laugh. "No. We'll just get one. It's going to be a hard choice."

We hang out a little while watching Lillie roll around in puppy heaven until finally, I make the call. "We've got to pick one, butter bean. Which do you like the best?"

Her mouth presses into a frown, and I'm afraid she might cry. Janet hops in and saves the day.

"I've got a little boy coming by later today. He's been wanting one of these guys, so you'd better pick the one you like best."

Lillie's eyes go round. "Is his name Louie?"

I swallow a laugh, and Janet pretends to think about it. "No… I think his name is Nicholas."

"That's good." She lets out a little exhale and returns to the small reddish dogs.

One has returned to the box and is rooting around in the blankets. Another has gone to the food bowl. Only one stands by her feet as if waiting to see what she'll do next.

"Him!" Lillie reaches down and picks up the small dog. "We'll call him Buddy."

"He might not be a boy…"

Janet scoops the little dog up and checks its bottom. "Buddy it is!" She presents him to me and walks to her kitchen. "I have their vaccination records I can give you."

"Are you sure you're giving them away for free? These guys are normally kind of expensive."

Janet only waves a hand. "Everybody's got a dog in Oakville. Nobody's going to buy one."

I don't want to argue her out of a deal, so I just agree. "Let's go, Lillie and Buddy."

Lillie holds the dog in her arms like a baby, and he puts his puppy head on her shoulder. It's the most adorable thing I've seen since… pretty much ever.

I put her in the booster chair and take a blanket out of my trunk. "Wrap him in this just in case he pees. He's probably never been in a car before."

"He won't pee, will you Buddy?" She's talking to him in her little sing-song voice, and I make the short drive to my house.

Fortunately, I have a fenced in backyard, and we spend the rest of the afternoon deciding where Buddy should sleep. I decide I'll have to buy a large kennel until he's house broken.

"We have to train him to use the bathroom outside." I'm on my laptop reading all about the breed. "He's supposed to be a very smart dog, so hopefully it won't take too long."

"I love him." Lillie is in the middle of my bed with her new baby, and as I research, both of them curl up together and fall asleep.

I cover them with a thin blanket and walk out to my dining room where I've set up an easel. I started a painting on the canvas I bought yesterday. At the moment it's just line sketches, but I plan to make it my version of Gustav Klimt's "Mother and Sleeping Child."

In my version, I want the mother to have distinctively Asian features, and I want the child to have golden curls and sweet green-hazel eyes.

I'm just laying down the eggshell background when I hear a knock on my door. This time I'm not terrified. I'm pretty confident I know who it is. He always liked to watch us playing together as if it gave him back something he'd lost.

I miss having him above us, looking down.

Opening the door, he glances up and gives me that panty-melting smile. "Can I see what all the excitement is about?"

"Of course." I reach out and clasp his hand. He threads our fingers immediately, and it feels so good. "Be quiet."

His eyes travel quickly around my small house as I lead him to my bedroom. He pauses a beat to study the painting, but I give him a gentle tug. Finally, he joins me outside my door, and for a minute we both stand watching Lillie lying on her side with Buddy curled up right beside her.

"Oh, man." Remi's voice is so warm. "That's the cutest thing ever."

"He's a Miniature Schnoodle. Lillie named him Buddy."

"A Schnoodle?"

Turning quickly, I launch into the speech. "Don't worry, he can stay here at my house, and I told Lillie she could come and see him as much as she wants—"

"Hey," Remi holds up a hand just in front of my lips. "It's okay. Whatever you want is fine with me."

Warm hands drop to my waist, and he pulls me closer. "Thank you for being so sweet to her."

My lips press, and I want to kiss him so bad.

I'm staring at his mouth when he speaks again. "I'd like to kiss you, too, but I'm afraid it might violate your rule... the one where we're supposed to be thinking about what we want."

I'm thinking about it... I'm leaning closer when a little voice interrupts our moment.

"Daddy!" Lillie sits up in the bed and we step apart. "Look what Ruby got for me! It's a puppy! His name is Buddy. He's a Schnoodle."

Remi gives me a smile and a light squeeze before going to his daughter. "I think Buddy is amazing. I've never heard of a Schnoodle."

"Isn't that a funny word for a dog?"

Buddy wakes up and starts hopping all around. "Lillie! He probably needs to pee. Let's get him outside, quick!"

She jumps up and runs with him to the back door. Remi and I trail behind her, watching as she walks around the small backyard talking to her little companion in the growing twilight.

"It feels right, doesn't it?"

Remi's voice is so full of love, it's like warm liquid in my veins.

I couldn't agree more.

Chapter 33

Remi

Lillie spends every afternoon at Ruby's house now that Buddy is in the picture, and I get daily updates of his house-breaking habits, how my daughter is teaching him to sit, roll over, speak.

According to Lillie, he speaks a lot.

According to Ruby, he's a smart little dog who's very good with children.

According to me, this is all fucking amazing.

We're like a new little family slowly forming.

Far too slowly forming if you ask me. Still, I hold back. I'm giving Ruby the time she needs to think.

Every day when I pick Lillie up before dinner, I can see the progress of Ruby's painting. She's added dark navy and maroon poppies around the border. The background is eggshell, with perfectly square brush strokes creating a pattern. The brushwork in the child's hair is so meticulous and loving, and the strokes down the mother's back... It's brilliant.

I'm not an art critic, but Ruby is fucking fantastic.

She's taking online courses to add art therapy to her skill set, and even though we're apart, she tells me about it while I wait for Lillie to tell Buddy goodnight when I pick her up.

It takes a half hour for my daughter to be sure *her* dog (who only lives at Ruby's house, she notes) knows she loves him and she'll be back again tomorrow.

I can't help thinking if this dog is really so smart, he's already figured it out.

Driving home, Lillie usually dozes, but tonight, she's unusually vocal. "Daddy, when you were in preschool, were there mean boys?"

I assume this is more Louie bullshit. "Yeah, they usually tried to do feats of strength and stuff like that. Why? Is Louie trying to make you eat something gross?"

"No!" She shrieks, her little nose curling. "I don't listen to Louie anymore." Then she gets quiet, and I can tell by her eyes, she's thinking. "What's feats of strength?"

"*Feats*. It just means boys trying to show off who's the strongest." *Alpha-male bullshit.*

"I think grown-up girls do feats of strength." She looks out the window as if she's done with this conversation.

Not so fast.

"What do you mean, princess?" She does a little sigh, and she's singing another Disney song I don't know. "Princess? Are grown-up girls being mean to you?"

My hackles are up, and I'm ready to get to the bottom of this.

Mamma bear? Meet Pappa bear.

"Not to me, Daddy." She laughs like that's ridiculous. In my experience, sadly, it's not so ridiculous. "I think some of the mommies are mean to Ruby."

If I thought the idea of someone being mean to my kid was bad, I had no idea how I'd react to someone being mean to Ruby. I can only guess it's because I sense it might be partly my fault.

"Did something happen, baby?"

"Huh uh." She shakes her little head no. "Ruby always wants to go home real quick. She never talks to Ms. Terry anymore. She says Buddy misses me."

A knot is in my throat, but I hide it. "I'm sure Buddy does miss you. You're his favorite human."

"And Ruby!" My daughter's voice is shrill and offended.

"Right—of course, I meant *and Ruby*. I just meant of the humans who don't live with him."

"Ruby's doing a painting. She says it's me and her."

The confession cements my resolve. I could see the resemblance as the days passed, but I didn't know for sure. Mother and sleeping child? Do I need to be hit over the head with a frying pan?

Lillie goes back to singing her Disney song as quickly as she stopped, and as always I'm amazed at how fast my daughter lets go of disagreements once they're settled. We should all be this way.

Back at the house, I pace in front of my computer. I've had this idea in my head since my conversation with Stephen, and it's only grown stronger with every passing day. It seems impulsive and ill-advised, but truth be told, Buddy cemented the deal.

Last week I ordered the ring, and tonight, I'll sit down with Lillie and ask if she's okay with what I'm planning to do. I'm pretty confident she'll be onboard with the idea.

Then I simply set the stage for it to happen…

Chapter 34

Ruby

The text from Remi blasts in my face. *Would you be able to take Lillie to school? Emergency errand. May can watch til you get here. Thanks.*

I've got to stop falling asleep with my phone in my hand.

Rubbing my eyes, I glance at the clock. *Seven fifteen!* I throw my feet out of bed. Buddy lifts his little head, seeming as annoyed as me at this unexpected intrusion.

"Come on, Bud." I grab him off the bed and carry him to the back door.

Thanks to my little helper, he's gotten to where he goes outside, does his business, and comes back when he's done. Lillie is taking responsible pet ownership very seriously. I just love that girl.

I especially enjoy the afternoons spent talking to her dad while she mothers Buddy like he's the only Miniature Schnoodle on the planet.

Stepping into old sweats and pulling on a turtleneck, I gather my hair into a messy bun and grab my mug of coffee. I'm going to have a chat with Remington about unscheduled emergencies like this. Yes, I'm still Lillie's nanny, but I'm not Miss "Drop of the Hat" girl. I wouldn't have stayed up all night finishing my painting if I'd known I was getting up at the crack of dawn.

Stopping in front of the easel, I smile. The portrait is similar to the original, a woman in a black dress with a sleeping toddler on her shoulder, but my woman's hair is shining black, her profile is mine, and the toddler is clearly Lillie. I have to say, I captured her angelic face and golden curls pretty damn well. I call it "Caregiver and Sleeping Child."

I love giving her care.

"Come on, Bud." I step into my black Uggs and scoop him under my arm.

Lillie will be thrilled to see her puppy before school. I also love spoiling that child.

Only because she's sweet about it.

If she were a little shit, I might not feel so spoil-ey.

Damn, I'm grumpy when I'm awoken unexpectedly.

"Lillie! Time for school."

"Ruby!" She squeals from upstairs, and Buddy goes bananas wiggling under my arm.

"All right, all right, Bud." I put him down, and he high-tails it to the stairs.

It's his first time in this house, but I swear to God, he scampers up those stairs like he knows exactly where his human lives. I stand in the grand entrance and watch his little apricot butt climb two flights, three flights, and take a sharp right at the top floor.

Half a second later, she's squealing his name. "Buddy!"

Lots of little-girl chatter and good mornings and she runs out on the landing holding her puppy as he strains to lick every square inch of her face.

She laughs so loud and squeal-ey, I start laughing, too.

"Don't drop him," I call, heading for the kitchen.

"I'm getting another cup of coffee. Hurry up before you're late for school."

"Hey, Miss Ruby! I've got to get to school." Matilda, the teen who lives next door gives me a wave before walking back to her house.

"Thanks, May." It's interesting to me how relaxed and easy being here feels without Eleanor's presence lurking around every corner. It almost feels like home to me.

Silly thought. I shake it from my mind.

A pounding of feet followed closely by the scuff of doggy toenails, and Lillie and Buddy are both in the kitchen. Lillie dances around in a sea-green skirt and matching mermaid tee. Her leggings have mermaid scales in the pattern.

"Hey, butter bean, take Buddy out real quick and make him pee before we leave for school. I don't want him going in my car."

She calls him and they both run across the living room for the patio door. I lean against the counter watching them go, wondering if puppies and preschoolers just naturally go together like peas and carrots — to quote Forrest Gump.

We're in the car, and I'm contemplating car line while Lillie plays with Buddy, who's riding right beside her in his little puppy seat belt.

"Can I bring Buddy in to show the class?" Lillie's eyes meet mine in the rearview mirror.

"No, baby, I'm not dressed to go inside today. Look at me." I've been making a point to dress executive nanny for every pickup since that black Friday.

"I think you look pretty."

I'm sure she's being truthful. Lillie has no concept of fashion yet.

"Yeah, but you're biased. I'd rather look a little less ratty when I go inside."

"Because of the mean moms?"

My jaw drops. "What are you talking about, Lil?"

She only shrugs and goes back to singing to Buddy. He's heard the entire soundtrack of *Lady and the Tramp*. I don't force her to elaborate. If I've said it once, I've said it a million times, little kids notice everything.

I'm at the drive, the moment of truth, and Lillie looks out the window. "Please, Mommy?"

Our eyes meet in the mirror, and I swear my heart stops beating.

Lillie looks down, "I mean—"

"Sure!" Affection tugs at my chest, and I think I might cry. "We can take Buddy to meet Ms. Terry."

I steer the car into the parking lot and help them both out of the backseat. Lillie holds my hand, swinging it as she skips, and Buddy rides happily tucked under her arm.

When we get to the door, I catch a glimpse of myself in the window and cringe. I don't look terrible, but I definitely look like I just rolled out of bed less than an hour ago.

"Oh, well." I exhale, squaring my shoulders. "Everybody has those days."

I pull the door open, and I see the Bitch Patrol in their little Gucci cluster gossiping outside Terry's door, likely judging every parent who drops off his or her kid. *I don't care.*

Fixing my eyes on the door, I walk with purpose to Lillie's class while she continues skipping, clutching Buddy to her side. The closer we get, the tighter the knot grows in my throat.

Their conversation fades to silence, and I brace

myself for Serena's slicing remark. "Well, look who it is." The sneer in her voice tenses my shoulders. "Late night at the office?"

Somebody fakes a laugh, but Terry steps out at that moment.

Lillie goes nuts, talking fast. "Ms. Terry! This is Buddy. He's a Schnoodle. He lives at Ruby's house, but she said he really belongs to me. I'm teaching him to do tricks, and it's really important to take him out after he sleeps because he can't pee in the house or Ruby goes, 'Oh no! Oh no!'"

She waves one hand over her head, dancing in place like I can only assume I did.

One time.

When Buddy started pooping on my favorite rug.

Her teacher is delighted, holding up both hands and laughing at Lillie's performance. I put my hand on my hip and grin. "Nice way to say thanks, Lil bean."

She's still dancing around when her expression changes, and she yells out, "Daddy!"

This time my heart really does stop in my chest. Turning, I see Remi striding up the hall in our direction looking hot as ever. He's only in jeans, a maroon tee, and dark gray blazer, but he seriously rocks the casual look.

"Perfect." I reach up and touch the mess that is my hair wishing the ground really did things like open up and swallow people. "What are you doing here?"

"I came to see my favorite girls." He gives me that signature grin, and I forget to care what I look like as I melt into a puddle.

Stopping beside me, he puts a hand on my lower back, pulling me against his side.

My body is hot all over, but I try to be cool. I'm acutely aware of the Bitch Patrol glaring daggers in our direction.

"What was the emergency errand? Nothing on fire, I hope."

He nods at Lillie and she hops over, taking his hand and looking up at me. "I had to pick something up at the store."

He releases me, scooping Lillie into his arms. "Ruby, I know you said we needed time—"

"Wait… What is this?" That knot has moved from my throat to my stomach, and it's getting tighter and tighter.

Remi presses on. "I learned the hard way how quickly life can change. We never know how much time we have, how much time we have with the people we love…"

I'm having trouble breathing. "Remi, what are you doing?"

"I talked to Lillie, and she said it was okay for me to say this…" My eyes heat. "We want to start sharing all our time with you."

He bends and puts his daughter down, whispering in her ear. She nods quickly then turns to me. "I'm going to class now, but Daddy wants to talk to you some more. You'd better take Buddy."

Kneeling, I pull her into a hug and take the puppy. "Thanks, sweetie."

Remi looks at the dog and his lips press into a funny smile. "Do you think he'll hang out with us if you put him down for a second?"

Blinking down to the little apricot face watching me, I nod, putting him at my feet. Sure enough. Buddy stands beside me looking up and down the hall. My eyes catch for a moment on the open mouths and wide eyes of Serena and her crew.

"Ruby, I wanted to say this in front of witnesses."

Stepping forward, I speak low in his chest. "You can't do this now. I'm not dressed for it."

"I think you look amazing." Placing his finger under my chin, he lifts my face to his. His eyes are like golden-hot caramel. "I've wanted to say this so many times... I love you, Ruby Banks."

That does it. I'm crying.

"Remi..." My voice is a high whisper.

That gorgeous smile touches his lips. "I love how smart you are and how funny you are. I love the way the light shines off your hair and sparkles in your eyes when you laugh. I love the way you get on your knees, right at eye level with Lillie when she wants to tell you something. I love how you don't back down when I say something you think is wrong... or when these bitches at school call you mean names..."

Serena makes a huffy "I never" noise, and I put my hand over my mouth to cover my laugh. A hot tear rolls down my cheek, and he looks at it with so much care, gently wiping it away with his thumb as he cups my face.

"You're strong and fierce and loving." He leans closer to whisper in my ear. "I especially love that sound you make when I kiss your pussy..."

"Remi!" I whisper, pushing his arm.

He only grins bigger, heat burning in his eyes. "I love that you're passionate about art and music and your work. Your dad was wrong—you're a strong woman. You're amazing. You're everything I want."

With that he steps back and reaches into his jacket pocket. Then he carefully lowers onto one knee. "You can't be Lillie's nanny anymore, because I want you to be my wife. I want to marry you. Will you marry me, Ruby?"

Blinking hard, I see he's holding the most

beautiful blue-velvet sapphire ring up to me. It's set in white gold with small pear-shaped diamonds on each side. My heart is in my throat, and I don't know how I'm still standing on two feet. Or maybe I'm floating off the ground.

Taking the ring, I slide it on my finger as he slowly rises to standing. "Is that a yes?" He's holding my hand. "I couldn't ask your father, because he's no longer with us. But I stopped by the church this morning and talked to your mom. She thinks it's a good idea."

My eyes go wide. "You talked to my mom?"

"It's the traditional thing to do." He does a shrug.

"And she thinks it's a good idea?" Her speech about him not being one of us is in my head, not that it makes one bit of difference. I'm a total goner for this man.

"She says we're a good match."

"Oh, Remi." I jump forward, putting my arm around his neck. "You want to make me yours?"

He laughs, lifting me off the ground, holding me under my butt as my legs wrap around his waist. "More than anything. Be my wife, Ruby. Be my lover for life. Help me take care of Lillie. I can't stand another minute of my life without you in it."

Hugging my arms around his neck, I study the gorgeous ring on my finger. "Yes... I will. Yes." I'm hugging him so close. His warm lips press against my neck, rising higher to my chin, igniting my panties, and before I lose all ability to reason, I quickly add, "In a year."

Remi draws back, frowning. "A year?"

His arms relax, and my feet slide to the floor as I try to explain. "We've only known each other a month, Remington. I can't just marry you like that. We have to at least be engaged a little while to be sure."

His brow lowers, and determination glows in his eyes. "I'm more sure of this than I've been of anything in a long, long time." His words are heat and warmth, and lightning in my veins. "But if it makes you happy, we can be engaged for a little while." His thumb is on my chin and his eyes focus hot on my lips. "As long as I get to kiss you."

"Definitely." Leaning forward, I peck his soft mouth. "Lots of kissing."

He presses my back to the wall as he cups my face in his hands. "I intend to kiss you everywhere, any time I want."

His mouth covers mine, moving my lips apart, and when our tongues meet, I ignite. My hands go around his neck, pulling him closer. His hands go to my waist, sliding beneath my crop top, over the bare skin of my back, pulling me even closer.

Everything is forgotten as I'm lost in the heaven of his arms, the love on his lips, the strength of his words, the satisfaction of his love. Lifting my head, our eyes meet in a moment so heavy with promise.

"I love you, Remington Key." He grins, and I know he's the love of my life.

I almost jump out of my skin when the hall erupts into cheers of teachers, children, and Lillie running to hug our legs, Buddy snug under her arm. Not even Serena North's sour-grapes face can rain on this parade.

I'm in the arms of my family, and even in a messy bun and sweat pants, it doesn't get any better than this.

The End.

———

Epilogue

Remi

Ruby didn't actually make me wait a whole year to get married.

I have my daughter and her best friend to thank for speeding up the timeline. After three months, she started looking at dresses. At four months, when she completed her art therapy licensure and returned to working at the clinic with Drew, I convinced her to let her small rental house go and move back into the McMansion with Lillie and me.

By six months, we were talking locations. I wanted a destination wedding, something like renting all of Cuixmala for a weekend and taking our family and closest friends.

Ruby decided that would be a better honeymoon destination, just the two of us. I couldn't even begin to argue.

Eleanor was a situation Ruby insisted she had to resolve.

After we were engaged, the two of them went to lunch. They returned to the house afterwards and continued an on-again, off-again heated conversation. Until, by the end of the day, they had become allies.

I was skeptical, but their friendship remains strong. Ruby said it took all her training as a therapist, but basically it amounted to Eleanor's fear that once

Ruby became my wife, she would be out of Lillie's life for good.

"I never wanted that," Ruby says, wrapped in my arms in the large, whirlpool bathtub in my master suite. "She said once we were married, there would be no place for her. Ma would be your mother-in-law, and she would be nothing."

The jets swirl foam from the bath salts around us, and a relaxing, lavender scent is in the air. It's soothing, but my hands are on Ruby's breasts, and the sensation of her in my arms, her hardening nipples, is giving me a semi.

"Eleanor will always be Lillie's grandmother. Nothing will change that." My lips press against the side of her neck, rising to behind her ear, and she shivers. "I would never dream of taking her family away."

Ruby nods, lowering her voice to a conspiratorial tone. "I also told her if she stopped pushing Lillie so hard, she'd never have to worry about losing her. Maybe she'll listen."

"In my experience, Eleanor does what she wants, regardless of what anybody says." Palming her breasts, I pinch her tight little nipples. "Now, the last thing I want to do in this moment is talk about my mothers-in-law."

My beautiful bride-to-be starts to laugh, and I slide my hands lower, over her flat stomach, until I'm cupping the space between her thighs, massaging her clit. Her head rocks back against my shoulder and she moans. "Remi…"

"What, beautiful?" I kiss her ear, pulling the shell between my teeth. "Are you wet for me?"

"Yes…"

Her hips slowly rock as I massage her, firm and

steady. I'm patient, watching my girl's breath grow faster. I feel her muscles tense, and I slide her thighs apart with my knee.

I position her so I'm right at her entrance. A thrust of my hips sends my tip into her clenching pussy. "Oh, fuck," I groan.

She's so wet and hot. It's delicious torture, but I do it again, just giving her the hypersensitive tip of my dick, teasing us both.

"Remi…" Her moves grow faster. She turns in my arms, slippery as a bar of soap, until she's facing me.

Now we're chest to chest, her small breasts floating in the water. Our mouths meet, tongues caressing, chasing, driving the heat between us higher as she straddles my lap.

Her hands grip the tub behind me, and I position my cock at her entrance. Then, with a swift drop, I'm sheathed inside her. We both moan at the incredible sensation, the clenching satisfaction of complete connection.

"My beautiful girl," I moan, sliding my hands from her hips up to her waist as she rides me. She's such a great rider. I'm trying to stay here with her and not get lost in the heaven between her thighs.

Grinding her body against mine, she bites her lip to keep from crying out. Her breasts rise out of the water, and she's moving fast. She's gorgeous to watch, the flush covering her breasts and rising to her neck.

My orgasm is tightening in my lower stomach, but I'm doing my best to hold out. It's hard with luscious insides pulling me, milking me. Leaning forward, I give her nipple a hard suck, a little bite.

"Remi!" It's a high whimper followed by a cascade of spasms through her core as she comes on my cock.

Her body breaks into shudders, and I let go,

pulsing and filling her, bucking up into her, groaning through the final waves of orgasm.

She collapses with her arms around my neck, and she's relaxed and smiling. "I love doing that."

"I love doing that with you."

Our lips meet, sweeter this time. I hold her to me so I can kiss her shoulder, nibble her neck, pull her lips with mine again as our tongues caress gently, languorously.

I'm so in love with this woman...

It brings us to today, to this lavish wedding ceremony right here in Oakville.

Stephen is in town as my best man, and Drew is Ruby's matron of honor. We have Ruby's mom, Eleanor, Dottie, Gray, Dagwood, a few people I don't know very well, and even Ms. Terry taking a role in the festivities.

We erected an arch and chairs in the town park square in front of the gazebo. It's spring, so flowers are blooming. Azalea bushes are giant masses of magenta, and wisteria hangs over our heads like lavender grapes on vines.

Drew and Mrs. B, as I've learned everyone calls Ruby's mom, added more flowers to the already bursting scenery. They let me know the wisteria, lilies, and camellias were added. I'm not an expert on flowers, but I think it looks like a technicolor rainbow straight out of any one of my daughter's favorite Disney movies.

I stand before the arch with Pastor Hibbert behind me and Stephen, Dag, and Gray at my side, and as much as I've counted down the days to this moment, my stomach is in knots as the music changes and everyone shifts in their seats.

First comes Lillie, the little show-stopper. She's

wearing a floor-length blue gown to match Ruby's engagement ring. It's designed to look like a princess with a full tulle skirt, and she has Buddy on a long leash as she drops petals down the aisle. When she gets to the front, she steps beside me, holding my hand.

Ruby wanted to be sure she was included, so she's taking part in the unity ceremony, lighting a candle to show our union as a family.

Dottie comes next, followed by Drew, also dressed in sapphire blue. They line up across from my groomsmen.

The music changes, and everyone stands. The Bridal Chorus begins, and when I see the white of her veil, I have to swallow the ache in my throat.

"Don't cry, man." Stephen is at my shoulder, and I exhale a laugh.

Ruby is utterly gorgeous. Her dress is fitted to her body, sleeveless, and floor-length, ending in waves of white satin. The veil hangs over her face and hair, but through the mesh, I see the light glistening off the tears in her eyes.

Fuck Stephen, I have to wipe away the mist. She's the most beautiful angel sent to bring me back to life.

Pastor Hibbert joins our hands, and Ruby bends down to take Lillie's small hand. My daughter looks up at her in wonder, and after the pastor's introduction, the three of us take our small candles and hold them together to illuminate the one larger candle in the center representing our new family.

Satisfaction calms my insides as I watch the yellow flame grow taller. I couldn't have imagined I would have this chance again, and I'm so fucking grateful.

Lillie goes to sit on her grandmother's lap, and Ruby and I take hands, reciting the words that will bond us together. I promise to love her, cherish her, protect her for the rest of my days. The words are so easy to say.

She looks up at me, and when she promises to love, honor, and care for me for the rest of her life, I know I'm the luckiest guy in the world.

At last we reach the part where I can remove that veil and kiss her beautiful lips. For a moment, I hold her in my arms, drinking in her beauty, making a permanent memory of this point in time, this time when I am given a second chance at love.

Our lips unite, our eyes close, and we're swept up in the bliss of union.

* * *

Ruby

Lillie touches her daddy's face before their dance, and my heart is just bursting. The music starts, and he leads her in a sweet version of "When You Wish Upon a Star."

My dance with Remi was equally magical. We glided around the space, me lost in his eyes to the strains of Elvis's "Can't Help Falling in Love." At the end, he kissed me gently, and I've been smoldering ever since.

Now, watching him with his daughter... Everyone's sniffing.

"You're making all your guests cry." Drew is at my elbow, and I put my arm around her waist. She's bouncing her new baby and smiling.

"You're just a softie," I tease. "Lillie picked this song all by herself. It's when the Blue Fairy brings Jiminy Cricket to life."

"That girl." My best friend blinks quickly. "She

really is adorable. It's the second most beautiful wedding I've ever seen."

That makes me laugh. "Can you even remember your wedding? I feel like I've been in a daze the whole day."

"You'll go back and watch the video in a few weeks."

The song ends, and Remi kneels down to hug Lillie. Everyone claps, and I expect the room to burst into partiers now that the official stuff is out of the way.

I'm surprised when my husband (squee!) motions for the DJ to give him the mic. The opening notes of Kenny Rogers fill the room, and my eyes go wide.

"He is not singing that." My stomach flips.

My mom hops up and starts dancing, flapping her elbows like a chicken.

Drew is laughing so hard, she's crying more. "Your mom should not be allowed to dance."

"No joke!" I shout.

Remi launches into the opening verse of "Ruby, Don't Take Your Love to Town," and I can only shake my head and focus on how great his voice sounds. The crowd goes wild with his moves and his singing.

When he finally finishes, begging for God's sake, that Ruby will please just turn around, I can't stand it anymore. I squeal at the top of my lungs like all the other females in the room.

The mic is returned to the DJ, and his arms are around my waist as the dancers fill in around us.

"That's a terrible song for a wedding!" I cry over the noise of K-pop.

"Your mother requested it." Remi grins, as if he can't tell my mother no.

My mind drifts to a moment before the ceremony,

standing with Ma and looking at my version of "Mother and Sleeping Child."

"You were always a gifted artist." She says it as if it's common knowledge, and not a dream I sat on for twelve years.

"You think so?" I can't keep the sarcasm out of my tone. "What happened to art being a useless degree?"

She only clucks her tongue. "Art is a risky degree. It takes a lot of luck and a lot of patience."

"You could've said that to me. I was old enough to understand that reality." It's times like this when I realize some old scars still ache a little — like a bad knee when a rainstorm is coming.

"It was a different time." She turns to me and smiles, arranging my veil, warmth flowing from her eyes. "You are very beautiful, Ruby-ah. Your father would be very proud of you." Her rare use of the diminutive makes my eyes heat.

"Thank you." It's the most I'm able to say.

She nods decisively. "Remington is a good man. He will make a good husband for you."

I couldn't agree more…

Now I'm in the arms of my husband, this beautiful man who gave me the courage to change my life.

Our crowd of friends flood the dance floor, jumping up and down, swaying their hips, pointing fingers disco-style, and pretty much dancing horribly to the music, but Remi and I are in our own separate bubble of love.

"I was just thinking…"

"What's that, wife?" His low voice calling me *wife*, thrills my insides.

"The first night we met, you said you wanted me to help you."

"You did help me."

"I did?" My brow furrows. "How?"

His eyes capture mine, intense and serious. "Well, for starters, you helped me not be like my dad—"

"But you were never like your dad. Everything you do with Lillie shows you're not like him. You were only grieving."

Long fingers smooth my hair back. "You helped me find my way back."

He pulls me close, and my eyes close as his cheek presses to mine. The music swirls with our friends around us, and I confess, as much as I adore Disney movies, I never believed fairytales really happened in real life.

This past year changed all of that.

I'm no longer an only child or even an insecure career girl, searching for meaning in my life. I'm a wife and mother. I'm using my art to help others at the clinic with Drew, which makes me financially independent—not that I need to be anymore.

I've met every goal on my list, with the benefits.

Lifting my chin, I kiss Remi lightly on the cheek, realizing he helped me as well. He's my living handsome prince, and together, we've saved each other.

* * *

Thank you so much for reading Ruby + Remi's story. I hope you laughed, cried, and fell in love with these two as much as I did.

Find out what happens when Drew falls hard for Gray, her brother's sexy best friend, in MAKE YOU MINE, available now!

It's a forbidden, second-chance, military romance you

won't forget. Keep turning for a special Sneak Peek...

STAY is coming June 16, 2019!

Stephen Hastings has a big brain and an even bigger ego.
When he crosses paths with sexy single mom Emmy Barton, he can't walk away without helping her get care for her young son...

Even if it means proposing marriage.
It's a matter of justice: It's not because Emmy is smart, sassy, and strong.

It's definitely not how the sunlight in her red hair reminds him of sunset in Bermuda...

Stephen Hastings solves problems.
He does not fall in love

STAY is a marriage of convenience love story that will make you sigh, swoon, and believe in the power of love.

* * *

Never miss a new release!

Your opinion counts!

If you enjoyed *Make Me Yours*, please leave a short, sweet review wherever you purchased your copy.

Reviews help your favorite authors more than you know.

Thank you so much!

* * *

Books by Tia Louise

Make You Mine, 2018
When We Kiss, 2018
Save Me, 2018
The Right Stud*, 2018
The Last Guy*, 2017
(*co-written with Ilsa Madden-Mills)

THE BRIGHT LIGHTS SERIES
Under the Lights, 2018
Under the Stars, 2018
Hit Girl, 2018

THE ONE TO HOLD SERIES
One to Hold, 2013
One to Keep, 2014
One to Protect, 2014
One to Love, 2014
One to Leave, 2014
One to Save, 2015
One to Chase, 2015
One to Take, 2016

THE DIRTY PLAYERS SERIES
The Prince & The Player, 2016
A Player for A Princess, 2016
Dirty Dealers, 2017
Dirty Thief, 2017

PARANORMAL ROMANCES
One Immortal, 2015
One Insatiable, 2015

On all eBook retailers, in print, and audiobook formats.

Exclusive Sneak Peek

Make You Mine
By Tia Louise
© TLM Productions LLC, 2018

PROLOGUE

Gray

I've heard people can change overnight.

I never believed it until that summer.

Gasoline, oil, dirty rags, grease, transmission fluid… the indelible scent of the garage. I don't even notice it anymore. I don't see the black under my fingernails that never completely washes clean. It's my life, and I'd never questioned it until that day.

"Hand me that socket wrench then get in the cab and spin it." A cigarette dangles from my uncle's lips, and the top of his overalls are tied around his waist.

I toss him the tool and climb into the cab of the ancient Chevy we're repairing. "Ready?"

My hand is on the key in the ignition. He holds up a finger, bending farther under the hood before stepping away and circling it in the air. I give it a crank, and it turns over instantly, settling into a low humming noise.

"There you go." Mack returns the cigarette to his lips and watches a few moments as the truck continues to idle. "Kill it."

I turn the engine off and climb out. "I'll write it up.

Starter, alternator…"

"Just charge for the alternator. I got that starter off an old Mustang. They don't have to pay me for it."

Walking to the office, I call over my shoulder, "You'll never make money giving shit away."

"I'm too old to start worrying about money."

I shake my head and go into the tiny room off the side of the garage. It's all windows, so I have a clear view of the 1961 cherry red gunmetal Aston-hero Classic Jaguar rolling into the shop.

Damn. The sight of it gives me a semi. "Holy shit."

The words are a sacred whisper from my lips. I know who it is. I've been admiring this piece of machinery since I was a little kid. I can't believe it's right here in Mack's garage.

"Grayson?" Mack's voice snaps me out of my daze.

I snatch up the clipboard holding the workorder for the Chevy and head out to where my uncle stands beside the sexiest of all sportscars.

"What you need, Carl?" Mack steps back as the elegantly dressed man emerges from the low ride.

He gives my uncle a cold nod. *Asshole.* "Just a tune-up. I'm planning to drive out to the lake this weekend, and I don't want to end up on the side of the road."

Mack chuckles, but I stay back until I'm called.

Carl Harris is a strange and hateful man. The old ladies say he spends his days drinking whiskey and staring at the photograph of his dead wife. I wouldn't know. I've never been invited inside his house, even though he's my best friend Danny's dad.

Speak of the devil.

"Hey, grease monkey. Got any bananas for me?" Danny charges out of the passenger seat and runs around to grab me in a headlock. "Who won the Kentucky Derby?"

I'm taller than him and stronger, but it still takes a minute for me to escape his grip.

"Charley Horse!" he cries.

I narrowly escape his elbow to my ribs. "Get off me, asshole."

Mr. Harris's voice is loud and sharp. "Daniel!"

My throat tightens. I didn't think he'd hear me swear. *Shit.*

"You're such an animal, Danny." That sweet voice gives me my second hard-on of the day.

Andrea "Drew" Harris walks around the back of the Jaguar dressed in tight white pants that show off her cute little ass and a top that stops right under her breasts, those small, luscious handfuls that seemed to grow overnight.

It also shows off the lines in her stomach, and I wonder what happened to the skinny little girl with stick-straight pigtails running around drinking Mountain Dew and bothering us.

It's like a sexy version of *Invasion of the Body Snatchers.* The aliens took little-kid Drew and replaced her with this grown-up bombshell, who now invades my dreams at night and leaves me with a tent in my sheets every morning.

I stand like an idiot beside Danny with my tongue figuratively hanging out as she walks up to us smiling.

"Shut up, Drew Poo," Danny yells before breaking into laughter.

Those four words flip the whole scene.

"You are such an asshole!" Drew yells, losing her cool.

I start to laugh. Even pissed, she's adorable.

"Andrea Rebecca Harris." Her dad's voice is

another sharp command, but it doesn't deter Drew.

Her eyes are flaming fire. "I was three years old!"

"Didn't stop you from shitting on my carpet."

"I was potty training!"

"Drew Poo," he sing-songs.

My sex-kitten teenage-dream turns wildcat. She snatches up the socket wrench and starts chasing her older brother around the plastic-covered cars.

"Stop this NOW!" Mr. Harris's face is beet red. He looks like he might have a heart attack. "Stop it!"

Danny dashes behind me, and I do the only thing I can. I grab Drew around the upper arms, holding her against my body as she struggles to get free. *Damn*, she feels so good.

She's soft in all the right places, and she smells like the beach and flowers and everything good. She does not smell like gasoline and oil and dirty rags.

I have to focus so my body doesn't betray how much I'm into her.

"Let me go, Grayson!"

"You can't swing tools around in the garage," I groan, giving her a shake. "Now drop it."

She struggles a moment longer before giving up the fight. The oversized wrench hits the concrete floor with a clatter. She twists in my arms and looks up at me, and for a minute, I'm lost in her blue eyes. I remember when she was four and a snake scared her in the brush behind her house.

She was crying, and I carried her in my arms to her mamma.

Fast forward eight years, and I remember comforting her after that pretty lady died. My mother died when I was even younger than her. It's what brought me to this town to live with my uncle in a garage.

This town where people treat us like dirt.

Holding her now, looking into her eyes, the way she's looking back at me, I'm struck by how much between us has changed.

"Boy!" Mr. Harris strides to where I stand with his daughter in my arms. "Let her go."

His tone breaks the spell. It banishes me all the way back to where I belong, outside his pristine world, hands off his princess daughter.

My arms relax, and Drew steps away from me. She's still looking at me that way, but I have to ignore it.

"They were fighting..." My voice dies in the face of her father's cold disdain.

"How old are you?" His words drip with malice.

"Seventeen. Going on eighteen."

"You're leaving for college in the fall?"

My uncle steps up beside me. "Grayson got accepted to state as well as the military college." His voice is friendly, I'm sure he's doing his best to ease the tension.

It doesn't work.

Drew's messed-up dad steps closer to me, so close his warm breath is on my cheek. "Don't you *ever* touch my daughter again."

It's low, a veiled threat.

I've never been threatened before, but I know it when I hear it. This man has nothing to lose but his legacy, and he's not going to let me put my oil-stained hands anywhere near it.

"I don't think Gray meant any harm." My uncle puts his hand on my shoulder, ducking. It's a submissive response, cowering in the presence of this old lion.

An old lion with a useless crown.

King of a forest that doesn't exist anymore.

"As if you'd teach him not to touch what he can't have." He's talking to Mack, but he's glaring at me.

"Come on, Carl." Mack's voice is placating. "You know it wasn't like that."

The man lifts a trembling hand, and a sheen of perspiration is on his forehead. I don't know what they're talking about, but he looks like he needs a drink. Whatever's going on, I won't cower to Carl Harris.

He returns to his car, pointing for his children to get in the vehicle.

"Didn't you want that tune-up?" Mack calls after him.

"I changed my mind. We're not going anywhere."

He can say that again. I hold steady as he fumbles with the keys to start the engine. As if drawn by magnetism, my eyes move to the clear blue ones watching me from the back seat with a very different expression.

Drew smiles, and heat fills my lower body. I smile back, watching as she drives away.

"Finish up that work order." My uncle starts for the T-bird waiting under the plastic cover. "And don't chase after trouble."

I tear my eyes off the beautiful blonde in the sexy sports car. I know he's right. I should stay away from Drew Harris. Nothing good can come of getting mixed up with her.

It's too bad I'm not very good at doing what I should.

* * *

Get *Make You Mine* Today!

───

312

Acknowledgments

I always find myself in this place, thinking about all the incredible people who helped me get to having a beautiful, finished novel, and just wanting to cry...

First, because of all the love and support of my amazing readers and friends. Second, because I never want to forget anybody as I thank you all.

For starters, thanks to my precious family, Mr. TL and my two daughters, for the love, for believing in me, and for PATIENCE. I love you guys!

HUGE THANKS to Dani Sanchez and Lulu Dumonceaux for all the incredible marketing and logistical support. You keep my brain straight when it's going in a million different directions, and you help me so much.

Even MORE Huge Thanks to Ilona Townsel for always being there, for dropping everything to help, and just for being the absolute best. You're my rock.

HUGE THANKS to my incredible beta squad... Becca Zsurkán, Ana Perez, Sarah Sentz, Clare Fuentes, and Tina Morgan—you ladies give amazing notes.

To my Mermaid VEEPs, Ilona Townsel, Jacquie Martin, Becca Zsurkán, Ana Perez, Clare Fuentes, Sheryl Parent, Jaime Long, Tammi Hart, Tina Morgan, and Ellie King. You ladies have no idea how much I love you all!

Harloe Rae... What would I do without you? I love you.

To all of my amazing author-buds, THANK YOU from the bottom of my heart. I know how hard it is, and I'm so so blessed to know you.

Special thanks to Shannon of Shanoff Formats for the gorgeous cover design. I love you. Thanks to Michelle Tan for your helpful tips. Thanks to Becky Barney for being my wonderful editor, and super thanks to Gemma Woolley for your proofreading talents.

To my MERMAIDS and my INCREDIBLE Promo Team, *Thank You* for giving me a place to relax and be silly.

THANKS to ALL the bloggers who have made an art and a science of book loving. Sharing this book with the reading world would be impossible without you. I appreciate your help so much.

To everyone who picks up this book, reads it, loves it, and tells one person about it, you've made my day. I'm so grateful to you all. Without readers, there would be no writers.

So much love,
Stay sexy,
<3 *Tia*

About The Author

Tia Louise is the *USA Today* best-selling, award-winning author of the "One to Hold" and "Dirty Players" series, and co-author of the #4 Amazon bestseller *The Last Guy*.

From Readers' Choice nominations, to *USA Today* "Happily Ever After" nods, to winning Favorite Erotica Author and the "Lady Boner Award" (LOL!), nothing makes her happier than communicating with fans and weaving new love stories that are smart, sassy, and very sexy.

A former journalist, Louise lives in the Midwest with her trophy husband, two teenage geniuses, and one grumpy cat.

Keep up with Tia online:
www.AuthorTiaLouise.com

68196889R00188

Made in the USA
Columbia, SC
06 August 2019